Natalie's Nighthawk

Nighthawk Search and Rescue Book 1

Amanda Zook

Contents

Dedication

For my Parents who instilled in me the love of books.
For Richard Bittinger, my English teacher at Hershey
High School for teaching me how to write.
And for Kris for giving me the support and freedom to
follow my dream.

Chapter 1

Late spring, twelve years ago

"A**WW, CRAP ON A Picasso!**" Natalie Ghannon muttered as she spotted the sleek vehicle approaching through the heat shimmering from the asphalt. Anyone could have come to her rescue. Why, oh why, did it have to be Graham Whitaker, the boy she'd had a crush on since she was twelve and he a mature thirteen.

As a senior in high school and one of the most popular guys in town, he was even more of a dream. A distant, unattainable dream that had her wishing he would notice her though she knew he never would.

He ran with the football team and dated cheerleaders. She spent her free time in the art room. He dressed to perfection in the latest styles when he wasn't wearing his football jersey. She wore baggy hand-me-downs that looked like they came out of the '80s. Her favorite the overall shorts she currently wore, covered with paint stains. Most days, she didn't care if she looked like a homeless person. But today?

She would kill Maddie for this.

Her sister, Madison, was supposed to be driving her home from the afterschool clubs they both participated in ... separately, of course. Maddie would never be caught dead in the art room. She might accidentally brush up against something and mess up her *perfect* clothes. Or get paint on her *perfect* manicure. Or muss the *perfect* hair on her *perfect* head.

A year older and about to graduate high school, Maddie was Natalie's complete opposite. She had perfect blonde hair styled to emulate whichever actress was currently popular, stunning blue eyes, and a perfect cheerleader's body. She had heard the term "striking" to describe her sister more than once. Natalie, however, looked more like the town recluse. Maddie's senior year was every girl's dream, Homecoming Queen, perfect grade point average, classic good looks. The center of the school's coveted social circle. Tons of friends, and hot guys always fawning all over themselves in the hopes of winning a date with her. Everybody loved Madison Ghannon. People couldn't be bothered to remember Natalie's name.

She knew she would never be a beauty like her sister. Her dark hair, pale skin, and the bothersome freckles on her nose were uninteresting. But right now, as she stood on the side of the road where her *perfect* sister had abandoned her, hair thrown up in a messy bun, stray strands stuck to the sweat on her neck, she longed to be more alluring. She wished the Earth would swallow her whole as she watched Graham's Mustang pull closer, a cloud of dust trailing behind.

Graham maneuvered the car over to the shoulder and rolled down the window on the passenger's side. Leaning over the center console, he looked at her over the top of his aviator sunglasses.

"Natalie?" Imagine that ... he knew her name. She didn't know why that stunned her so much since they'd been neighbors for all of her seventeen years. "What are you doing out here?"

Trying not to fidget as the cloud of road dust settled around her, Natalie answered, "Walking home."

"Walking home?" He looked incredulously at the surrounding miles of soybean fields. "It must be, like, ten miles to home! And it's a hundred degrees out."

"Gee, I hadn't noticed." Wiping sweat off her forehead, she knew he didn't deserve her sarcasm, but she couldn't help herself. He reacted to her foul mood with a slight lifting of the corner of his mouth. *God, those lips!*

"Have you been walking all the way from school?"

"No. Just since my sister kicked me out of her car." She pushed a sticky strand of hair behind her ear, fidgeting again.

Stop acting like such a moron! And stop looking at his lips! She tore her eyes away from his mouth and looked down ... right at his crotch. He was wearing a pair of khaki cargo shorts which hugged him just right.

No, don't look there either. She dragged her eyes higher, where they landed on the outrageous pectoral muscles obvious beneath his black t-shirt. *Seriously, what high school boy has muscles like that?* Panicking and not knowing where to look—everywhere her eyes landed made her blush—she closed her eyes and took a deep breath.

While she tried to control the chaos in her brain, he took his sunglasses off and asked, "Why'd she do that?"

Natalie tilted her head, curious why he cared.

She needed him to drive on. Even though she lived with one, she didn't know how to communicate with the beautiful ones. She always felt awkward around them. As if every flaw in her appearance, every freckle was screaming out—*Hey, look at me! Look how I don't fit in!*

It was even harder to communicate with Graham because he was one of the leaders of the beautiful ones. Her crush on him made her extra self-conscious, and she could feel the heat rising up her neck. Staring into his ice-blue eyes, she wondered if he knew about her crush. Her eyes dropped to those perfect lips again.

Inwardly groaning at herself, she forced her eyes away from those lips before she answered, "She seemed to take offense to me ratting on her to our parents about her new boyfriend." Their parents definitely *would* object to Maddie's twenty-three-year-old tattoo-covered motorcycle riding bad boy rebel without a clue as an acceptable boyfriend.

Graham gave a short bark of a laugh. Even that was sexy. "And did you? Rat on her that is."

Natalie couldn't stop the sly smile, "Not in the way she thinks."

Seeing that sly smile, Graham was intrigued. He watched her delicate fingers fiddle with her hair again, shoving a piece that had blown in her face behind her ear. He was hot and tired after soccer practice but spotting his neighbor walking along a desolate road surrounded by farmland had made him curious. Not to mention his protective instincts were activated; he knew he could score some major hero points for stopping.

"How so?" he asked.

"Well, I didn't tell my parents directly, per se." That devious smile that he was starting to find extremely adorable lifted one corner of her mouth again.

Natalie wasn't beautiful like her sister. Far from it, in fact, but she had a certain charm that was cute. A flush caused by the heat accentuated the soft smattering of freckles across her nose, and her smooth, almost black hair shone with streaks of fire when the sun caught it just right. She probably didn't even know how fascinating those red highlights were in the sun.

"I didn't tell my parents," she continued. "But I told Chloe while her mom was within hearing range. And Chloe's mom and my mom are friends." Natalie shrugged, the sly smile still evident. "I guess word traveled through the mom grapevine."

"So, Maddie got mad and just left you here? That was kind of bitchy of her." Graham thought Maddie was a grade-A bitch, unless she was trying to flirt. Graham thought he might be the only boy in school who hadn't dated her. He'd never even been tempted to, finding her fake and full of herself. It didn't surprise him that Maddie had tapped out the pool of boys in the high school and had started looking elsewhere.

"She'll eventually realize how much trouble she'll be in for this, then she'll be back." Natalie was far more forgiving than he would be. She didn't even seem mad; she was so blasé about the situation that he wondered what it would take to actually piss her off.

"How 'bout we teach her a lesson?" She tilted her head slightly to the right, the sun caught the fire in her dark hair. A slight hitch in his chest caused his breath to catch, and all the blood suddenly headed south. A teenager, that particular area was always flooded with a little extra, but this was the first time it had ever happened at such an alarming speed. "Get in," he croaked, gesturing to the passenger seat. "When she comes back and can't find you, she'll panic and think you've been kidnapped or something." Now he had the sly smile.

"Diabolical." She shrugged slightly. "Okay!"

Once settled and underway, he strangely didn't want their little interlude to end. Natalie sat hunched in the seat as if she were trying to fold into herself. He didn't understand why she was nervous; they'd known each other since birth and had spent hours together constructing Lego masterpieces as kids. Of course, they hadn't had much to do with each other since they'd entered the double digits; different interests had taken them in different directions. Playing as many sports as possible was his obsession. And she ... well, he wasn't so sure what she was interested in and should probably remedy that. They had been close friends when they were younger, that they had drifted so far apart made him sad.

"Seems like you've had a rough afternoon. How about we get some ice cream?"

"Oh! You don't need to bother." One hand nervously clutched the seat belt across her chest. "I'm sure you want to get home. You're probably hot and sweaty from practice."

That was an understatement. The heat had made practice unbearable. "All the more reason to get some ice cream. It will help cool me down."

She shot him a look that said she questioned his motive ... or his sanity. If he was honest with himself, he questioned his motive too. He wanted to talk to her, she was real, and for some reason, he felt comfortable with her. More than he had with any of the girls he'd dated. "What do you say? My treat!"

"Okay." She smiled at him causing that strange hitch in his chest again. He shifted in his seat to alleviate the pressure in his shorts.

After placing their order at the drive-thru of the local Dairy Queen—a hot fudge sundae for her and a chocolate-dipped cone for him—he told her he knew the perfect place to enjoy their snack, driving to a secluded spot that overlooked the southern shore of Lake Michigan, just outside of their little town.

"Oh! I didn't know this was here!"

"Most people don't." It was the perfect place *because* nobody knew about it. He came here often when the world became too overwhelming. Especially lately, when the pressure to pick the right college, and the right career, weighed heavily on him.

"Come on." Taking a blanket out of the trunk, he spread it over the sand in front of the car. They sat and finished their ice cream in silence. The weather was perfect here next to the lake. A breeze coming in off the water combined with the shade from the trees made the temperature much more bearable than on the wide-open soccer field.

"Sooo," Natalie drew out the word. "How many girls have you brought here?" she teased.

He laughed. "Funny you should ask ... you're the first."

"Sure, I am," she said skeptically. He couldn't blame her for the cynicism. He had dated quite a few girls in the last few years.

"No, really! You are!" She rolled her eyes, the intense emerald shade sparkling in the sunlight. "Really, it's the truth!" He'd never brought anyone here before, not even his friends. This was *his* place, a private spot for thinking.

"So why do I get the honor of being the first?"

He shrugged; he had no answer for her. They weren't close, at least not anymore, he'd simply felt a tremendous need to share something special with her.

As they finished their ice cream, Graham watched her out of the corner of his eye. Her profile wasn't striking but was pleasant. Not a classic beauty like most of the girls he hung out with, she was pretty. What made her immensely intriguing was that she seemed unaware of her allure.

He took in the fine details of her, his cock twitching uncomfortably as he stared at her toned legs beneath the shorts of her overalls. All that silken skin he was itching to touch. He'd never had a reaction like that to a girl's legs before.

He forced his eyes to move up to her face. She had a slim, straight nose, Cupid's bow lips, and delicate cheekbones, one of which bore a bit of white paint. Amused, he reached out to touch the dab of paint. "What's this?"

Startled, she reached up to touch the spot too. "What?"

"Looks like paint."

"Oh. Probably is," she blushed. "I was finishing up a project in the art room."

"I forgot you were an artist." When she lowered her hand, he noticed the black marks on it. They looked like pencil smudges from the side of the pinkie finger on her left hand down to her wrist. He grabbed her hand for a closer look. "And this?"

"Happens to most left-handers. But more so for me because I spend a lot of time sketching."

"I'd love to see your work sometime."

Her face lit up; obviously, she loved the subject. His cock throbbed even harder, seeing that smile again. Knowing he needed to control that, he moved his arm across his lap to hide the insistent bulge.

"I've got my sketchbook here." She reached in her bag and pulled out a large leather-bound book.

He opened it and glanced through. The first few pages were close-up drawings of eyes and wings, breathtaking in their detail. Each tiny, delicate line in the feathers was precise. And the eyes ... it was incredible that she'd captured a reflection in an eye ... with a pencil.

Then came the sketches of the birds; some perched on branches, others wings spread wide in flight. Drawings so fine and intricate that they looked ready to fly off the page.

"My new favorite subject right now is birds. I love all the fine lines in the feathers. And the eyes! Bird's eyes always seem to hold the knowledge of the world. Fascinating creatures." Her voice faltered, a blush hitting her cheeks. Eyes drawn to the soft color traveling up her face from her chest, she was the fascinating creature.

He tore his gaze away from her and flipped to another page in the book. This bird was smaller and perched on the side of a tree about to take off. Mostly brown and white with a black cap on its head, its feathers so finely detailed he ran his finger over them as if to feel their softness.

"Chickadee," she explained. "He's my favorite. In part, because I just like saying 'chickadee.' But also because of how small they are. Their coloring is so striking, with the little black cap." *Just like her with her cap of dark hair.*

He gaped at her in incredulity. "These are amazing! I didn't realize how talented you are. You should sell these! I bet people would buy them by the dozens."

She looked out at the dark clouds that were approaching across the water with a far-off dreamy look. She smiled shyly at him, swiping a loose strand of hair behind her ear with pencil smudged fingers. "Maybe someday."

The pair spent the next hour talking. Natalie had never chatted so freely with a boy before, and he wasn't shy about sharing things with her. They talked about everything, her art, his college prospects, their families, and their childhood memories of each other. It was a welcome distraction from the loneliness that usually plagued her, and she didn't want it to end.

They drove home in silence; the storm they had watched approaching across the lake had finally caught up with them, forcing them to leave the beach. They were lost in their own thoughts as Graham drove; watching the sky turn an eerie green. The hairs on the back of Natalie's neck rose as they got closer to their development, and the wind increasing dramatically. Graham battled the gusts to keep the car on the road. And then there it was, as they turned on to their cul-de-sac.

The tornado was immense, Natalie had never seen one this close before and it both fascinated and terrified her. Graham slammed on the brakes, bringing them to a skidding stop. They watched helplessly as the tornado spun closer to the houses on their street. Debris flew everywhere around them. Branches rained down on the car. Lawn chairs, plants, pots, and a trampoline flew past them. Anything in yards that hadn't been tied down was now a projectile flying through the air. A large branch suddenly smashed into the front of the car, cracking its windshield. They jumped, and Graham threw the car into reverse to get away from the soaring debris as quickly as possible.

Still, their attention was on the spinning vortex. It passed quickly through Mrs. Thompson's yard, turning suddenly as if to stroll down the sidewalk, directly toward their own houses at the end of the cul-de-sac.

Chapter 2

Present Day

"ARE YOU SURE ABOUT this?" Maddie asked, slamming the car door behind her. "What if he doesn't help us?"

"He'll help us."

"How can you be so sure?"

"I just am." As her sister gaped at her, Natalie took a deep breath and walked confidently to the door of the building that housed the headquarters of Nighthawk Search and Rescue.

Of course, Maddie was confused by her sudden confidence. It had been a long time since Natalie had shown anything close to confidence. But she had to at least appear that way. He had to help them; they were out of other options; they needed him.

"This was your idea, remember?" Natalie continued. "I had no idea this group even existed until you mentioned them."

"I know. But they are big-league since the Marcus Rayne rescue. What makes you think they'll help us with our problem?" Rayne was a famous actor who had made it big starring in a superhero movie. While hiking a few months ago, he'd had an accident and had needed to be rescued.

"They'll have to." Natalie paused with her hand on the door. He'd help her. She was sure of it. A tiny niggle of doubt crept in. It had been twelve years; he likely didn't even remember her. She shook off the thought; it wasn't about her. They needed help, and she wasn't going to accept no for an answer. Taking a deep breath, she pushed open the door.

"Can I help you?" the young woman behind the desk asked as they entered.

Natalie glanced around the room, empty except for the desk the receptionist sat behind; the walls were full of large, framed photographs. One picture showed men in reflective vests and helmets carrying a stretcher down a forest trail. Another was of a similar group scaling a cliff with ropes and harnesses. Yet another focused on men in a large black inflatable motorized boat in what appeared to be a flooded-out neighborhood. Scattered among those were the typical "You can do it" inspirational posters.

"I'd like to speak to Graham, please." Natalie wanted to take a closer look at a nearby shelf that held awards and brochures; a chance to learn about the man whose help she was seeking.

The petite blonde gave her a once-over before turning back to her computer. "Do you have an appointment? Mr. Whitaker is very busy today and doesn't have time to meet with groupies."

Natalie glanced at Maddie in confusion. *Groupies?* Maddie shrugged, just as confused.

"Um ... I don't think you understand." Natalie's confidence was dwindling as the blonde receptionist stared at her. "I'm a friend of Graham's ..."

"I'm sure you are," the blonde gave them a cursory receptionist smile, barely suppressing her skepticism. "But Mr. Whitaker is currently in a session though I'd be happy to make an appointment for you."

Exasperated with the woman's dismissal, Natalie tried a different tactic. "You don't understand. We need his help. Two little kids ..."

"Maddie? Natalie?" a deep voice to their left called out, interrupting her attempt to appeal to the blonde's sense of decency.

"David!" Maddie addressed the man who had just entered the room. Graham Whitaker's brother was more handsome than Natalie remembered. He was tall, probably around six feet, his dark hair cut short suited him, as did the dark scruff that adorned his face. Maddie, her limp barely perceptible with the new prosthetic, walked over to David and embraced him. "Look at you all grown up! You've aged well!" she complimented, giving him a once-over.

"Look at you," he parroted. "No more wheels?"

"Nope. I graduated to titanium!" She lifted her pant leg to show him the titanium prosthetic.

"Congrats! That is so cool! Looks good on you. You've aged extremely well yourself!"

"Thanks," Maddie blushed. Briefly, Natalie wondered how David knew Maddie had been in a wheelchair since he had moved away right after the tornado. She was under the impression that none of the Whitakers had been in contact with her family since then. She felt her stomach knot. Maybe she was making too much of that day by the lake. It had only been a few hours, definitely not the magical unicorn moment that she continually measured all moments against.

"What are you doing here?" David asked after returning Natalie's hug hello.

"We need your help," Natalie blurted out. "I mean ... we were hoping we could get Graham's help. Two of my students have gone missing ..."

"Say no more," David pulled a radio out of his pocket. "Graham," he said into the device. "You're needed at the main office."

"Now?" a voice squawked back. "I'm a little busy at the moment."

"It's an emergency."

A sigh was heard through the radio. "Can't you handle it?"

"I think you are going to want to handle this one," David replied with a wink to the sisters.

"Fine!" the exasperated voice replied. "Be there in two minutes."

"Copy." Putting the device back in his pocket, David gestured for them to follow him into a conference room. The room was a typical fishbowl office space with a long, oval polished wood table and windows taking up two walls. Natalie moved to the windows on the side opposite the door and looked out over the grounds.

The facility was more impressive than Natalie had imagined. There were half a dozen buildings spread across the grounds resembling a college campus. Instead of students in the usual college attire, men and women in various types of training gear milled around.

Under a grouping of trees between the main building and a large four-story building, a crowd sat at a set of painted metal picnic tables enjoying a coffee break.

That's where Natalie first spotted him, the man of her childhood dreams. He looked about the same as he had that day by the lake if a little wiser and older. And more ... muscular? Just ... more.

Her heart beat erratically as she watched him separate from the group and throw a leg over a nearby ATV. Lucy and Colin were counting on her; she shouldn't be swooning at the mere glimpse of him. She reminded herself that she needed his help, not his obviously toned body.

But her thoughts betrayed her, flashing back to that day. The day Graham Whitaker had given her that first kiss.

Twelve Years Ago

The conversation moved to other topics after he'd studied her sketches. During a brief pause in their banter, they stared across the water, where dark clouds were building up. "Looks like a storm's coming," Natalie stated.

"They were calling for storms this afternoon."

"Right." A gust of wind whipped her hair into her face. She pulled out her hair tie and fought the wind to redo her bun. "Sorry to hear you and Laney broke up."

"I'm not," he replied with a smile that made her stomach flip. Those lips of his were too much. "She was way too into herself."

"How many girls have you dated?" It was a bold question for her, but if the rumors of dozens were true, she wanted to understand what he was doing here with her.

A corner of his lip turned up in amusement. "A few. You?"

Natalie lowered her head, blushing furiously. She grabbed her sketchbook from where he'd left it and clutched it to her chest, though it made an inadequate shield. Turnabout was fair play, she supposed; still, she wasn't sure she wanted him to know the answer. But then, who cares what he thought about her answer. She was fine with it. Happy, even, that she had never—

"It's none, isn't it," he guessed, interrupting her thoughts. Flicking the corner of her sketchbook repeatedly, she felt every bit of confidence deflating. "That's cool," he went on to reassure her. "You know who you are and what you want. None of the flitting around from guy to guy. You strike me as someone who doesn't play those games. I respect that," he finished quietly. Clearly, he'd been played with too many times.

"I'm sorry, girls can be such bitches."

"Not all of them." His intense blue eyes met hers as he brushed a finger down the paint streak on her cheek, the corners of his mouth curling into the sexiest grin she'd ever seen. A furious heat rushed through her body.

The wind picked up again, blowing a few dark strands of hair that had escaped her bun again to tangle in his fingers. He fingered a strand gently before dropping his hand.

"Guess you've never had that first kiss either." He gazed across the lake. She felt the blush explode across her cheeks. This was not a conversation she wanted to have with the hottest guy in school. Though she was fine with never having had a boyfriend, it was still embarrassing. "I remember my first kiss," he mused. "I was so nervous. Thought I was going to screw the whole thing up."

That surprised Natalie. He seemed the consummate ladies' man. So confident when it came to dealing with the opposite sex, it amazed her to think that he could be just as insecure as the rest of them.

A rumble of thunder in the distance was followed by a stronger gust of wind rolling through again. The dark clouds were almost upon them. "We'd better go." Was that disappointment she heard in his voice or was she projecting her own feelings onto him? "Looks like we're going to get dumped on."

He stood, and she followed suit, bringing the blanket with her, folding it as they walked to the Mustang. "You know, Chickadee ... I could do it if you want," he said after she placed the blanket in the trunk. Confused at what he'd just called her, she tilted her head to look at him.

She didn't understand what he wanted to do. "You know ... be your first. Your first kiss, I mean." He sounded flustered.

She chewed on her lower lip as an unfamiliar tingle traveled through her body. She wondered why he would make such an offer, what his motive might be.

"I won't tell anyone. I promise." That made the decision even harder. On one hand it would be nice to get the first kiss out of the way so that when she did meet somebody worthwhile, she wouldn't be so nervous about a simple kiss.

But on the other hand, this was Graham, the most popular guy in school who could very well be making fun of her. But it would be really nice kissing him. A dream. One she'd had for a long time. He could make her fantasy come true today.

Her thoughts were a disorganized jumble of trying to fathom his motive.

He cupped her cheek, drawing her eyes to his as electricity shot through her body from his touch. "What's the worst that could happen?"

His ice-blue stare was intense. She swallowed past the lump that had suddenly formed in her throat as her nerves quaked, causing her knees to weaken. "Okay," she muttered, eyes widening as it dawned on her what she'd agreed to do.

He grinned that killer sexy smile that made her body quicken and leaned closer to her, the atmosphere around them crackling with energy. The wind whipped up, and Natalie slowly closed her eyes. Then she felt his lips gently on hers, his hand still on her cheek. It was a sweet kiss. A chaste kiss. A fleeting touch of lips accompanied with a spark of awareness.

Then it was over. Feeling disappointed, she opened her eyes as he pulled away from her. He stared at her with wide eyes; lips parted slightly. He appeared stunned at what he'd just done. She lowered her head in embarrassment and started to inch back from him, but he suddenly reached out and grabbed her face with both hands.

"Wait." His eyes glistened with an icy heat.

Then he leaned in again, his lips crashing down on hers. At the sudden feel of his tongue along the seam of her lips, she gasped, allowing him to slip inside her mouth. Their tongues dueled, sliding against each other. Her heart was a wild thing, blood rushing recklessly through her veins. He had one hand on the back of her neck beneath the messy bun in her hair; the other hand slid down to the small of her back. Her arms hung uselessly at her sides until she came to her senses and wrapped them around his neck. With just the gentlest of pressure, he pulled her closer to him so that their bodies were touching from breast to pelvis. She wanted to soak it all in, breathe in his intoxicating scent until every moment, every touch had been committed to memory.

Natalie was in new territory as his tongue did magical things in her mouth. She was floating yet heavy all at once. His mouth on hers was exquisite. Her heart fluttered like the wings of the birds she loved drawing and felt as if it would burst from her body in flight. She hadn't known that a simple kiss could be this wondrous.

A loud metallic thunk broke the spell. They stepped apart, both confused by the sound, breathing heavily as they stared at each other. Then came another thunk. And another. Hail!

The storm had finally caught up to them. Laughing as they were pelted with tiny chunks of ice, Graham slammed the trunk closed, and they raced into the car. "I guess mother nature is trying to tell us it's time to go home," he joked.

Suddenly shy around him again and slightly embarrassed by how her body reacted to that kiss, Natalie could only manage a small smile.

Present Day

She closed her eyes briefly as the memories swamped her, opening them again just as Graham reached the building and entered through a door to the right of the conference room. *Breathe!* A shiver chased through her body. She had to get her jitters under control. He's a friend. Not a god. Oh, but that body!

Stop it! She wasn't helping her kids by fantasizing about the one man who could rescue them.

Cautioning herself to keep breathing normally, she heard the blonde say, "In there." And then he was there behind her.

"What's this all about," he started to ask David. Then, "Maddie?"

"Hi, Graham." Her sister greeted him first, allowing Natalie more time to get her frazzled emotions in check. Hearing that smooth voice again after all these years was messing with her composure. He returned Maddie's hug, and that's when he noticed her, his dazzling blue eyes slamming into hers.

"Chickadee!" Before she knew it, she was in his arms in an overwhelming hug, and all the control she had been struggling for vanished. She was right about the body. He was all hard, toned muscle. The outdoorsy scent of him filled her senses as he squeezed her tight.

"Chickadee?" Natalie heard Maddie's whispered question to David. How could she have forgotten the nickname he'd given her all those years ago. It made her heart soar that he hadn't forgotten.

"Long story," Graham replied to Maddie as he released Natalie while never breaking eye contact with her. She viscerally felt the absence of his heat as he stepped back from her. His intense gaze checked her over. "You haven't changed a bit," he said as he reached up and lightly touched her chin, turning her head slightly to the left. "Except, no paint." He softly ran his fingertips down the side of her right cheek, and she had to stifle a moan as the feeling of his calloused fingers on her skin turned her insides to jelly.

"Not today," she replied quietly, forcing her body to suppress the shiver his touch generated. Even after twelve years, he still had a magnetic power over her. She was trapped in his gaze, unable to look away even if the room were to erupt around her. He was the same but different. His dark blonde hair was cut short and brushed to the left, his eyes still an intense icy blue. He was fit and tan, with a smooth square jawline that made her fingers itch for a touch. Her heart stuttered as the corners of his lips quirked up into that sexy grin that was all his. *Damn that grin.*

"Too bad." He held her gaze a moment longer before he blinked, breaking the spell that ensnared her, and stepped back away from her. What was that she had seen in his eyes?

Clearing his throat, he asked, "What's going on? Why are you here?"

"Right," Natalie silently berated herself for getting distracted. "Two of my students from Lake Haven elementary - Lucy and Colin, brother and sister - have been missing since Friday morning when they never showed up for school." It was now Sunday morning. Two days. Two whole days and not a sign of them. And she should know since she and most of the rest of the town had spent those two days searching for them.

At a gesture from Graham, David sat down behind a computer terminal situated in the corner of the room. On the wall in front of her, a satellite image projection appeared of Lake Haven, a small town on the southeast shores of Lake Michigan.

"Tell me everything you know. And if you can, indicate on the map the relevant areas."

Natalie studied the overview of the town, trying to step inside the map to orient herself. She pointed at a small cluster of houses. "Lucy and Colin O'Donnoll, ages five and ten, live here. They walk to school, which is here." With a few clicks of the keyboard, two circles appeared around the areas she indicated. "Somewhere in between the two, they disappeared." Graham placed a comforting hand on her shoulder as her voice caught on the last word.

"What areas have been searched already?" Graham asked, studying the map.

Natalie pointed to an area to the right of the O'Donnoll house, and a blue X appeared over the section. "Most everyone has been focused here since it's so close to their house."

"But you don't think that's the right spot?"

"No." She pointed to a larger area on the left on the map, across the street from the house and closer to the school. "This is mostly forest and pretty dense. There are a few trails through it, but if you don't stick to the trails, it's easy to get turned around and lost." A green circle appeared around the forest area.

"Why do you think they are there?"

There was a very good reason she thought they were in those woods, but the Sheriff hadn't believed her when she went to him with her theory. She hesitated, afraid Graham would dismiss her notion as well.

"Natalie overheard some of the kids talking," Maddie supplied when Natalie faltered. "Apparently, there is a bully."

Natalie nodded before finding her voice. "Donnie has been giving Colin a hard time for a few weeks now. According to the other kids, Donnie and his 'gang' wait here," she pointed to the map at a spot just south of the school at the edge of the forest. "They like to tease Colin because he walks his sister to school every day. I think Colin got fed up and attempted to take a shortcut through the forest to the school. It was incredibly foggy on Friday morning and I have no problem believing that they got lost in the fog; it was so thick. But I can't imagine why they weren't able to find their way out after the fog lifted. Something must have happened." Her breath hitched again. Her students were her "kids", she loved each and every one of them as if they were her own. To think that something may have happened to two of them was heart-wrenching. Losing Lucy would be especially devastating, that little girl held a very special place in Natalie's heart. Even at five years old, Lucy had more artistic talent than most of the fully-grown artists Natalie knew.

"So why aren't they searching there," David wondered.

Maddie snorted. "The sheriff didn't believe Natalie when she told him." Maddie was still angry at Sheriff Dodd and his stubbornness. She couldn't fathom how a tip like the one Natalie had given would be ignored. He hadn't sent any of his deputies out to the area. "Ass," she hissed, her anger still bubbling on the surface.

"Okay," Graham started all business now. "David, send the relevant maps to my phone."

"On it," David confirmed with a thumbs up.

"I'm going with Natalie to Lake Haven. I need to grab some supplies." He was moving quickly, and Natalie was impressed by his efficiency. "I'm gonna need the truck if you could follow as soon as you tie up things here."

"How about you and Natalie go in your truck, and I'll drive David up in Natalie's car," suggested Maddie.

"Yeah. Okay, good." Natalie watched him, wondering if he was running through scenarios and the difficulties he might face. He studied the map closely, and with the click of a device Natalie didn't know he was holding, he zoomed in on the area on the map where she believed the kids had gone. Scanning it inch by inch, he concentrated on a small section where there were fewer trees. With a few more clicks, he magnified it, seeing what appeared to be the remains of a long-forgotten house.

"Any idea what this is?" he asked.

Natalie studied the spot. "At one time, Lake Haven was a mining town. I think there are still some remnants of people's claims from those days." Nearly two hundred years ago, people had flocked to Michigan's Upper Peninsula for the large deposits of copper found there. Some intrepid explorers had headed farther south, hoping other areas of Michigan would be just as plentiful. They were unsuccessful.

"That could explain why they haven't been able to find their own way out yet. Maybe they fell into an old mine shaft."

Maddie gasped. "That would be terrifying!"

"I'd like to talk to the bullies," Graham went on. "They might have seen where the kids entered the forest. Think you can arrange that, Natalie?"

"I'll call Donnie's mom on our way and have them meet us ... is at the school a good place?" He nodded.

"I need to grab a few things, and then we can get going. David, can you print out a topo of that area?

"On it," he said with another thumbs up.

"Bring it with you when you come. Let's go, Natalie." He grabbed her hand, and together they left the conference room. The secretary's eyes shot down to their clasped hands, a shocked expression flashing in her eyes which she masked quickly when he paused to fill her in on the situation.

Graham headed down a long hallway. Natalie peered through a narrow window in one of the doors they passed. Three rows of long tables and chairs crowded the room. A handful of men, all wearing matching t-shirts with an identical insignia on the breast pocket, sat at the tables, each intently studying whatever or whoever was in front of them. Natalie assumed this was one of the instruction rooms that Nighthawk used to teach Search and Rescue techniques and certifications.

After passing two more rooms set up in similar configurations, Graham ushered her into a large office at the back of the building. His office had framed pictures scattered around the room, some of himself on a mountain somewhere, and others of him and David in exotic locations. There were medals and awards filling the shelves against one wall. She gaped at the sheer number of accolades he had received.

Her eye was drawn to the wall opposite the shelves, and she gasped. There, framed in a place of honor, was Natalie's drawing of a nighthawk.

"You thief," she huffed, unable to control her smile. He paused in the process of shoving water bottles and granola bars into a backpack to glance over his shoulder at her.

He chuckled quietly. "Guilty." Zipping the bag, he came to stand beside her as she stared at her drawing. "You could say it's inspired me all these years. I never forgot the ornithology lesson you gave me that day, Chickadee."

Flooded with overwhelming feelings that she'd sift through when she wasn't so worried about her kids; she spoke quietly, her eyes focused on the drawing. "I thought I'd lost that sketchbook."

"I found it a few months later under the seat in my car. It must have fallen out of your bag."

"Humph," was all she could manage.

"Come on, Chickadee." He grasped her hand again. "Let's go find your kids."

Chapter 3

T HE RIDE TO LAKE Haven took less time than he'd thought. All these years, she'd merely been thirty minutes away. Never guessing they'd both settle in the same area, close to the lake they grew up loving, he'd always assumed she'd stayed in Indiana.

As Natalie placed the call to have the bully meet them, he thought about that moment when she spotted her drawing. He'd forgotten it was there and hadn't considered how she'd react to seeing it hanging on his office wall. He thought she'd notice all his awards if anything. A small part of him had hoped she would, although he couldn't fathom why. The sheer number of awards embarrassed him most days. That wasn't why he did what he did. It wasn't why he'd chosen search and rescue as a career. He hated displaying them, but David insisted, saying they would look attractive to potential clients.

He still hated them. But he wondered why, then, he'd been keen for Natalie to see them?

A twinge of guilt about the drawing hit his gut. He hadn't meant to keep the book all these years, but he couldn't bring himself to part with it. He smiled as the memories from that day came back to him.

Twelve Years Ago

Natalie indicated the bird on the page he was looking at in her sketchbook. It was a large bird that she'd captured in flight. Wings outstretched, its eyes alert as if hunting for prey.

"This is a nighthawk. They are distinctive because of the white line that goes across the tips of their wings, which you can only see when they are flying. The beaks are different too. For a bird this large, they have unusually tiny beaks, perfect for catching the insects they eat in mid-air." She looked up to find him smirking at her. "Sorry. Sometimes I get carried away."

"Don't be sorry. I like listening to you," he told her honestly. Flipping to another page, he traced the wings of the nighthawk that she'd drawn. The image was so lifelike he could almost feel the downy softness of the feathers under his fingertips. "This is remarkable," he whispered.

"I once read a Native American story about the nighthawks."

"Really?" He looked up at her becoming snared in her emerald eyes. His breath caught at their beauty. Clearing his throat, he asked, "Can you tell it to me?"

"Um, let me see if I remember it." She closed her eyes, and he took a deep breath, released from the spell of her stunning eyes. "There was an old man who did ... um something ... to a stone. I can't remember exactly what the man did." She shook her head.

"That's okay." He placed his hand over hers where it lay on the blanket. His thumb softly stroked the smooth skin. He liked the feeling of her tiny hand under his.

He watched her as she told her story. The sun had picked up the red in her hair, glimmering like fine strands of fire. The faint smattering of freckles across her nose looked like a sprinkling of brown sugar that he wished he could taste. His eyes were drawn to her lips as she spoke. They were pink and perfect. He watched, transfixed as the words formed on her lips. Her voice wrapped around him, enmeshing him in a calm he'd never felt. He could easily become addicted.

"The stone grew angry because of what he had done." She continued her story staring down at their hands, her long lashes concealing her gorgeous eyes. "It rolled after the old man, chasing him down the mountain till, eventually, it bowled over top of him. The stone came to rest, sitting on his back, trapping him. The old man cried out for help many times over."

As she talked, she flipped her hand over, intertwining her fingers through his, and he was struck with how tiny they looked. Graham curled his fingers and gave her hand a squeeze. Her answering squeeze shot straight to his cock.

"Finally, hearing the cry as he soared freely above the Earth, the nighthawk rushed to help. He flew up into the sky, so high he was barely a black speck to those below then came straight down, gaining speed as he went. A single-minded determination was his focus as he aimed for the stone. He dealt that stone an awful blow breaking it into two pieces. The blow was so great that it spoiled its beak, forever changing its shape, making it small and deformed. His head was also jammed into his body, shortening his neck. But the old man was free and so grateful to the nighthawk that he offered to make him different from other birds; make it so it would always be known for the savior it was. He took the fine white powder left from the broken stone and sprinkled it onto the bird's wings in spots and stripes, declaring that no other bird would have such spectacular markings on his clothes. All the nighthawk's children would dress similarly, flying, soaring, and dipping over our heads. They would be proud to show off the beautiful white stripes on their wings, proud of their dress, and proud of the ancient ancestor who risked himself to rescue another."

Graham watched a blush rise up into her cheeks as she met his enamored gaze. He couldn't control the reaction he had listening to her. She was unlike any girl he'd ever met. Her voice soothed something deep inside him, and he felt the stresses of the last year ease.

"That is a nice story. So, he is a hero and was rewarded for rescuing the old man. I love stories like that." Reluctantly, he forced himself to look out over the water before he completely freaked her out with his unrelenting stare. He knew that he had a way of making the girls around him tongue-tied, but with Natalie, this little chickadee, it was the other way around. He was becoming so enamored with her that he was now the tongue-tied one.

Present Day

That day by the lake was a tangible memory to him, one he kept with him always. And when he was starting up his search and rescue training business, the drawing had inspired him. Nighthawk Search and Rescue. He had named his company after that drawing and the story she'd told him.

The fact that he was sitting in his truck beside the artist that had held an important place in his heart for so many years was a wonder to him. His little chickadee; the nickname still suited her. She was still little, probably five foot four, and she still had that lovely cap of dark hair that now fell in waves around her shoulders instead of the messy bun from that day twelve years ago that he'd always pictured her with.

He knew he should have looked her up years ago, but he'd been afraid he'd find her married with kids. He'd never been sure he could deal with that reality. It had been better to live with his fantasy. Shit! For all he knew right now, she *was* married. He stole a glance at her left hand. He couldn't just come out and ask. Though he felt like he was still that inept eighteen-year-old; he knew that would be awkward. Once again, she had him tongue-tied.

As Graham pulled up in front of the school, he chided himself. He needed to get his head back in the game and not on his living, breathing dream sitting beside him.

Natalie introduced Graham to Donnie and his mom, Diane. The boy, to his credit, looked miserable and was more than willing to answer all of Graham's questions. The guilt he was feeling was palpable. He admitted to teasing Colin unmercifully every day before school and had, in fact, been stationed at his usual spot that Friday morning when he saw Colin and Lucy veer off into the woods to avoid him and his buddies. Donnie even showed Graham and Natalie exactly where, admitting to chasing them through the trees for a short time until the fog made it too difficult to see, and they lost their prey.

As he finished with his story, a sheriff's vehicle raced into the lot. Graham had asked his Receptionist/Administrative Assistant, Lauren Phillips, to call the local law to let them know that the Nighthawks were joining the search. Leaving the engine running, Sheriff Dodd hefted his weight out of the SUV.

"What's this all about?" he blustered, the buttons of his uniform shirt straining to contain his girth, his eyes narrowing in on Natalie. "I told you, Miss Ghannon," he said, pointing his bulbous finger at her while spittle flew out of his mouth. "There is no reason to believe those kids are in these woods." The man was the epitome of smarmy, and Graham's hackles rose to defend Natalie.

But before he could, Donnie stepped up between the Sheriff and Natalie, fists clenched. "I saw them, Sheriff Dodd. That morning. They went into the forest." Even he was outraged that the Sheriff was such an ass.

"Look, I'm just here to help," Graham interjected. "I'm sure your resources are stretched pretty thin." The word had spread that a Nighthawk was here to help, and the parking lot was quickly filling up with townsfolk.

"I'm sure you wouldn't want to turn away more searchers, would you, Sheriff Dodd?" Natalie stated loudly. Sheriff Dodd glowered at Natalie, and Graham could tell he knew full well she had bested him. He obviously couldn't say anything without the whole town thinking him an ass. The Sheriff's eyes darted around at the gathering crowd, and Graham could see the moment he realized he had to save face somehow in front of all the potential voters if he wanted to keep his job with election season just around the corner.

"Of course not," the Sheriff conceded, running an agitated hand over his bald head. "Obviously, the more searchers, the better. Since you've come with your own manpower," the Sheriff indicated David, who had just arrived. "Why don't you start in these woods while my men continue their search behind the O'Donnoll's house?"

Graham heard Maddie's snort of derision behind him. "Absolutely. Here's my cell number where you can reach me if you find them." He handed the Sheriff his business card. Then he turned to David, completely dismissing the incompetent Sheriff. "Let's take a look at that topo map you brought."

A young deputy walked over to Natalie. "Sorry about this, Natalie. Sheriff's got tunnel vision when it comes to this case for some reason. I'm glad you brought your own group in. Dodd wouldn't listen to reason, and we were stretched too thin doing his bidding. Otherwise, I would have been in these woods long ago."

Natalie introduced Graham to Deputy Ian McClintock, who thanked him for helping out. Then he excused himself to smooth over the Sheriff's ruffled feathers. Natalie explained that everybody knew if you needed anything, Deputy McClintock was your man.

Graham felt a wave of jealousy momentarily as he observed Natalie converse with the deputy. They seemed to have an easy rapport. Were they friends or something more? The deputy was good-looking, he supposed. The man's hair was darker than his own but styled similarly. His dark blue eyes looked down at Natalie with kindness and familiarity. Together they made an attractive couple. His stomach knotted as the jealousy flared. He realized that he should never have stayed away from her for so many years. He'd only been back in her presence for a few hours, and he was already feeling possessive.

Fuck. He pulled himself out of his musings and turned to talk to his brother, desperate to shake off the jealousy.

Graham and David were poring over possible places to start their search when two large SUVs pulled into the lot, and five of his best Nighthawks plus Lauren spilled out. "I guess Lauren filled the guys in on what we were doing," David said as the men joined them.

"Thanks for coming guys." He gave them the sitrep as the townsfolk prattled on around them. He could hear snippets of their conversations. The same conversations people always had about the Nighthawks. Most of the talk centered in awe and wonder.

He was used to the chatter about him, but it had become ten times worse since the Nighthawks had rescued the actor six months ago. That had given them national attention, and his face had been plastered on all the major news networks for days. Graham had been forced to break his own rule about news interviews so the speculation about him and his Nighthawks would die down. He cringed even now, thinking about that interview.

Natalie seemed oblivious to her neighbors' fascination with him as she spoke quietly with a young couple. He was thankful for that. He didn't want her thinking he was some stupid, superstar celebrity. As he spoke to his men, Natalie led the couple over to him.

"Graham." She lightly touched his arm to get his attention. Of course, all that did was intensify his awareness of her and the warmth her tiny hand on his arm generated. "This is Milly and Daniel O'Donnoll, Lucy and Colin's parents."

"We can't thank you enough for this." Daniel, who wore a Lake Haven Fire Department t-shirt, grabbed Graham's hand and shook it enthusiastically. "When Diane called us to tell us the Nighthawks were coming to help, well, we could hardly believe it. But here you are! All of you," He gestured to the group of men. "Thank you so much." Mrs. O'Donnoll, who was clutching her husband's arm for support, also shook his hand but could only squeeze out a quick "Thanks" past her tears.

Thankfully, Lauren arrived and drew the parents away. A wiz with family members, she had worked for the Red Cross when he first met her. They had often worked the same disasters and had struck up a friendship. Graham eventually convinced her to leave the Red Cross and come work for him, and he'd never regretted a minute of it. She had a way with people that was nothing short of miraculous.

After sending his men off to search key locations he thought the kids might have wandered to, he went to his truck to grab his gear. Natalie met him there. "Anything I can do to help?" she asked.

"Well," he mused. "I usually employ the buddy system with the Nighthawks, but I seem to be a man short. Wanna be my buddy?"

Her entire face lit up, which was fascinating to him, and just as it had twelve years ago, the blood in his body shot south at an alarming speed.

"Absolutely!" she answered, reaching up to throw her long dark hair into a ponytail. He watched as she lifted her hair up, mesmerized by the smooth skin of her neck. He imagined what it would be like to place his mouth there.

Fuck. Twelve years and he still couldn't stop fantasizing about her.

Snapping himself out of his reverie, they set off in the direction of the ruins he had noticed on the satellite image map. He kept his eyes glued to the trail, looking for any evidence of humans passing nearby recently. Anything from overturned brush, broken branches, or footprints left in the dirt to a scrap of material snagged by a twig could indicate someone had walked through the area.

Determining if it was the children was the trick. There was no real way of telling if any of the signs his tracking skills spotted was from the missing kids. It was a weekend, which meant there was a chance that plenty of hikers had been in these woods recently, but Graham figured most of them would stick to the marked trails. Would the children do the same, or had they veered off the trail and been unable to find their way back?

After searching quietly for a while, Natalie said, "So, I couldn't help but notice everybody's reaction to you." *Shit. Here come the usual questions.* "Heard someone mention Marcus Rayne. They seemed infatuated with your group. What's that about?" Marcus Rayne was the actor he had rescued off the side of a cliff after the man had fallen twenty feet while hiking and broken his leg. Rayne had been so grateful that he'd made a sizable donation to the Nighthawks, which ran largely off the generosity of people and fundraisers. They never accepted payment for any rescue.

"Don't you watch the news?" Frankly, he was incredulous that she hadn't heard about that particular rescue. He was still popping up in the news cycles. Especially now that Marcus' newest Titan superhero movie would premiere the following week. It was big news to them. The superhero needing to be rescued by a team of real-life superheroes was an entertainment reporter's wet dream.

"No. I don't bother with the news too often. It's all so depressing."

"Marcus Rayne fell down a cliff while hiking in the Upper Peninsula a few months ago and broke his leg. My Nighthawks got him out."

"Bet there was more to it than that," she remarked, ponytail swinging as she walked. He absentmindedly grabbed her hand to help her over a fallen log, tingles shooting up his arm. He heard her breath catch. She must have felt the connection too.

"Just another day on the job for us," he stated, reluctantly releasing her hand. He hoped that would satisfy her curiosity for now. He didn't want to go into it.

They walked in comfortable silence till she asked, "So ... about my drawing?" He winced; she was going for all the gut punches.

"Ummm," he stammered.

"I'm glad you kept it and that it inspired you. You named your team for it, right?"

"Um ... Yeah. I couldn't help but notice the similarities between your story of the rescue of the old man and a typical search and rescue team; doing what is right, risking their lives for someone else. My Nighthawks also race out to help when there is a cry for aid. The search and rescue motto is 'So others may live', and we strive to answer any call for help."

"And there's always plenty of those." A depressing fact, but true. He sensed her mind had turned to the missing kids and the disaster that would hit the town hard if there wasn't a positive outcome.

"Hey." He stopped walking and faced her. The fiery highlights in her hair were shining in the sunlight streaming through the trees. Placing a hand on her cheek, he looked into her eyes and reassured her, "We *will* find them."

She nodded once, blinking back her tears and taking a deep breath. After pushing a loose strand of hair behind her ear, he slid his hand slowly down her arm and grasped her hand again to continue walking. His eyes were always searching, his senses attuned to his surroundings. Still, he couldn't help but appreciate the feeling of her small hand in his. Somehow, it just fit.

Upon arriving at the ruins Graham wanted to search, they fanned out looking for anything that might indicate the kids had passed through. There wasn't much left of the old homestead. A stone chimney and a few crumbling walls. There was a hole in the ground at one corner of the house indicative of an old root cellar.

Outside the house, the forest was attempting to take the land back and young saplings were thriving. There was so much new growth that he just missed falling into a well some poor homesteader had dug. He peered through the holes in the plywood cover someone had thrown over it, unable to see the bottom. Impressive dig. He called out to Colin and Lucy, shining his flashlight into the dark pit. He prayed they weren't down there. He didn't think they were since the ground around it was undisturbed and the cover still intact. If they had trudged through here, there would be some indication. He searched for the usual signs of human disturbances, but there was nothing.

He glanced toward Natalie; she had stopped dead in her tracks, her head slightly tilted to the left as if listening to something. He quickly crossed to her. "What is it?"

"I don't know," she answered slowly, squinting into the woods ahead. "I thought I might have heard ... music? Is that possible?"

"Don't know. Maybe."

"Could it be one of your team?"

"Not a chance. We are trained to use all our senses when on a SAR mission. My guys would never be listening to music."

"Hmmm. Can we maybe go in the direction I heard it?"

"Sure. Lead on."

After a few steps, she stopped. "There. I heard it again."

"Can you pinpoint more accurately where?"

"This way," she continued.

It wasn't long before Graham started to hear the music too. "Is that ... Christmas carols?" Natalie asked, hope lacing her voice. "Is someone singing Christmas carols? Could it be them?"

They were moving faster now through the undergrowth, growing closer to the sound. They could hear "Frosty" clearly, but still couldn't locate exactly where it was coming from.

Natalie called out their names and nearly collapsed in relief when they heard a faint "Here!"

"Oh my God. It is them!" she squeaked. "We hear you! Where are you? Keep talking so we can find you!"

"Here! Here!" they cried. "We're down here!" Natalie would have kept walking, drawn to the frightened voices, had Graham not reached out to stop her. There in front of them was a large drop-off, a cave-in of some old mine. Graham had been afraid of this.

He peered over the edge and spotted the little girl standing near her brother. She looked none the worse for wear, tired and dirty, but alive and well. "We're here, kids. We're gonna get you out."

"Miss Ghannon?" Lucy asked, her voice small and shaky.

"Yes, Lucy, it's me. I'm here with my friend Graham. He's gonna help me get you both out of there and home to your parents. Are you okay? Are either one of you hurt?"

Colin, who sat propped against the side of the hole, answered, "A few scrapes and bruises, but we're okay. Just cold and hungry."

"I bet," Natalie called back.

"Tell her about your ankle," she heard Lucy hiss to Colin.

"Shhh. It's okay, Lucy. I'm okay," Colin reassured his baby sister.

While Natalie comforted the kids, Graham studied the ground. If there was a mine shaft running under them, they could be susceptible to another cave-in at any moment. Placing a quick call to his team to give them his coordinates, he reached into his bag for his coil of climbing rope and harness. Donning his harness, he anchored the rope to the nearest sturdy tree. Then, grabbing his pack, he clipped into the rope and sent the loose end into the hole, his mind filled with calculations and safety procedures.

"Wait here for my team," he said to Natalie. She was staring at him, worry etched on her expressive features. "Don't worry," he stroked her cheek softly, wishing he didn't have his climbing gloves on so that he could feel the smoothness of her skin. "I'll get them out."

She nodded, and he slowly lowered himself down to the kids. It took seconds for him to reach them, and Lucy flung herself into his arms before he could detach from the rope. "You must be Lucy. I'm Graham." He chuckled as her little arms squeezed him tightly. "I've heard a lot about you."

"You have?"

"Yup." He tweaked her nose before setting her on her feet. Colin, he noticed, hadn't moved from his spot sitting against the side of the shaft. "Miss Ghannon has told me quite a few stories about her two best students." He knelt down near Colin, his pack between his knees. Reaching in, he pulled out two water bottles handing them to the kids. Colin opened his and handed it to his sister, taking hers for himself. Ever the big brother, Graham noted. He knew that feeling well. He'd always done the same when it came to David.

After they drank their fill, Graham handed each of them a granola bar which they devoured quickly. "What are those?" Lucy asked him when he pulled out the silver emergency blankets.

"These are special blankets to keep you warm." He shook one out of its packaging. "They are called space blankets. The astronauts use these in outer space."

"Cool," she chirped. He handed her a blanket, asking her to cover her brother with it, and wrapped her in the other. Then he studied the area the kids had stumbled into. The sun was going to set shortly, so he took out the small but powerful lantern he carried.

As far as mine shafts went, this one was not very impressive. Dug by hand a hundred or so years ago, the area they were currently in was just large enough to stand in, mostly due to the cave-in. The side that wasn't covered in debris had a tunnel that looked just big enough for a man to crawl through. Not his idea of a good time.

"Okay," he started as the kids ate a few more granola bars. "We're going to wait here a few more minutes till the rest of my team catches up to us. Then we're going to figure out a way to get you both safely out of here."

"You're not going to leave us, are you?" Colin tried to mask the note of panic in his voice. Obviously, the kid had been scared but had bravely kept it together for his sister.

Graham noticed the open lunch boxes beside Colin that still had some food inside, little half-eaten bites. Looks like the boy had been smart enough to ration their food. Graham was impressed. And he bet Lucy got the majority of the food.

"Nope," he answered Colin. "I'm staying right here with you two. We're in this together now."

"Oh. Okay. Good," Colin sighed, relieved not to have to be the brave one alone anymore. Graham looked the kid over, his blonde hair mussed and full of dirt, and dark circles under his eyes. A sure sign he probably had been too busy protecting Lucy to sleep much. But underneath, deep lines of pain were etched into his young face. He recalled Lucy muttering something about his ankle. The blanket didn't quite reach his feet, and Graham visually assessed the ankle in question. Definitely swollen. Possibly broken.

Tapping into his paramedic training, Graham reached into his pack for his first aid supplies. "Okay, Lucy," he said to the little blonde girl. "Let's get those cuts cleaned up."

"Are you a doctor?" she asked.

"No. A Paramedic," he answered as he cleaned the deepest cuts on her hands and arms.

"My daddy's a fireman. He sometimes has to doctor people too." Graham nodded to let the girl know he was listening as she prattled on about her father. After placing a bandage on a particularly nasty cut on the little girl's cheek, he turned to Colin.

"You're next."

"I'm fine," Colin balked, not wanting to look weak in front of his sister.

"Sorry. Nonnegotiable," he replied. "Hey, Lucy. Why don't you see if Miss Ghannon is still up there? Ask her if my team has arrived yet."

"Kay." She bounded over to a spot closer to the big hole to yell up to Natalie.

The look of relief on Colin's face spoke volumes. "Let's take a look at that ankle," Graham said softly. As gently as he could, Graham tended the ankle. Unable to tell at this point if it was broken, he wrapped an ace bandage around it, shoe, and all.

Since Lucy was still distracted chatting with Natalie, Graham moved on to the boy's hands. The fingers were scraped, bloody and raw. He had noted earlier that Colin kept his fists clenched while Lucy was around. The more he saw, the more his admiration for the brave boy grew.

"You tried to climb out, didn't you?" he asked as he cleaned and wrapped each finger with a bandage.

Colin nodded. "Kept slipping. Couldn't get a good grip."

"Is that how you messed up your ankle?"

Another nod. "It was so foggy I didn't see the hole until Lucy was already falling. I tried to stop her fall, but the ground gave way under me, and we both fell in. I wanted to climb out, get help, but ..."

"You did all you could," Graham assured Colin. "Are you a scout?" Colin nodded. "Is that where you learned to ration your food? I noticed the lunch boxes; that was really smart."

"I didn't know how long we'd be down here."

"You've got more survival instincts than some of my best Nighthawks." Colin beamed. "And the singing! That was genius."

"Lucy started that. She loves to sing. Especially Christmas songs. It kept her calm."

"Well, it worked. Miss Ghannon heard you from pretty far away. Without that, we might not have found you so soon."

Colin looked confused and disappointed. "I ... I thought someone would have found us long ago. Why did it take two days?"

"Well, the Sheriff had everybody looking in the woods behind your house. He figured you would have gone in there. It wasn't until Miss Ghannon began talking to some of your classmates that she learned about Donnie."

Colin made a disgusted sound in his throat. "I don't like him."

"Believe it or not, it was Donnie who helped us find you. He showed us where he lost you in the woods. I think he feels really bad about what happened to you."

"Sure," Colin said sarcastically, taking another chug from his water bottle.

"Anyway," Graham continued, "Miss Ghannon figured the Sheriff could use more manpower to search, so she came and got me this morning."

"Aren't you that guy who saved Marcus Rayne?"

Graham groaned inwardly. He was never going to get away from that. "Yup."

"And you came for us?"

"Well, when Miss Ghannon told me her kids were missing, I didn't hesitate."

"I didn't know she knew you."

"We grew up together. She was my neighbor. Can you believe today is the first time I've seen her in twelve years?"

"Really?"

"Yup. Sure did miss her," he mused.

"Hey Boss!" Finch, a Nighthawk teammate, called down to him from above. "You okay down there?"

"Absolutely!" he called back. "But I think my new friends would like to get out of here. Got a way to do that yet?"

"Working on it."

A few minutes later, Graham had strapped the kids into modified harnesses and was watching as they were hoisted out of the hole. Lauren had arrived with the O'Donnolls, and he could hear Lucy excitedly chatting to them as Lauren handed the girl a cookie. All was right with their world again.

Hours later, the Nighthawks, along with Natalie and Maddie, were enjoying dinner at Jolene's, a local Lake Haven watering hole. Atticus Mobey, who went by Finch in honor of his *To Kill a Mockingbird* namesake, was regaling the women with stories of some of their exploits. And of course, much to Graham's chagrin, they wanted to know all about the rescue of Marcus Rayne.

Finch, the Nighthawk helicopter pilot, had spent the first ten years of his adult life in the Air Force, having enlisted straight out of high school. He had a curly mop of red hair on the top of his head with the sides trimmed close. His hazel eyes shined with mirth. "And then he says to the boss man, 'Your life story would make a great movie. I'd like to buy the rights.' You wouldn't believe the look on boss man's face." He made a face somewhere between shock and disgust to illustrate.

The whole table erupted in laughter. "What did he say to that?" Maddie wondered.

Jude Riker picked up the thread of the story. "He looked at the guy for a moment as if he couldn't believe he'd just said that." Jude, formerly with the Army special forces, was a large, intimidating man with straight brown hair that was cut close to his skull. He was big and muscular, and his bulging biceps stretched the sleeves of his black t-shirt to their limit.

"Then he just walked away," finished Evan Cole, a former police officer. Sick of the politics, he'd left the Chicago police force but not before he'd taken several of Nighthawk's training seminars on his department's dime. It simply made sense that he made the transition to full teammate and fellow trainer. "The man could have been a multimillionaire, and he just walks away." Evan's face was expressionless under his brown hair, his blue eyes shuttered. He was quieter than the rest of the group, more reserved. Not as relaxed as the others.

"Not only that," Finch remarked, sending a frustrated hand through his curls as they fell – as usual – across his brow. "But the Nighthawks could have been fully funded for the rest of our lives!" He shook his head. He still couldn't believe Graham had turned down that offer. "What was the boss man thinking?"

"He gave us a sizable donation," David said, coming to his brother's defense.

Another teammate, Logan Cain, raised his beer in salute. "Cheers to that!" The table erupted in huzzah's all around, the clinking thuds of beer glasses ringing out across the bar. Logan was a former SEAL, his demeanor making him seem dark and brooding. He had brown hair with eyes that matched that dark vibe. There was an undertone of sadness in the man, one he didn't talk about with his teammates.

"Well, if this isn't just about the best-looking table I've ever had here!" cried a lovely redhead as she approached their tables. "Maddie, introduce me to your admirers."

"Everyone," Maddie said, getting the attention of the table. "This is Jolene Pritchett, proprietor and burger-making genius. And one of the best micro-brew masters in Southwest Michigan. The brew you are currently enjoying was designed by Jolene."

"You flatter," Jolene teased. "And yes, my mother was a Dolly Parton fan. And no, you can't sing it to me." Everyone laughed thinking she'd obviously heard too many joke and bad renditions of the song at her expense.

Maddie started to name everyone around the table. Finch stood up and inclined his head to Jolene; his old-fashioned manners so ingrained they often made the rest of the group look like assholes. "You made this?" he indicated his drink.

"That and a few others," Jolene answered with a wink swiping a stray strand of red hair behind her ear. Everyone praised her talent. She did make a decent beer.

"Heard the kids were found." Natalie nodded with a broad smile, her joy at the kids being found safe uncontainable. "Well, thank God for that. I'll let you all get back to it then," she said as she sauntered back to the bar. The men started teasing Finch for his obvious infatuation as they caught him staring after her. They all got a kick out of his unrelenting impeccable manners when it came to the opposite sex, but they'd never seen him so flustered before.

"I've heard you don't take any payments for the rescues you do," Maddie said, continuing the conversation that Jolene had interrupted. She sat on the other side of the table from Natalie between David and Finch. "How do you fund such an elaborate operation?" Maddie was a freelance bookkeeper; finances and numbers were her life. He couldn't fault her for being curious about the Nighthawk's finances.

"Donations mostly. But our training sessions and certification classes also help to offset the costs," Graham answered from his position next to Natalie. As he explained to Maddie how his operation stayed afloat, he casually sat back in his chair. Taking a slug from his glass, he stretched his right arm out across the back of Natalie's chair, his fingers lightly brushing her shoulder. He hid a smile behind his beer when he felt her tremble through his fingertips.

"You should watch the 20/20 interview Graham did a few months ago after all the Marcus Rayne hoopla," Logan said. "He explains how we operate in detail."

Natalie heard Graham groan. "That stupid interview. I should never have done it. It's sure to haunt me for the rest of my life."

"I did see it," Maddie exclaimed, ignoring Graham's complaint.

"What?" Natalie cried. "You didn't tell me anything about it."

"Where do you think I got the idea to ask them for help in finding Colin and Lucy?" Maddie replied.

"You haven't seen it?" Graham asked, aghast. "I thought the entire world had seen it by now."

"No. I told you I don't watch the news much," she replied. "I'm just surprised my own sister didn't tell me about it. I would have liked to have seen it."

"I bet you can still find it on the internet. Just search Graham's name," Jude supplied.

"Yeah, look," Finch said, holding up his phone. "It's one of the first stories that pop up under his name!" Graham rolled his eyes and groaned at his men. They all knew how much he hated that video, and they never passed up an opportunity to tease him about it.

"You should watch it, Natalie," Maddie told her. "I found it quite informative," she continued with a wink. *Fuck.* He forgot they had shown Natalie's nighthawk drawing in that interview. He'd referenced the artist as a "special friend" several times. He was suddenly glad she had never seen it.

"We also hold a few fundraisers throughout the year," Graham explained, desperate to change the subject.

"Yeah," Wyatt "Tin Man" Tinsley groaned. "Graham makes us dress up in those monkey suits." Tin Man, a former Ranger, was another good-looking Nighthawk. Especially when he smiled, and his dimple appeared to the left of his mouth.

"Not only that," Logan lamented. "He makes us schmoose too."

"But with your natural charisma, you do it so well, Cain," Tin Man teased. Logan shot a dark look at him. Tin Man winked back and blew him a kiss. His dark eyes rolled at the taunt.

"He may have the charisma," Finch mocked, "but I'm the one that looks the best in those monkey suits. All the women with their husband's big wallets flock to this magnificence." He spread his arms wide to flaunt his perceived good looks.

Chapter 4

A S THE MEN CONTINUED to tease each other about who's charm could bring in the largest donations, Natalie glanced across the table where Lauren was staring at her. There was something in that stare that unnerved her, but she couldn't place what it was making her feel. She smiled and inclined her head to Lauren to try to put them both at ease. Lauren's eyes flashed briefly to Graham's fingers brushing Natalie's shoulder, then away without returning the friendly smile. Natalie couldn't help but wonder what she had done that would cause the other woman to dislike her. Perhaps she was reading too much into the situation. She must be more tired than she thought. Natalie had spent the last two nights searching for and worrying about Colin and Lucy. Maybe the exhaustion was just catching up to her.

Natalie tried to stifle a yawn as the conversations from the group buzzed around her, but of course, Graham noticed. He leaned in closer to her, his lips inches from her ear as he asked, "Tired?"

Suppressing a shiver, Natalie nodded. "How 'bout I drive you home."

"You don't have to do that," Natalie replied. "I live close by and don't mind walking. You stay and enjoy your friends."

"I'll walk you then," he insisted.

"But your friends ..."

"I see them every day. I'd like to spend some time with you, catch up on what you've been doing over the years." She was filled with pleasure at hearing those words. She would love nothing more than to be with him a bit longer. She'd get to know him and learn all he'd done over the last twelve years, but she was terrified thinking that he'd also want to learn about her. There were parts of her history that she'd rather not think about.

Giving her no room for argument, he stood up, drawing the attention of the group. Grabbing her elbow to help her stand, he explained to them all, "I'm going to walk Natalie home." The Nighthawks nodded and returned to their conversations.

"You okay?" Maddie asked, concerned for her baby sister. She knew the ordeal of the last few days had been stressful.

"Just tired. I haven't slept well since the kids went missing," Natalie explained. "Do you want to come with us?" Natalie and Maddie shared a duplex, each with their own side and had worked hard to refurbish it to suit their needs.

"Do you mind if I stay here a bit longer?"

"I'll make sure she gets home safely," David supplied.

"Not at all," Natalie assured. "Have fun. It was nice meeting all of you," she said to the group of Nighthawks. They all returned the sentiment.

"Ready?" Graham held his hand out for her. As she slipped her fingers into his, her gaze once again met Lauren's cold stare.

Before she could think more of it, he was steering them toward the door. Graham still held her hand as they walked to her house and chatted about nonsensical things. It was a perfect October evening. The kind of weather that was neither too warm nor too cold. But there was still a slight bite to the air that indicated winter was coming, especially in the breeze coming off Lake Michigan.

Lake Haven was a quaint town in southwest Michigan. During the summer, it was filled with tourists from big cities like Chicago, who were drawn to the sugar sand of the lakeshore. The charming shops at the top of the bluff that overlooked the lake only added to the delightful Lake Haven experience. All of them had some variation of the Haven name, which Natalie found utterly captivating. From Brew-tiful Haven, the coffee shop, to Haven in Ink, a tattoo parlor; Haven Vine, the wine tasting shop, was located next to Torch of Haven, a candle shop where customers could not only buy premade candles, but also mix their own wax colors and scents. The whimsical shop names always amused her.

When they approached the front steps of the duplex only two blocks from the main part of town, Natalie said, "This is me on the right. Maddie's place is the left side." She tried to see her home through Graham's eyes. The porch stretched across the front of both halves. They had removed the fence that split it so that they both could enjoy the whole space. There was a welcoming assortment of seating spread across the deck, including a porch swing at the end of Natalie's side. Since it was fall, Maddie had replaced the summer flowers in the pots scattered around with a few colorful mums and pumpkins sat on the steps waiting to be carved for Halloween. It was a quaint, welcoming space. Each spring, the sisters worked together to get their garden cleaned up and blooming. And each fall, they worked to put it to sleep for the winter. Natalie loved those simple days. It was hard work, but so worth it. Most of their summer evenings were spent lounging on this porch.

"I hadn't realized you two lived together," Graham said.

"Together but separate," Natalie explained. "The duplex is technically two separate houses, but Maddie and I cut a doorway in our laundry rooms so we can easily get to each other's place. And we share the front porch, the gardens, and the deck out back."

"It's nice."

"It works for us. After the tornado, I spent so much time taking care of Maddie that it just made sense for us to share a place like this. We each have our own space but can still be there for each other when needed. And believe me, that has come in handy – for both of us." She flashed briefly back over four years ago when Natalie had been the one to need Maddie's help. For a moment, her vision clouded as she remembered that day. She could still taste the fear on her tongue. Still caught up in the questions. How had things gone bad so fast with her ex? How had she not seen the desperate madness that lived inside him until it was nearly too late?

"Do you want to come in?" Natalie asked, shaking herself out of her morose thoughts. She was holding her breath for his answer but not sure how she wanted him to answer. Her fears were embedded so deeply that she wasn't sure she could ever escape them. After that experience, she'd never wanted anything more with anyone; but she thought that perhaps this man with his intense blue eyes that shone with kindness might finally be the one to help her heal.

She was shocked at where her thoughts were going, she must be more tired than she'd thought. It was the first time in twelve years that they'd seen each other. She might have fallen for him a little bit that day at the lake, but her feelings had had twelve years to cool down, fizzle, and die. Yet, when she looked into his eyes ... when he smiled at her, she couldn't help but wonder "what if."

"It's such a nice night. How 'bout we sit on that great swing for a little while?"

"I'd like that."

Graham sent the swing into a gentle motion as they sat in silence for a moment, his leg brushing against hers, sending little tremors through her body. Crickets serenaded them as they rocked. "I really can't thank you enough for your help today."

"I'm glad I could help. I could tell those kids meant a lot to you."

"Most of my students mean the world to me but with Lucy, it's different. She's only five, but her talent is years beyond most masters. I look forward to harnessing and molding that talent, helping her grow."

"Do you enjoy teaching?"

"I do, though I sometimes wish I had more time for my own work. I'd love to open my own studio someday, maybe give private lessons to kids like Lucy."

"So why don't you?"

"I don't know. For many years, I was busy taking care of Maddie, so I focused on finishing my degree and getting a steady paycheck. But she's been doing so well ... amazingly well actually, that maybe I *can* start planning for my own dreams." It hadn't occurred to her until that moment that she probably could have her own studio. It was a realization that would need some serious mulling over.

"I hope someday you achieve everything you want."

Natalie blushed. She'd never once in the last twelve years imagined she deserved to have her own dreams fulfilled. She loved her job, loved teaching, and every aspect of it. She couldn't imagine a day without seeing their smiling faces. The joy they experienced while they created something from their own imagination fulfilled her. Some days, though she hated to admit it, she yearned for more.

"It certainly looks like you've achieved some success of your own," Natalie said. "Your complex is impressive."

"It's taken a long time to get there, and we still have a long way to go. But I'm happy with it. It was a group effort. Those guys tonight have done more for Nighthawk than I can ever repay. I've been very lucky."

"Have you been interested in Search and Rescue since the night of the tornado?" That day, that *night* was etched into both their memories. Briefly, they flashed back to the moment when from his car, they watched as the tornado barreled down on their neighborhood.

"In a way. I just didn't know I could do it for a living at that time. I had intended to be a business major or an engineer. I hadn't decided yet. But in my first year of college, I joined a group of other students for spring break. We headed out to Illinois to help people recover from flooding. It was our job to remove the old, moldy drywall from houses that had been affected and replace it with new. But while we were there, the rain started up again.

"It was crazy. One minute we were just doing our job, the next, the street was completely flooded again. The river encroached, flooding the houses we had just repaired. We were suddenly trapped. The house next door had an old rowboat in the driveway. We 'commandeered' it to get out."

"Interesting way to put it," Natalie smirked.

He smiled. "As we went along, we saw people everywhere, trapped on porches, on roofs, on anything high they could get to while the water continued to rise. We took as many as we could, got them out, then went back for more."

"That was very brave," Natalie told him, impressed by his giving nature.

He shrugged. "We just did what was right. They were all so grateful. It made me feel … important, I guess. I don't know how else to put it. It was an awesome feeling to have helped so many people."

"I can understand that. It's kind of how I feel when a student finally 'gets it.' A joy every teacher loves to experience."

"Exactly," he smiled at her, happy that she understood so easily. "Eventually, I met a guy who was with the National Guard and we got to talking about that feeling. He told me as a police officer in Chicago, he had taken some special training courses for search and rescue so that summer, I found a place that offered similar courses and was hooked."

"Why did you decide to open your own training facility?" Natalie asked beyond curious to learn his story.

He smiled sadly. "I've spent most of my adult life traveling the globe. Pitching in on some of the biggest disasters. I've been on many missions; digging people out of whatever situation they've been trapped in. The skills I've learned have enabled me to save lives." He paused and sighed sadly. Natalie grew concerned, noticing his furrowed brow. "Then there are the recovery missions. So many recoveries. So many that I couldn't save. The tsunami in Indonesia was the worst. I needed a break from it all and thought I could share my skills with others. I discovered there was a need for the type of training I could offer in this area."

Natalie reached for his hand, entwining her fingers with his and squeezing gently in sympathy as they rocked slowly back and forth on the swing. "I'm sorry you had to go through that. I've heard stories about how horrible the tsunami was, but I never realized you were there. I can't imagine what you've seen." She shivered slightly, whether from the chill in the air or from imagining the horrors of that disaster, she couldn't say.

"Cold?" he asked in concern.

"No, just a little chill," she replied. He let go of her hand and placed his arm around her shoulders, drawing her closer to his side, sharing his body heat with her. It was a sweet, almost romantic gesture. She couldn't hold back the contented sigh as his warmth enveloped her.

The tender sensation of Natalie leaning into his warmth as he wrapped his arm around her had the magical effect of chasing away the images of bloated bodies he'd seen in Indonesia. He felt more than heard her sigh of contentment, struggling to contain his own groan as desire rushed through him.

Shit! Even after twelve years, she still had a devastating effect on him. He flashed back to that kiss by the lake. A kiss he'd measured all other kisses against for the last twelve years. All of which fell short of the passion and heat of that one simple kiss.

Twelve years! Graham felt an overwhelming regret at the loss of all those years. He didn't understand how one afternoon by the lake could have changed him so dramatically. He had dated through the years, of course, but they had all left him feeling flat; nobody could measure up to his little chickadee.

He'd spent the last twelve years thinking he was crazy. It wasn't possible to fall for someone in one afternoon; that was just crazy. Then he saw her standing in his conference room earlier today, and something clicked. The others he'd dated never felt right because they weren't Natalie. It terrified him to think that he'd found his other half, and he still didn't know if she was married or not.

"Can I ask you a question?" she queried quietly.

"Absolutely." He knew he would answer anything, tell her anything, give her anything if he could keep her by his side a little while longer.

"Why did you never come back to visit?" The town they had both grown up in was about an hour south of Lake Haven, over the border in Indiana at the bottom point of Lake Michigan. After the tornado, he'd had to move farther away from the lake he loved and had never gone back. He would never understand why he didn't go back. "I mean, after the tornado and you guys left to live with your grandmother, I thought surely I'd see you again, especially at your graduation. I looked for you," she finished softly, looking down at her lap.

The tornado had left his house uninhabitable, so he and his family had spent a few days crashing with friends, helping with the clean-up in town. He had kept an eye out, hoping to see Natalie around, and had found out what had happened to her sister, after which he'd assumed she'd spent most of her time at the hospital.

Eventually, his family was forced to salvage what they could and move to live with his grandmother until they could rebuild. By the time the house had been rebuilt, Graham had been in college and then gone off on his search and rescue endeavors. He'd barely had time to visit his parents during those years. And when he'd been ready to start up Nighthawk, his parents had moved to Virginia. "They let me finish up the school year by correspondence. I got my diploma by mail and never made it to graduation."

"Oh," she said feebly. "You had lots of friends here. Didn't you want to reconnect with any of them in twelve years?"

"No," he answered honestly.

He watched as her face fell. She was unable to hide her disappointment at his answer. The whole truth was there wasn't anybody he wanted to see again from his hometown except for his little chickadee, and that had shocked him. He'd allowed his fears and insecurities to keep him away, telling himself that it had only been a few hours he'd spent with her that afternoon. A few hours and one scorching hot kiss.

"Well, there was one person," he admitted, squeezing her shoulder. Her face brightened hesitantly. He loved that he could read her expressions so easily. "But I was terrified to see her again, afraid I'd be disappointed." Throughout the years, he'd thought of her often. But then his thoughts had turned to images of her happily married with a litter of kids. Those thoughts depressed him so much that it was easier to just stay away from her.

"I don't understand," she said, her brow creasing.

"I was afraid I'd find her happily married with two point five kids."

"Ha!" she snorted. "Couldn't be further from the truth."

"Really?" He asked hopefully. Even to himself, he sounded like a lovesick schoolboy.

"Really. I was engaged once. It ended badly." She shivered again, and a dark expression clouded her eyes. He wanted to delve into the reasons for the dark look, but he could see the exhaustion weighing on her. He should go and let her get some sleep, but he couldn't seem to pull himself away from her.

Graham heard voices drift towards them and moments later, David and Maddie came into view. Natalie stood up quickly. "I didn't realize it was so late, I really should get to bed. I've got school in the morning."

"Okay," he said, already missing her warmth immensely. He knew he couldn't stay away this time. He couldn't go another twelve years without seeing her again. "I'd like to see you again. How 'bout I take you out to dinner tomorrow night?"

She blushed but grinned with pleasure. "I'd like that."

"Great! Pick you up at seven?"

"Can we make it six since it's a school night?"

He smiled. "In that case, I'll have to make sure to get you home before curfew."

They joined Maddie and David at the steps to say their goodnights. Graham longed to kiss her but didn't want to embarrass her in front of her sister. He told himself it was too early for kisses. He couldn't just kiss her after knowing her again for one day and then leave. He needed to do this right.

"Don't be a stranger," Maddie was saying to David.

"Oh, I'll be back. Especially now that I've found the best burger joint in the state!" They all laughed as the girls turned to go in while the brothers walked quickly back to the restaurant where they'd left the truck.

"So ... what was that between the two of you?" David asked.

"What?" Graham feigned indifference.

"The intensity off the two of you was hot!"

"I don't know what you're talking about." Graham wasn't ready to share with David. It was too new. Even he didn't entirely understand what had happened today. It would take some mulling over.

"Right," David drew out the word.

Chapter 5

PROMPTLY AT SIX THE next evening, Graham was at Natalie's door, his stomach in knots. He'd been unable to sleep the night before, the day by the lake endlessly repeating through his mind. As he escorted Natalie to a quiet booth in the corner of Jolene's, his anxiety surprised him. He was unaccustomed to feeling unsure in any situation. He'd placed the Natalie he knew from that afternoon on a pedestal for so many years that he was afraid the Natalie of today wouldn't compare. He was worried too, that if she were everything he'd remembered and dreamed, he might do something to mess it up. After placing their orders, Graham took a deep breath to calm his nerves, and asked about her teaching.

"I love it. I really do," she explained. He sensed her hesitancy.

"But ..."

She smiled. "But I do miss having more time to work on my own things. As I said, I'd like to open my own studio and take on the students who genuinely wanted to be there."

"So why don't you?"

"Money. Time. There's never enough of either."

He could understand that. It had taken a substantial amount of capital and a generous inheritance from his grandmother to start up Nighthawk. He and David had been shocked to discover their battle-axe of a grandmother had been a multi-millionaire. She'd horded away an inheritance, investing wisely, building her portfolio until she had a nice fat nest egg, the majority of which was left to her grandsons upon her death. It made sense to the brothers to pool their money and build Nighthawk together. David, having been a business major in college, had the wherewithal to invest wisely, which had allowed them to build Nighthawk slowly.

They still relied on the generous donations they received to keep the day-to-day operations running, as well as the fees they charged for their training sessions, but they'd occasionally had to dip into their investments to add to their business. So far, they'd been able to develop an urban rescue training area that consisted of buildings that looked like they'd been destroyed by various disasters. The previous summer, they'd added several climbing facilities, both indoors and out. There was also a large building they used for offices and classrooms, and the four-story dorm complete with dining hall and industrial kitchen.

After the first year of operations, Graham found that the groups that came to the Nighthawk complex to train benefited from on-site lodging. He'd had the dorm built, his men affectionately calling it "the barracks," since most of them had a military background. Over the years, a few of the Nighthawks had stayed at the barracks until they could find their own apartments.

Graham had purposely bought the land they were on because of the woods and river that ran through it, allowing them to do SAR training. So far, it had worked well, and they were becoming fairly successful. They had been able to tap into the area's first responders' - police, fire, and others - need for proper training and were currently branching out to the surrounding states' first responders as well. It had been a lot of hard work and had required a lot of time, but it had been worth it. He now had an excellent group of guys that he worked closely with and was able to spend most of his time passing on his knowledge of SAR while still going out on the occasional rescue, as he had for Natalie's students. Every now and then, he and his fellow Nighthawks deployed to wherever they might be needed. It allowed him to put the horrors he had seen behind him.

"Ahh, the great struggle every human battles against," he sympathized. "Do you still get to do your own art?"

"Sometimes. Not as much as I wish," she lamented. "I'm working mostly with oil paints these days. It can be slow going with everything else that interferes. Taking care of Maddie all those years restricted the time I could dedicate to my art. These last few years though, she's been doing so well that I find myself having more free time."

"She is lucky to have you." He'd made her blush again. He loved seeing that bit of color flood her cheeks; it was endearing. He studied her across the table. Her hair hung long and loose around her shoulders, and he longed to run his fingers through the silken strands. When she had answered her door, he'd nearly fallen to his knees in front of her. She was wearing a tight little denim skirt that left just enough bare leg to ramp up his desire. She'd paired the skirt with a white blouse that hugged her curves so perfectly he wanted to reach out and touch her to make sure she was real. He stared into her glorious green eyes, fighting the urge to lower his to the enticing glimpse of cleavage her blouse revealed. But the pull was irresistible.

The waitress chose that moment to bring them their meals. Both were burgers; his piled with a generous portion of bacon, and hers loaded with cheese that was melting out the sides of the bun. Both looked amazingly tasty, and he couldn't wait to sink his teeth into his.

"Can I ask where your parents were? Didn't they help take care of Maddie?" he asked around a bite of the juicy burger.

A flash of anger moved through her eyes. But there was a resigned sadness beneath the anger. "About a year after the tornado, the day after I graduated from high school, in fact, they moved to Florida. Maddie and I decided to stay here. I went off to get my degree while Maddie learned to deal with her new reality. My parents generously paid for everything, an apartment for us, food, tuition. Everything we needed," she intoned sarcastically.

"Except for their time and love," he guessed. How sad for the two sisters. He'd been lucky with his family. He still had the love and respect of his parents. They had moved to Virginia following the death of his grandmother, but they still visited each other as often as they could. They had been beyond supportive of his Nighthawk dream.

"It was harder for Maddie, I think." She dabbed her lips with her napkin, and he'd never been so jealous of a napkin before as he watched the material drift across her mouth. "She went from being their darling girl to their pariah. In her mind, she lost her leg and her parents' love and struggled with that for years."

"Must have been hard for you too, taking up the slack for them," he said reluctantly, pulling his gaze from her lips.

"I'd spent most of my life being the black sheep in the family, so I knew how to help Maddie deal with it. She was in a dark place for a long time. I'm proud of the woman she's fought so hard to become, she's an inspiration." The love and respect she had for her sister shone from her face. He understood that since he and David also had a close relationship.

Graham's phone buzzed, indicating a text had come in. He hated to do it, but he took the phone out to look at it. Never knowing when the team would be needed meant that he made sure to answer every text that came through. It was David. A group of kayakers had gone missing on the river and the Nighthawks had been asked to help in the search. His heart sank. He hated to do this to Natalie; he didn't want to cut their evening short.

"What is it?" she asked, sensing his disappointment and frustration.

"I have to go."

"Oh," she said, her face falling as she sipped her beer.

"I hate to do this to you. I was having such a great time, but I never know when the Nighthawks will be needed. There's a group missing on the river. I have to go," he finished reaching for his wallet. He signaled for the waitress to take his credit card. "Stay and finish if you want. Or I can take you home real quick."

"I'll leave now as well." She stood and grabbed the light jacket she had worn. Her disappointment was almost as palpable as his. When he pulled up to the front of her house, he got out to walk her to her door.

"Do me a favor, text me when you're done. Doesn't matter what time. I ... I'd like to know when you're safe."

He leaned in to kiss her cheek. "Sure thing, chickadee. I'll talk to you later," he added as he headed back to his car. He was thinking of seriously killing his brother for calling him in on this one. But Graham understood his skills would be needed.

"How was your dinner?" David asked Graham as the zodiac raced down the St. Joseph River, Logan at the helm. The three of them stood behind the console windshield at the bow of the Rigid Inflatable Boat - otherwise known as RIB - eyes scanning for the lost group of boaters.

Graham snorted. "Short."

"Sorry about that." David paused to study a cluster of trees more closely. "So, what is going on with the two of you?"

"Is this really the time?" Graham asked as he scanned the river for the missing kayakers using the large spotlight to illuminate the area.

"I think so."

"Me too!" shouted Logan over the roar of the outboard motor. They had decided to use their smaller RIB since it was reported that only five men were missing. Even with the three Nighthawks, there would be plenty of room for the kayakers. Being a former SEAL, Logan was the ideal choice if a water rescue was needed. He was in his element in the water.

"Seriously though, Graham," David continued. "I am a bit surprised that you two clicked so fast. I thought you hadn't had much contact with her since elementary school."

"That's not exactly true," Graham relented, knowing David would never give it a rest.

"What does that mean?" David shone his light into another area of thick foliage.

"We spent some time together when I was a senior."

"Really? But I thought you were dating that other girl. What was her name? Kelly? No Callie, right?"

"Laney. Yeah, no. I dumped her."

"Not surprising." Graham had been notorious for dating and dumping during high school. "But Natalie wasn't your usual type back then. Bit of an outsider, wasn't she?"

"She was," Graham said with a slight smile remembering Natalie as she was that day, so unlike any of the other girls he'd ever socialized with. Maybe that was why he'd been so fascinated with her then. She was interesting and smart. He'd enjoyed talking with her much more than he'd ever enjoyed talking to the ditzy girls he'd dated in high school. Hair and makeup, who was dating who, that was all they wanted to talk about. It grew tiresome very quickly. But with Natalie, the conversation had been stimulating.

"And you dated her? How did I never know?"

"No," Graham stated, unable to hide his amusement at his brother's bewilderment.

"No what?"

"No, we didn't date."

David shot him a look of confusion. "I don't get it. Why do you seem so interested in her now? And that hug you gave her. I'd never seen you so happy to see an old flame before."

"She's not an old flame. We just had a nice afternoon together."

"One afternoon?" Logan wondered, unashamedly eavesdropping.

"Did you sleep with her?" David asked as his eyebrows shot upward.

"Of course not. We just talked."

"You shared one afternoon together and just *talked*?" Graham found it amusing that David was having such a hard time grasping that concept. The brother David had known as a lady's man in high school, would never have spent an afternoon just talking to a girl.

"Yup," he answered, failing to stifle his laugh.

"When was this?" David was still trying to understand.

"The day of the tornado."

"Seriously?"

"What tornado?" Logan asked at the same time.

"The tornado that destroyed our house when we were in high school," David answered. "Wait. I remember. She was there, wasn't she? She's the one you talk about in that interview, isn't she?"

"She's the 'slow your panic' friend?" Logan was equally as bewildered as David.

"Yup," Graham answered simply.

"Holy hell!" David cried, grabbing his hat before a gust of wind knocked it off his head.

"Isn't she an art teacher?" Logan asked.

"Holy hell!" David shouted. "It's her nighthawk drawing, isn't it?"

"Yup."

"Holy hell," he swore again. "I need to sit down." He plopped down hard on the bench seat behind him.

Logan shot Graham a look over his shoulder. "You named your company after her drawing?"

"Why?" David still couldn't understand. No one could understand. Graham could hardly understand most days why one afternoon spent talking to a neighbor changed him so radically. His only answer was the girl herself. She must have been something special back then. Graham wondered if she'd still be just as special today. He was looking forward to exploring that thought further.

Graham shrugged in answer to David's question. "We talked. She told me a story about nighthawks, and it stuck with me. She stuck with me."

"Understatement," Logan muttered under his breath. "I had a friend like that growing up too," he told them sadly.

"What happened?" Graham could sense that there was a story there.

"Same as you, I guess. We lost touch." Graham didn't think that was all. There was something behind the sadness in his eyes. A loss that had buried itself bone-deep. Graham could sense Logan was troubled about something in his past, but he was closed off about it. Maybe, someday, the SEAL would open up to them. He'd learned long ago it wasn't healthy to let things fester.

David swept his light upriver. "Why didn't you ever tell me?"

He shrugged again, having often wondered that himself. He figured he had wanted to keep that unusual time to himself. It was precious to him. He'd felt guilty for not telling his brother and business partner since they usually shared everything with each other. Why, then, had he never told David the truth about that day? He didn't have an answer.

David shook his head in disbelief. "And you never slept with her?"

"Nope. Just a conversation. Well, that and a kiss."

"Ha!" David exclaimed. "I knew there had to have been something else. Damn, if she's that important to you, what are you doing here now? We could have handled this one without you."

"I know, but it's my job."

"Shit, there's your superhero complex again."

"What are you talking about?" Graham was shocked at the tone in David's voice.

David sighed. "You have this need to always be the one to save the day. It's admirable, but you are allowed to have a life of your own."

"You've trained us all well," Logan added. "We can occasionally handle a mission without you. Especially those of us with special forces training." Logan grinned, his amusement that Graham thought they couldn't do the job without him shining behind his eyes. "I know that," Graham insisted.

"So, maybe we need to make some changes. We've spent so much of our time and energy developing Nighthawk, building our reputation, that maybe now that we are doing so well, it's time for us to loosen the reigns a bit." David had a valid point. But SAR had been his life for so long that he didn't know how to let go. He'd never forgive himself if he did, and something happened that he could have prevented. For a chance to spend more time with Natalie, he just might consider it.

"Two o'clock, guys!" Logan shouted.

The brothers both looked ahead to the right, seeing the kayakers waving their hands in the air to get their attention. Logan maneuvered the RIB closer to the men who were relieved someone had spotted them and doubly grateful it was a team of Nighthawks. They were all uninjured and dry, just lost. They loaded the men into the RIB, tied the kayaks together to the back, and took them to their launching place. It took another hour to get back to the Nighthawk's dock and securely store the boat.

Graham looked at his watch. It was too late to call Natalie, but he'd promised her he'd let her know when he was safe. He typed a quick text as he made his way to his truck.

The text came through at two in the morning, allowing Natalie to finally relax enough to fall asleep. Her dreams were filled with the man who currently occupied way too much space in her head. It had been only two days since they'd reconnected, but she already felt like she knew him better than she'd known her ex-fiancé. She'd never felt like her ex had truly let her in; that should have been her first clue to the type of man he would later show himself to be.

Natalie had been disappointed when Graham had had to cut their evening short, but she'd also been extremely proud. He did important work. She had firsthand knowledge of that since he'd found Colin and Lucy so quickly, a feat the Sheriff was still complaining about even as he took credit for the decision to bring the Nighthawks in. Of course, the entire town knew that for the lie that it was.

After he'd dropped her off last night, she'd done an internet search and found the interview everyone had been talking about, curiosity getting the better of her. It was an hour-long episode of 20/20 featuring Marcus Rayne's rescue and Graham's life history. She, of course, knew at least half of his history, but the rest was fascinating. What was most surprising was how predominantly *she* featured in that history even though he'd never named her. Graham told the reporter how a "special friend's" advice to him while helping save his brother after the tornado, had stuck with him ever since.

Twelve years ago

Natalie watched in horror as the tornado made a beeline straight for Graham's house. It was like a living thing, eating up everything in its path, leaving nothing unscathed. Roof shingles and siding torn off houses on both sides of the street. Trees pulled out by the roots and flung far. Even cars didn't escape the destruction. The image of a two-ton car being tossed around like a toy would forever be imprinted in her memory.

The tornado shifted slightly right as it barreled towards their houses. Natalie's house was to the right of Graham's, the vortex sucking the siding off the side of the house. Her favorite tree in the front yard was reduced to kindling. But it was watching what was happening to Graham's house that was the most heartbreaking. The whirling creature cut through the house, as if it entered through the front door and walked straight to exit out the back door. Walls disappeared, windows, furniture, books, electronics, stairs – everything gone. The only thing remaining after the tornado wreaked its havoc was one outside wall, the back corner, and a small section of roof attached to that wall.

"I think my brother was in there," Graham blurted out in horror. Natalie stared at him. She didn't know how anybody could have survived that. She gave a brief thought to Maddie and her parents, though she didn't think any of them had been home, but the damage there wasn't as devastating as it was at Graham's house. She didn't have any time to think about her family as Graham had thrown the car into gear again and was speeding toward what was left of his house, not caring about the debris he was crashing through as he raced to get home as quickly as he could.

Slamming the car in park, Graham threw himself out the door to race to his brother, Natalie right on his heels. She noticed the remaining wall trembled, ready to collapse, and instinctively knew it wouldn't be a good idea to enter. She yelled for Graham to stop, but his focus was entirely on getting to his brother. It wasn't until she placed herself directly in front of him, set a palm flat on his chest, and screamed for him to stop that he finally paused.

"You can't go in there right now!" she cried. He made a choked sound of denial; his eyes wide, darting around, and unable to focus. His thoughts were completely on his brother. "Look," Natalie indicated the precariously wobbling wall. "That might come down any time, and if you are in there when it does ..." she let the thought trail off, too disturbed to even think about it.

"The sirens went off before the tornado, right?" she reasoned. "David probably heard them. Where do you guys go when the sirens sound?" She could tell Graham wasn't hearing her. He was too panicked, too worried to focus on her words, his breathing way too fast. "Graham!" she yelled louder. He looked at her, eyes wide, the pupils dilated. Okay. She had to get him to focus. Had to get him to understand before he did something stupid and got himself killed. "Where would David go when he heard the sirens?"

She could see reason slowly return to his brain. "Umm ... basement. Yeah, the basement. That's where we were always told to go."

"Okay. Basement. Good," she was thinking out loud. How were they going to get to the basement with the piles of debris all over? Not to mention that unstable wall. "Where ... where are the basement steps?" It had been a long time since she'd been inside the Whitaker house and couldn't recall exactly where the basement had been.

"Umm ..." he muttered.

His eyes darted to the house; she was losing him again. "Graham!" she shouted. "The steps! Picture your house in your mind and find the basement steps!"

"Right. Basement. Steps ... There!" He pointed to an area in the middle of the house.

Okay, progress. But if they started digging to get to the steps, they ran the risk of moving the wrong thing and having that wall come crashing down on top of them.

"I've got to get him out!" Graham was moving toward the house again.

"Graham!" she shouted once more. He stopped abruptly. "Stop and think! Slow your panic! I know you want to get to David as quickly as possible, but fast is not always best. You can't help him if you are freaking out!" She was desperate to make him understand.

He still wasn't getting it. He was too worried about David. Too distracted. Natalie grabbed his face between her hands and forced him to look at her. "Slow. Your. Panic." She enunciated each word until she could see them sink into his unfocused brain. "You must think!" she reiterated. She used her hands to turn his face to the unstable wall. "That wall. It could collapse at any time. You'd be no help to your brother if you are in there when it does." She couldn't help the shiver of fear that swept up her body at the thought of being crushed by that wall.

"Right," Graham sighed. "Right. What do we do? I can't just wait here. He might be hurt." He was trying so desperately to hold in his panic, Natalie's heart went out to him.

"I think ... I think we need to find a way to stabilize it. Shore it up somehow." She thought she remembered something about how to do that. Something about bracing pieces.

Natalie looked around her. Searching for inspiration. To her left, she spotted some long two-by-fours that must have come from someone's home workshop. Those might do. She pointed at the boards, explaining her plan. Graham caught on quickly and went to work. Finally having something for his panicked brain to concentrate on helped to keep him focused as they gingerly braced the damaged wall with the long planks. Natalie ignored the splinters and cuts as they worked quickly and efficiently. Once they were satisfied that the wall was stable, at least for now, they got to work on finding the steps to the basement.

After what seemed like hours but was, in fact, merely minutes, they uncovered the hole to the basement. The stairs, for the most part, were still intact.

"David!" Graham called as he carefully placed a foot on the first stair. They were both unsure if the stairs were safe or if they were damaged somehow, and if the first weight that was placed on them would cause them to collapse.

"I'm here!" a voice called back. And suddenly, he was there. Standing at the bottom of the staircase. He smiled up at them, a look of hero worship for his big brother. Reassuring themselves that the stairs were safe, David raced up and threw himself into Graham's arms. The brothers *hugged each other tightly as Natalie fought the lump of emotion that had lodged itself in her throat. She was happy for them, but she couldn't relax until she found her own family.*

Present Day

Natalie's words, as Graham had stated in that stupid interview, had indeed stuck with him. 'Slow your panic' had been his mantra all these years. Every search. Every rescue, every training mission, he recited those words. He wondered, not for the first time, if Natalie knew the lasting impact she and her words would have on him from that day forward. *If she watched the interview, she probably figured it out, asshole.*

His mind drifted back to that day after the tornado as he listened to Finch intone about tracking skills and sign cutting to a group of policemen from Grand Rapids. Yes, he and his family had lost their home and all their belongings that day, but they had each other. He and Natalie had managed to save David. And Graham was eternally grateful for her help. He was very lucky.

But Natalie, it seemed, hadn't been quite so lucky. Losing his favorite skateboard seemed insignificant to all that Natalie had lost. Even though her house had suffered minimal damage, the tornado had shattered the Ghannon family. He regretted that he hadn't been there for Natalie like she was for him. He wished with all his heart that he had been able to return her sister to her whole as she had with David. But it wasn't until the early hours of the next morning that they'd found the mangled car and Maddie unconscious inside.

Graham had been too focused on himself and his own family to realize the turmoil and distress Natalie had gone through. Even all these years later, he still didn't know the whole story. How *had* Maddie lost her leg? And he asked himself why their parents would leave Natalie alone to deal with it all. She seemed to have accepted their abandonment, but he felt compelled to be angry at them on her behalf. He couldn't imagine his parents or David ever deserting him. Not for anything. The tornado had taught them all about how precious life was. Graham's family lived life to the fullest every day.

The buzzing in his pocket brought Graham back to the present. He smiled as he saw it was a text from Natalie. She was asking him to call her. He excused himself from the training seminar and stepped out into the hall, dialing her number.

"Hey, Chickadee. What's up?"

"How did it go last night?" she asked.

"It was good. We found the kayakers quickly enough. They had just gotten turned around and couldn't find their landing spot." The group of morons hadn't thought to bring a compass with them. Or GPS. Or even their cell phones. *Who does that in this day and age? Idiots.*

"That's good. I'm glad they were safe."

"Me too."

"Umm ... the reason I wanted to talk to you ... and you can feel free to say no," she rushed on to assure him. "My principal has asked me to ask if you would be willing to do an assembly for the kids. You know, general stuff, about what you do."

It amused him that she was rambling. She clearly felt awkward asking him. He quickly answered to put her at ease, "I'd love to." He'd done numerous assemblies for different schools. He mostly focused on teaching them basic survival skills like the ones Colin had learned in scouts. But sometimes, especially with the older kids, they got curious about some of the big disasters he'd assisted with, and they were always full of questions.

"That's great! We were wondering if next Friday would work for you. Or if it's too soon, we can schedule it for another time," she sounded flustered again. "It's just that we were going to have an award ceremony for Colin. We wanted to recognize his resilience and bravery. We thought if you could be there too ..." she trailed off.

"Friday's good. I'm free all day." He could audibly hear her sigh of relief.

"My principal will be so relieved." After finalizing the plans, he hung up and slipped his phone back into his pocket. As he returned to the training room, his thoughts again drifted to his little chickadee. Ten days. He could wait ten days to see her again. Couldn't he?

No, he couldn't. He stepped outside the room again and hit the phone symbol next to Natalie's name, calling her back immediately.

She answered on the first ring. "Is something wrong?"

"Yes," he stated. "I can't wait until next Friday to see you. Have dinner with me again."

"Oh ... well ... okay," she spluttered.

"Great! When are you free?"

"I could do this Friday if you want."

"Perfect. Pick you up at six?"

"Okay. See you then."

Graham smiled as he walked back into the training room. He hadn't felt this exhilarated for a date in ... forever.

Chapter 6

H E DID SAY HE'D *pick me up at six ... right?* Natalie paced the floor in front of her fireplace. It was only ten minutes past six, and he was late with no text or call informing her that he was delayed. *Maybe I got the time wrong. Or the day?*

But then another thought crept into her head. Maybe he'd been hurt on a rescue and couldn't call her. Maybe he was lying in the hospital right now. Or worse.

Panicked at the direction in which her mind was taking her, she wished she had a phone number for his teammates to find out. Maybe one of them knew about their planned date and would try to contact her. Surely David would. If something had happened, she needed to know.

She shook her head. No, he was fine. Just a few minutes late. No need to panic. He was skilled at his job. Nothing would ever happen to him ... right?

It was the unknowns about his job that were messing with her head right now. How dangerous was search and rescue work? Natalie had no clue. She needed to remedy that if this—thing—between them was to go any further.

But even if the job was+ dangerous, would she let that keep her away from building something with him? She wanted to say no ... emphatically. But the truth was she didn't know. It was all so new. His Nighthawk life was so different from anything she'd ever experienced.

She never once thought about the men and women who searched debris for survivors after disasters. The monumental task those rescuers faced at every disaster was mind-boggling. And that was Graham's world. A world she *needed* to learn more about. Otherwise, the unknown would drive her bonkers.

Like it was right now—now that he was fifteen minutes late.

Natalie continued to pace, trying to get images of death and destruction out of her brain. She was reasonably sure they were not a daily part of his life. It was probably most often lost kayakers or lost hikers. Not to mention the training he gave other groups; he was a teacher just like her. Simple. Many disasters happened in a year, but he certainly didn't charge into all of them.

After thirty minutes, she heard a loud rumble that caused the windows of the house to vibrate. Natalie went out to the porch, wondering what could possibly be making that noise. It sounded far away but grew closer as she stood there. Soon, she could make out the distinctive *whop whop whop* of a helicopter.

Curious, it wasn't often a helicopter flew over Lake Haven. Especially not as low as this one was flying. The skids were just barely missing the tops of the trees.

It flew over her house before it reached the elementary school and there, it dropped behind the tree line until Natalie couldn't see it anymore. Maddie had joined her on the porch by that time.

"That was weird," Maddie was looking down the street in the direction the helicopter had flown. "Wonder what that was all about?"

Natalie shrugged. "No clue."

"I hope it wasn't one of those medical helicopters."

"I haven't heard any emergency sirens, so I don't think it would be." After a few minutes, the sisters watched as the helicopter rose into the sky, disappearing.

Once the noise had dissipated, Maddie looked at her sister, eyeing the outfit she'd chosen. She'd kept it casual. Dark jeans and a forest green sweater with a wide neckline that allowed it to hang off of one shoulder. Her hair was loose, curling in soft waves over the bare shoulder. "You look nice."

Natalie nodded, wringing her hands. "I'm so nervous."

"You don't need to be nervous. He's obviously into you if the number of texts and phone calls is any indication. If anybody deserves to have more with someone they click with, it's definitely you," Maddie told her, squeezing her hands.

Graham had been calling her every night since she had asked him to come to her school. He'd also sent her an occasional text. Mostly mundane things. A few times, she'd receive a selfie of him either on the climbing wall or at a rescue site. Or a picture of a lovely flower he'd found growing wild while out on a job. It was sweet, the attention he was giving her. She looked forward to his phone call every night. He was easy to talk to, and he wasn't shy about sharing things about himself with her. It was a nice change from what it had been like with most of the guys she'd dated, especially her ex.

"Just take it one day at a time. And don't be scared. I'll be here for you if it doesn't turn into something; but I have no doubt it *will*." She waggled her eyebrows as she continued. "I bet sex with a body like that would be *hot!*" Maddie fanned herself, making Natalie erupt into a fit of giggles.

Natalie smiled at the woman who meant more to her than anything. She relaxed her grip on her own hands to clasp Maddie's, unable to deny that sex with him *would* be hot. If she still remembered a simple kiss from twelve years ago, having a full-blown sexual experience with him would probably be epic. A shiver raced through her at the thought.

"When's he picking you up?"

"Thirty minutes ago."

"Oh, hun, I'm sorry." Natalie couldn't stand the pity on her sister's face. Graham wouldn't stand her up. She was pretty sure of it. But then her mind flashed back to the type of guy he'd been during high school. It didn't seem like he was still that guy who dated a lot of women during those high school years, but then again, she barely knew him though her instincts screamed that he wasn't that guy anymore.

"He probably just got held up or called out for a rescue or something," she gave voice to the thoughts that had run through her head in the past thirty minutes.

"Wouldn't he have contacted you somehow?"

She shrugged her bare shoulder. "I'm sure he would have if he could." She didn't mean to sound so despondent when she said that. Not having gone on many dates, she didn't know the protocol for being stood up. *Stop*, she admonished herself. *It's only been thirty minutes!*

Maddie's eyes flashed to a spot behind Natalie, her lips turning up at the corners. "I have a feeling your night is gonna improve."

Natalie turned around to see what had captured her sister's attention. Graham was running towards the house. He looked rumpled in his black cargo pants and black Nighthawk tee, a small backpack hanging from one shoulder, but he was a welcome sight. Releasing the breath she hadn't realized she'd been holding for the last thirty minutes, she watched as he took the six porch steps in two to reach her.

"I'm so sorry I'm late, Chickadee." He took hold of one of her hands and leaned in to kiss her on the cheek. Natalie inhaled the masculine scent of him. He smelled like the outdoors, pine and fresh air mixed slightly with sweat and hard work. His hair was mussed like he'd been caught in a windstorm. He was dirty and unkempt but the best-looking thing she'd seen in a long time.

He stepped back from her squeezing her hand, then turned to her sister with a nod. "Maddie."

"Nice to see you, Graham. Everything okay?"

"It is now." he looked at Natalie as he answered. She could feel the heat of a blush work its way up her cheeks.

"You always show up for your dates dirty and smelly?" Maddie asked, wrinkling her nose.

"Maddie!" Natalie hissed.

Graham chuckled. "Yeah, sorry. We just got back from a rescue in the UP."

"I figured," Maddie remarked. "Wait ... was that you on that helicopter?"

"Yeah. Finch dropped me off. I didn't want to leave my lovely date waiting any longer."

Natalie blushed again, wondering if she would ever stop blushing around this man? A man who took a helicopter to get to a date, definitely a first for her.

"Holy shit!" Her exclamation elicited a bark of laughter from him. "You didn't have to ... I mean ... you could have canceled. We could have gone out another time. I imagine you're exhausted after the rescue."

"Nope. If I can use your bathroom for a bit, I'll be raring to go."

The thought of Graham using her shower had her blushing once more. *Gah! Don't think about him naked in your shower!* But the image wouldn't leave her brain. All those sleek muscles slick with soap, water forging a path over the ridges and valleys of his body. Her lady bits started to stand up and take notice at the direction her thoughts were going.

"Natalie?" Graham asked with a smirk, pulling her back from her wandering brain.

"Right ... shower. Sure. Go ahead." She mentally slapped herself. Could she sound any more like an idiot?

"Thanks, Chickadee. I won't be but a few minutes. Then we can get a bite to eat."

"Sounds good."

"Have fun, you two," Maddie said with a wave as she went through her own door.

"You can use the shower in my room. It's bigger than the guest bath. Last room at the end of the hall upstairs. Towels in the closet."

"Thanks, I'll be quick."

Natalie watched as he took the stairs two at a time and breathed a sigh of relief. He was okay. And he'd been in such a rush to see her he'd had the helicopter drop him off here. *Holy shit. How hot was that?*

Graham rushed through his shower, anxious to get back to Natalie. He was itching to spend the evening with her, despite the exhaustion that pulled at him. The rescue had been a challenging one. A group of teenagers and their boat had been trapped in the rocks at the base of a cliff along the shore of Lake Superior. The waves were strong, not allowing for a water rescue. They'd had to rappel down and pull the kids out with ropes. Thankfully, everyone was uninjured. It had been grueling work for his team. But there was no way he was going to cancel on Natalie.

The guys had laughed when he'd asked Finch to drop him at the parking lot of the elementary school. He accepted the teasing, knowing that he'd have the last laugh when they each eventually found someone they were as eager to see.

Clean and dressed in a red Henley and jeans, he found Natalie in her kitchen. He didn't notice the layout of the kitchen, being too busy taking her in. She was sexy as hell with a dark green sweater exposing one creamy shoulder. A shoulder he had the sudden urge to place his lips on. The blood rushed to a certain part of his anatomy as he stared at her bare skin. *Was she not wearing a bra?* There was no strap. More heat rushed through his veins.

"You must be hungry," she smiled as if she knew exactly where his thoughts had gone. "Where should we go for dinner?"

He yanked himself out of his shoulder fantasy. "Pretty sure the Nighthawks planned to head to Jolene's as soon as they got cleaned up, so I'd rather go somewhere else. Somewhere for just the two of us."

Her eyes sparkled like emeralds as her mouth curled into a sexy smile. "Okay. Lake Haven has a few decent places, but aside from Jolene's, the next best is Pizza Haven. And it shouldn't be too busy this time of year. You can forget about that place during the summer, it's always packed."

"Sounds good. Let's go." He grabbed her hand to lead her out of the house, and she nabbed her purse and keys off the counter as they went. He waited on the porch while she locked the door behind them, breathing in the fresh lake air.

"We can walk there from here, but if you are tired, we can drive."

"A walk sounds perfect," he replied as he took her hand again. He couldn't stop himself from reaching for her. Her hand felt so small and right in his larger one.

They headed down the sidewalk toward the center of town. The restaurant was quaint and perfect, set on the bluff overlooking Lake Michigan.

As the hostess directed them to a table, a small voice called out to them. "Miss Ghannon!"

"Lucy." Natalie stopped at the table where the small girl, frantically waving to get their attention, sat with her family. "How's my favorite five-year-old?"

"Not five anymore. Today's my birthday! I'm six now!" She climbed up to stand on the seat of the booth until she was eye to eye with Natalie.

"Well, that sure is cause for celebration!" Natalie thumped a finger against her chin as she exaggerated thinking. "Hmm. I'm afraid I don't have any present to give you right now."

"That's okay, Miss Ghannon. A hug is the best present you can give a person." Wise words from the mouth of a six-year-old.

"That is very true, Lucy." She opened her arms wide, and the tiny girl threw herself into the embrace, giggling as Natalie twirled her around. Placing Lucy back on the bench beside her mother, Natalie turned to the others at the table, "You all remember Graham Whitaker?"

Lucy's dad stood to shake his hand. So did Colin, a miniature version of his father. After greeting the mother, Natalie laughed at something Lucy whispered into her ear. "Well, I'm not exactly sure," Natalie told her. "But you can ask him if you'd like."

Lucy turned to him, eyes solemn. "You're a Nighthawk, right?"

"Yes, I am," he answered.

"Miss Ghannon says that's a bird."

"That's right."

"Then ... can you fly?"

He swallowed the laugh that threatened to escape. "Only with help."

Lucy tilted her head as she studied him. "Good to know," she replied seriously before a big smile lit her face. "Can I have a birthday hug from you too? After all, I'll only turn six once."

Graham chuckled. "Absolutely." He caught the little girl as she leapt into his arms and gave her a squeeze. "Happy birthday, sweet girl."

"Okay, Lucy," her mother said as he set her back on the bench. "Let's let Miss Ghannon and Mr. Whitaker get their own dinner now."

"Okay." Lucy plopped back down into her seat. She gave them one last wave before picking up a slice of pizza and taking a huge bite.

Graham and Natalie said their goodbyes to the rest of the family before he gently guided her to their table. He briefly imagined what it would be like to have a little girl as precocious as Lucy. A little girl with gorgeous green eyes. The thought didn't scare him as much as it might have before Natalie came back into his life.

Having placed their orders, Graham reached across the table for Natalie's hand. "I'm truly sorry I was late tonight, Chickadee."

"Graham, you don't need to apologize. I understand. I worried about you, but I knew you would eventually let me know what was going on."

Hearing her say she had worried about him sent an unfamiliar jolt through his system. A not so unpleasant jolt if he were honest with himself. It felt nice to have someone outside his immediate family worry about him.

"You were worried about me?"

"Well ... yeah. Briefly." An adorable rosy blush colored her cheeks. "But I think most of the worry stemmed from not knowing exactly what you do."

"I can understand that. Tell you what, I have a session to teach tomorrow morning; how 'bout you come to the complex in the afternoon, and I'll give you a tour and explain our operation to you. Then maybe you'll understand more about search and rescue."

Natalie's face lit up. "That sounds great. I'd like to learn about what you do."

Her smile was infectious. He couldn't help smiling, pleased she was eager to learn his business. They arranged to meet at two the next afternoon as the waitress delivered their pizzas. After taking a bite and savoring the unique blend of spices, he thought about the worry he'd caused her. He knew his work could be dangerous at times. Not as dangerous as a deployed soldier, but some rescues could be treacherous.

The rescue of those teenagers today had been tricky work, especially with winds pushing them into the side of the cliff. If he hadn't had confidence in his team or his equipment - which they meticulously inspected after each use - he could see how an outsider might think his work was dangerous. But that was why his Nighthawks trained daily, preparing themselves for any and all situations.

Still, he'd hate to cause Natalie to worry unnecessarily every time he went out on a rescue. Showing her around the Nighthawk complex would certainly help alleviate some of that. He hoped.

"So, I have this insane desire to learn everything about you," he grinned. "You've ... um ... never been married, right?"

"That's right."

"But you said you were engaged once. Can you tell me about it?"

Graham watched as her expression changed from open and happy to completely closed-off and shuttered; darkness clouded her eyes. "Umm ... the usual, I guess. He wasn't who I thought he was." He could tell there was more to the story than that. Something had happened to put that look into her eyes. It was hard to pinpoint, but it almost seemed like fear. Had she been abused? If that were the case, Graham would love nothing more than to hunt the bastard down and give him a taste of his own medicine.

"Well, I guess it's good that you found that out before you went through with the wedding," he stated.

She gave him a small smile that she tried to hide behind her drink, not quite making eye contact with him. Graham decided to let the subject drop. It was clear she wasn't ready to talk about it, but the day would come that she would share everything with him. He was sure of it. Just like the day would come when he would share everything about himself with her. Even his dark parts.

They left the restaurant and strolled along the bluff, enjoying the last few rays of the sunset over the lake. At an overlook they leaned against the rail, letting the sound of the waves calm them. Graham inhaled deeply, the fresh, clean lake air filling him with peace.

"I can't believe I've never visited this town before. It's so peaceful here."

Natalie smiled. "I love it here. I couldn't imagine living anyplace else."

"Could you imagine if I had visited here and we ran into each other on the sidewalk?"

"Do you think we'd recognize each other?" she quipped.

"If you were smiling, I would definitely have recognized you in an instant," he confessed, placing his palm against her cheek, his thumb sweeping across her lips. "I have never forgotten this smile."

Sweeping a curl of long dark hair out of the way, he exposed the creamy smoothness of her delicate shoulder that he so longed to taste. His hand moved of its own accord, tracing the line of her collarbone with his calloused fingertips. He drifted closer, lured into her captivating gravity.

A shuddering breath escaped as his fingers glided over her skin, hypnotized by her lavender scent filling his senses. His hand traveled higher, over the slope of her jaw, until he was cupping her cheek. The heat of her deep blush radiating into his palm as she leaned into it. Her hand grasped his wrist, her nails digging into his skin. His muscles tensed with the desire to crush her to him.

His eyes were drawn to her lips, mesmerized as her tongue slowly traced the Cupid's bow. His cock twitched, straining against his pants. He angled closer until only a whisper of space separated them. His gaze flickered from her lips up to her eyes, dilated with desire until the black pupils nearly obliterated the emerald of her irises.

Unable to resist the pull, he brushed his lips against hers, allowing them to linger longer than might have been appropriate. He pulled back slightly and met her eyes, seeing his hunger reflected in them. She smiled, and that was it. He was starving for more of her.

"Shit, Natalie," he murmured, and her eyes flared. He brushed his thumb across her lower lip. Her tongue reached out to trace its path. All his blood rushed south, his cock aching in its confinement. He wanted her, more than he had ever wanted anyone.

Taking a hesitant breath, she started to pull back, dropping her eyes shyly until he took her face in both hands. "Wait," he rasped. Bright eyes widened as his lips crashed to hers again. As it had twelve years ago, her gasp of surprise allowed him entrance, and he delved right in to savor her.

It was just as he remembered. Just as powerful. Just as phenomenal. Their tongues reacquainted themselves, and he slid his hands to the back of her head into her hair. Silky strands tangled around his fingers. As he tilted her head to plunge deeper, a soft moan escaped from within her, a sound that resonated in his gut.

Voices nearby reminded him they were in a public place, forcing him back to his senses. He pulled back and stared down at her, his fingers still twisted in her hair. He was sure the heat shining in her eyes mirrored his own.

Natalie must have heard the approaching voices too and stepped back slightly. He let his fingers comb through her long dark strands until they dropped to her shoulders. Running his thumb across the smooth skin of that bare shoulder in a soft caress, he willed his cock to relax before he embarrassed himself.

"Darn people," she muttered. "Can't they tell we're having a moment here?"

Graham couldn't help himself. He threw his head back and laughed. "I know ... right? Damn inconsiderate of them." He dropped his hands from her shoulders and took her hand before she could pull further away. "Come on. I'll walk you home."

At her porch, they kissed again. And again. Graham would have loved nothing more than to be invited inside, even knowing it was too soon. Determined not to mess this up, he forced himself to tamp down his libido and step back from her, promising he'd see her tomorrow.

After listening for the click of her lock, he climbed into his truck, grateful that the guys had dropped it off. He had a feeling it would be a while before his smile would fade. He drove off in preoccupied ignorance of the shadow that had watched them from across the street.

Chapter 7

T HE FOLLOWING MORNING WENT quickly, and it was soon time for Natalie to arrive. He tried to pretend he wasn't anxiously waiting for her as he prowled the parking lot, but the Nighthawks weren't fooled. They all knew their boss was smitten, but he didn't care what they thought. He was as eager for Natalie to learn about him and his world as he was to learn all about her.

Finally, she arrived, and he watched as she climbed out of her car. She wore black and looked sexy as hell. No more paint splattered hand-me-downs for her. Black jeans paired with a black sweater hugged every one of her delectable curves. Black leather boots completed the picture, their low heels bringing her an inch closer to his height. Unable to help himself, he leaned in, kissing her briefly. She flashed him her brilliant smile, and his chest clenched. Rubbing a hand over the spot, he took her hand to lead her out of the lot.

"Ready to see my world?"

"Absolutely. Can't wait."

He and his brother had spent six grueling years building Nighthawk from nothing and he was anxious to discover what she thought about the place – more so than with anyone else he'd given a tour to. He tried to see it through her eyes. For the most part, the Nighthawk complex resembled a college campus. There was a building that held several classrooms and their main offices. Behind that the barracks and dining hall. Finch, Logan,

Tin Man, and Evan also had rooms at the barracks, finding it easier to stay there than find their own place. Until recently, Jude had also stayed there.

The barracks was a four-story building, containing the dining hall and kitchen on the first floor, three other levels housed the rooms, ten to a floor. The bathrooms were shared dorm-style and located in the middle of each floor. Clients were good about cleaning up after themselves, though they had a cleaning company come in once a week. Graham had been relieved when the day had come that he no longer had to do the weekly cleaning. After the first year of operation, they'd finally been in the black and able to hire outside help.

The kitchen was part of a buffet-style dining hall complete with a cook and staff. Chef Layla immediately doted on Natalie once she and her staff had been introduced and promised to make her something special for dinner that night. The cook was like family to Graham, so he was pleased the two women were forming a friendship.

The hands-on training areas had Natalie in awe. Graham took her first to the urban search and rescue training area, which, to the untrained eye, looked like a disaster. What had once been a strip mall now lay in a disorganized pile of rubble. The mangled mess of a building was designed to look like it had once held a restaurant, a clothing store, and a salon.

Next to the strip mall were single-family homes that appeared to have been hit hard by disaster. A few mangled mobile homes that Graham had been able to purchase after they had been through a catastrophe, completed the area that the Nighthawks called Calamity Village.

After nine-eleven, most of the country had become painfully aware of how unprepared they were for terrorist attack. Therefore, complexes like Nighthawk were seen to be needed and were sought after.

Graham showed Natalie how they used the buildings of Calamity Village to train their clients. "Someday, I hope to add K-9 SAR training," he was telling her as he climbed around on the debris. "I've worked with a few organizations over the years. The work they do is remarkable. Their senses are so much more attuned than the average human. I've seen a SAR dog sniff out a person that we had passed over numerous times."

Near the village was the Pile a disorganized pile of wood, concrete, and rebar resembling a large trash heap - included several pockets where "victims" could be found and rescued by the men and women in training.

Next, he showed Natalie the warehouse where they kept their equipment. The front part of the building was lined with floor-to-ceiling shelves. They held everything from bottled water and energy bars to lanterns, ropes, tents, and blankets. Anything they could need on a rescue was stored in the warehouse. At the back of the long concrete building was the repair room. There they could look their equipment over after each use to make sure it was sound for the next mission.

Natalie had wandered over to the shelves that held their high-tech. Graham was raising funds for the purchase of several new devices to aid in searches. One in particular, the snake, with a small camera attached, could slither through small cracks in search of victims. Future tech for search and rescue was exciting but damn expensive.

Graham took down a device and turned it on. "This is a thermal imager, a special camera that can detect infrared heat signatures." He handed it to her saying, "Point it at me. You can see on the screen there a large reddish-white blob. Body heat shows up that color. Comes in handy when we don't have access to K-9s."

"How far away can you see with it?"

"For a good reading, and to understand what you are looking at, no more than one hundred feet. But we can't rely completely on this one device. It might show a warm spot, but it could just be a gas line or water heater. Or even an animal. False positives are frequent when using it on its own; that's why we pair it with other equipment, both high and low-tech.

"And new technology is being developed every day," he continued, returning the device to its assigned spot on the shelf. "There is a place in Texas where they are testing the use of a special type of AI that can squeeze into spaces the average human can't, to spot people who might be trapped. It can film the area around the victim, allowing the SAR crew to safely develop a plan of action to get that person out." He hoped to have equipment like that someday.

"Robots to the rescue," Natalie quipped.

"Respect the robots," he teased. "They may be our over-lords someday."

After showing Natalie the docks and RIBs they used for water rescue training and the occasional real-life rescue; Graham took her to their newest facility. The climbing gym was built the previous year, complete with locker rooms and gym equipment that comprised half of the building. The various climbing walls allowed them to train for any sort of rescue, be it mountain, cliff, deep hole—like the one Colin and Lucy had fallen into—or building. Anything that would require ropes and climbing to reach a victim. David, being an avid climber, had insisted they build the facility. It had been a quality addition to Nighthawk. Most of their clients came to them with absolutely no ropes knowledge. After taking Nighthawk's climbing courses, they could adequately handle all aspects of climbing and working with the ropes. David, of course, was particularly proud of these courses.

The Whitaker brothers were expert climbers, but David was a step above, a natural on any terrain. Graham was often in awe of his brother when he watched him climb.

"This is all so fascinating. How often do your rescues require climbing skills?"

"More often than you would think. Mostly it depends on how hazardous the terrain is. We don't have very many mountain ranges here in Michigan, but we do have the bluffs overlooking the lakes. And the UP has some excellent climbing areas where people can sometimes find themselves in trouble if they are not careful."

"I didn't know climbing was such a big business. I've heard of the occasional climbing gym like this, but I didn't know people climbed cliffs and mountains like they do these walls."

"Unfortunately, it's not only the occasional climber we're called out for." At her look of confusion, he went on to explain about yesterday's rescue. "Since Lake Superior was having a fit, the water was too rough for a rescue by boat. We had to climb down to them. They were uninjured and had some climbing experience, so we helped them climb up, and they had a blast, which was a nice change."

"Other rescues don't go that well?" Her voice was full of concern.

"Sometimes, no. Some of the people we rescue have been injured. That's when we use the baskets." He pointed to the human-sized litter propped up in the corner. The steel-framed piece of equipment could hold around nine hundred pounds and was outfitted with nylon webbing and straps to hold the victim in as they were extracted. The "victim" they used to train with, whom the team had affectionately dubbed Manny, lay slumped nearby. They'd put Manny through the paces too many times to count.

Her brow furrowed. "How ... how dangerous is it ... for you and your team?" She stumbled through her words.

He looked down, meeting her eyes that swam with apprehension. "I won't lie and say it's not dangerous." He placed his hands on her shoulders. "But that is why we train. We work hard, so we are prepared for whatever we face. And my Nighthawks are some of the best. Some are former special forces members who have more advanced training than me. I'd trust any one of them with my life."

Her expression relaxed as some of her unease quieted. "Thank you for showing me all this. And for helping me understand your life. I'll still worry about you but not nearly as much now." She smiled up at him, causing his heart to skip as he smiled back.

Noting it was close to dinner time, Graham slid his hands down her arms and entwined his fingers with hers, pulling gently. "Let's go see what Chef Layla has come up with for dinner."

She moved to follow him and tripped over the edge of one of the floor mats falling into him. He caught her, wrapping both arms around her pulling her closer to his body. She flushed that beautiful pink color.

She was gorgeous and like a breath of fresh air in this gym full of the stench of man sweat. The lavender aroma that had been torturing him all afternoon filled his senses. Unable to resist, he leaned in, burying his face in her neck just below her ear. Inhaling deeply, he groaned.

Drawing his lips up her neck to her ear, he whispered, "You smell so good." He nipped her earlobe gently before pulling back to meet her gaze. Awareness flared just before he lowered his head to take her lips. He hesitated millimeters from her lips before she closed the distance meeting him in a scorching kiss.

Her arms snaked around his waist to rest on his back as she moaned. A sound he inhaled deep inside. He tightened his arms around her pulling her closer, her breasts pressed against his chest. Her hands clenched against his back, her nails digging into his back, but he felt no pain, only pleasure as he explored the wonders of her mouth. His hands moved of their own volition, discovering the contours of her body until they came to a rest on her ass. He squeezed the perfect globes before pulling her even closer.

Natalie gasped as he pressed his erection against her stomach. Graham thrust his tongue deeper into her mouth. Tasting and delving into every crevice. He couldn't get enough of drinking her in, and she met his ferocity with a fervor of her own. Her desire for him was more of a turn-on than his own desire for her.

Knowing he needed to put a stop to this before he lay her down on the mats to have his way with her, he slowed the kiss down. Giving her lips one last nip, he raised his head. Her eyes drifted opened and the haze of desire slowly lifted. She placed her fingers against her lips as if stunned by what had just happened. Then her lips tilted in a dreamy smile.

Feeling more proud of himself than he should for putting that wistful expression on her face, he squeezed her in a tight hug. Graham rested his cheek against Natalie's temple, enjoying the lavender fragrance of her hair until the annoying trill of his cell phone drew his attention away from her.

"Whitaker," he answered after swiping to receive the call. Pausing to listen to the caller, he replied, "On our way." Putting his cell back in his pocket, he kissed Natalie on her head and told her dinner was ready and waiting for them.

Again, Graham took her hand, and together they walked slowly back to the dining hall; neither of them anxious to end their time alone.

Chapter 8

FRIDAY DAWNED DULL AND dreary but did nothing to dampen Natalie's disposition. She should question why she was in such a good mood, but she refused to delve that deeply. She was coming to appreciate the feeling of anticipation and the excited flutter her belly gave every time she thought about seeing Graham again.

It hadn't been two weeks since they'd reunited. She needed to calm down. Today she needed to be a professional, not some lovesick schoolgirl. As she walked into the school building, the anticipation of being near him again had her grinning from ear to ear, especially with the goodnight kiss they'd shared at her car after her tour of Nighthawk flashing through her mind.

Dinner in the dining hall had been entertaining as the Nighthawks took advantage of the fact that she was there to tease their boss unmercifully. Each of them shared stories of their boss that ranged from funny to poignant. It was the latter that nearly had her in tears a few times as she came to understand how much of a hero Graham truly was. He and his Nighthawks were heroes and deserved every accolade.

But it was those kisses that refused to let her mind focus on her work. First, the scorching kiss in the gym, followed by one at her car as she prepared to head home. She had been so ready to offer to stay with him that night, even knowing it was too soon, his kisses had that effect on her. Her lips still burned with the memory of the passion.

"You look like the cat that ate the canary," her principal, Letty Scott, said, having caught Natalie mid grin. Letty was the youngish grandmotherly type everyone wished they had. No one knew her true age; some thought her to be in her late fifties. Others placed her closer to retirement age, even as she stubbornly refused to ever leave her post. When asked why she hadn't retired, her answer was always the same, 'I'm not done yet.' She treated all her teachers as if they were her kids, with love and respect while also being the battle-axe leader they all looked up to. Letty dressed like Mr. Rogers, with sneakers and a cardigan around her plump body. Somehow the look was endearing. "How can you be in such a good mood when it's only October, and we are already expecting our first snow of the season," she lamented. Natalie had forgotten that a few inches of snow were expected.

"Maybe I like snow."

"I like snow too, but not this early!" Letty complained as she headed into her office, sneakers squeaking on the tiled floor. Natalie laughed, heading down the hall to her own classroom. Snow and Graham. Now there were two things that pleased her enormously.

Natalie turned the corner into the hall where her classroom was located, and there he was, leaning against the wall by her door, a large duffel bag at his feet. Cue the tell-tale flutter that always affected her when he was near. Handsome as always in a pair of tight-fitting jeans that hugged everything! The baby blue sweater he wore with the Nighthawk logo on the left did nothing to hide the muscles across his chest and arms and accentuated those ice-blue eyes that were fixed on Natalie as she walked closer to him.

He smiled at her as she approached. "Morning, Chickadee."

She smiled back. She couldn't *not* smile when he looked at her like that and called her by that sweet nickname; her heart raced. "Morning. You're here early."

She fidgeted awkwardly with her teacher ID lanyard, suddenly apprehensive. She was dressed nicely enough in her black slacks and green silk blouse, an outfit she had spent far too much time picking out. Usually, she didn't care what she wore, but somehow when it came to Graham, she did.

"Thought I'd get the lay of the land before we started," he said with a wink. "Got a few things I want to set up." He indicated the bag at his feet.

"Let me set my things down, and I'll take you to the café-audi-nasium."

"The what?"

She laughed. "That's what we call the gym that is also the cafeteria and the auditorium. It's a multipurpose space." She set her bag down on her chair and her Tervis cup on her desk.

He snorted. "Then why not call it the multipurpose room?"

Natalie paused; *why don't we call it that?* "I have absolutely no idea." Graham chuckled.

Natalie watched as he took in her home away from home. She'd worked hard many years to set up her room just right. Posters of all sorts filled the walls, the color wheel took up a prominent spot at the front of the classroom. One wall was reserved for posters of some of the most recognizable masterpieces. Another wall was covered with works of her current students. Throughout it all, inspirational quotes about creativity were spaced. The room was colorful and cozy.

In the center of the room were six long tables, each with six chairs. The center of every table held a plastic caddy with glue, scissors, markers, crayons, and anything else a young budding artist would need. And of course, each table was splattered with paint. Natalie tried to clean up as much of the paint at the end of the day as she could, but the look of chaos the paint created signified the creativity that took place in this room each and every day.

One corner of the room held other much-needed supplies. Rows of construction paper stored by color in specific slots. One cabinet was full of large glue jugs, jars filled with a colorful assortment of pipe cleaners, boxes of crayons and colored pencils. Another held the paint, both in bottles in every color of the rainbow, and in the rectangular plastic boxes that the fledgling artists used regularly.

She was proud of the work she did at Lake Haven Elementary; helping young minds find their creative side was most rewarding. She loved the mess, the chaos caused by each new project; watching the outcome of the creativity of those young minds made it all worthwhile. No two visions were the same and that fact gave Natalie enormous satisfaction and pride.

"So, this is where the magic happens." Graham wandered over to the wall that displayed her current students' works, observing each piece.

Natalie smiled at his description. Some days it was like magic. Other days she wished she could run and hide in her studio. But she always returned, year after year. The joy of watching the little ones create feeding her inspiration.

"It's like I stepped back in time to my own childhood," he mused, taking in a haunted house project the second graders were working on for Halloween. "I remember doing a similar project." He grinned and turned to face her. "Bet my mom still has it saved in a memory box somewhere."

Now wasn't that just the sweetest thing ever. She doubted her mom had any such memory boxes. Natalie learned long ago if she wanted to preserve any of her childhood, it would be up to her to do so.

"Come on. I'll show you where you can set up."

Natalie finally had a free period late in the day to sit in on Graham's presentation. She'd heard so many good things from her students that she was beyond curious. When she walked into the café-audi-nasium, she noted that he had the attention of each and every fourth and fifth-grader. No small feat. They were enraptured as he displayed the items necessary for survival in the wilderness for them.

"Who's excited for the snow tonight," he asked the group. Little hands everywhere popped up and an excited twitter rippled through the room. "Me too," he confessed laughing.

"Now, if you were going outside to build your epic snow fort, what would you need to stay warm?" he asked.

Hands shot up. He pointed to one fifth-grader who called out 'boots.' Nodding approval at the girl, he pointed to another hand, 'heavy coat,' that voice shouted. This continued until everyone had exhausted their ideas.

"Good!" he praised the room. "Now, what if you and your family were going for a long hike in the snowy forest. What else would you need? Hint, I bet you'd find a few of them on this table." He gestured to the table where he had displayed a variety of possibilities. Kids started shouting out all the things they thought would be useful. Almost every item on the table was named.

"Now, let's flash forward to summer vacation!" There were cheers from the crowd. Everyone looked forward to summer break. "You are on the same hike with your family in the same woods. What would you need then?" The kids were shocked to realize they would need most of the same items plus a few extras like bug spray. Natalie watched Graham as he explained the usefulness of each. He was a natural in front of a room full of kids and it was obvious he was enjoying himself. There was no question why his SAR training facility was becoming so popular; he was a natural instructor.

"Okay, you've been hiking for a while, and suddenly you realize you can't see your parents anymore. What do you do?" The kids all looked at each other. "I'll tell you something someone told me long ago that I tell myself every time I'm in a scary situation," he said, glancing at Natalie. "Slow your panic." The room was so silent one could hear a pin drop. Graham continued to hold Natalie's gaze. "Works every time."

Natalie's heart fluttered. It still amazed her that he remembered those words; she certainly hadn't. And the fact that he used them as a personal mantra was remarkable. She wished she had remembered them, they'd have come in handy that awful night with her ex. Shuddering, she pushed the unwelcome memory away.

He turned his attention back to the room, "Every time I find myself in a situation that becomes a little too scary, I just say those words to myself. Slow your panic. It allows me to slow my breathing and think; because if you are freaking out, you can't think. So, if you're lost, slow your panic. Who knows what else you should do?" Answers came quickly. Graham praised each answer then, as a group, they decided the most important thing they should do was stay put, but only if they were in a safe spot. Help would always come to find them if they stayed in one place. Then Graham went on to explain the Nighthawks' role in situations like that. It was the perfect segue for him to discuss all that his team could do and the different roles each team member played. The kids were fascinated.

Graham pushed a button on the remote that had been in his hand, and the screen behind him lit up with pictures of some of his rescues. There were images of him with the Nighthawks scaling impossible cliffs, strapping victims into what he called a litter. Sometimes those litters were hauled up to a waiting helicopter. Another image showed the litter being hauled down using a complicated rope system. There were also pictures on the water showing the team using more ropes to pull people out of rushing water.

Natalie stared at one picture where Graham's head was barely above water, fighting the rushing currents, a small child wrapped under one arm. An image popped up of Graham standing atop a pile of rubble as a search dog explore the area for signs of life. The discipline and strength required for his work was extraordinary.

The last image was his rescue of Marcus Rayne and it had the kids all cheering. Then Graham began to answer questions. Anything ranging from how many mountains he had climbed to did he have a girlfriend asked by the curious group of students, and he answered every question with great patience, Natalie laughed when he answered the girlfriend question with "I'm working on it.". After they had exhausted themselves with questions, Graham asked for their undivided attention again.

"I have something very important I need to do now for one very special person." The room hummed with the whispered mumble of curious adolescents. "This person has shown remarkable bravery and strength in the direst of circumstances." Again, the whispers, as the kids looked around for who he meant.

"This person did everything right in a situation that would have paralyzed even the most experienced of hikers with fear. Using their intelligence, resourcefulness, strength, and bravery, they did the extraordinary; they slowed their panic and got themselves and someone else through a dire situation." The room was beyond curious now. Natalie glanced around the room, trying to spot the boy, knowing exactly who Graham was talking about. In the corner with Letty were Mr. and Mrs. O'Donnoll and Lucy, their faces alight with pride. This would be a moment Colin would remember forever.

"I'm talking, of course, about a good friend of mine," Graham continued, pausing for effect; "Colin O'Donnoll!" The room exploded in cheers, the sound echoing off the gym walls till Natalie felt she'd gone partially deaf. "Colin? Can you come up here?" The boy's head popped up in the crowd. He stood there a moment, looking awkward and shy before he hobbled toward Graham. The ankle, thankfully, had not been broken, just severely sprained.

When Colin reached his side, Graham put an arm around the boy's shoulders. Waiting till the room quieted down, he continued. "My good friend Colin did everything right and that enabled him to save not only his own life but the life of his sister." Everyone cheered for their classmate. "And even though he'd been injured, Colin still managed to protect Lucy. He slowed his panic and used his smarts. He did something we on the SAR teams call rationing. He knew they didn't have much food, and no idea when they would be found. So, he rationed their food, eating just a bit at a time to make it last as long as possible. Though they were in a hole in the ground, Colin still managed to erect a structure to keep the elements off of them, allowing them to stay dry and warm. These are things that I usually teach to people three times his age."

Graham reached into the big duffle bag on the table beside him. "Colin O'Donnoll, in honor of your bravery, resourcefulness, and strength, I present you with this Medal of Valor." The medal hung on a red, white, and blue ribbon and had a dazzling gold sunburst with the word Valor in raised letters across the top. The Michigan seal in the center of the sunburst in bright, bold colors made it look official. Graham made a grand ceremony of placing the ribbon around Colin's neck. The boy stared at the medal in awe as the room once again burst into cheers and applause. Lucy rushed up and gave her big brother a huge hug. Colin, still looking stunned, stood frozen while his classmates lined up to offer their congratulations.

Natalie teared up as she watched Graham place the ribbon around Colin's neck. She had never witnessed something so selfless; she was pretty sure that the medal was one of his. She felt herself falling just a little bit more for the man as he stood back to applaud the boy while his classmates crowded around to get a closer look at the fabulous medal.

Letty sidled up next to Natalie. "If I were thirty years younger," she leaned in to whisper to Natalie, "I wouldn't hesitate to snatch that man up; he is something special."

"That he is," Natalie answered, wiping away a tear. "Did you know he was going to do that?"

"We had talked about honoring Colin in some way, but I never imagined he'd go all out like that!" Letty also had to wipe away a tear or two. "Where do you suppose he got the medal?" she mused.

"I'm pretty sure it's his," she answered. Letty's eyes widened, and her jaw dropped open. Natalie understood the Principal's surprise; there weren't many people who would give up an honor they'd won for a child. Graham was the type of man who wouldn't hesitate to give something with that importance to honor someone else.

Chapter 9

G RAHAM FELT NATALIE'S EYES on him and glanced over
after he'd been hugged by Mrs. O'Donnoll for the
thousandth time. There was an expression on her face
that he was dying to interpret. He watched as she
reached up and wiped a tear away while chatting with
Miss Letty—the woman wouldn't let him call her anything
else; it was Letty or Miss Letty. The teachers finally managed to shoo the students back to their classrooms, an
intricate dance of organized chaos.

Graham extracted himself from the grateful O'Donnoll
family and joined the two ladies at the back of the room,
dodging excited youngsters as he went. As soon as he
reached them, he was enveloped in Miss Letty's ample
bosom for a huge hug.

"You are something else," she enthused. "On behalf of
everyone here at Lake Haven Elementary, I thank you for
what you've done for our student body today. I've never
seen so many little faces give somebody their unwavering
attention for so long. You must be magical," she finished
in wonder, hugging him again.

"Just doing my job."

"You are something else." She reiterated as she wiped
away another tear before rushing off to help with the
students.

"She's right, you know," Natalie started. "You are something else."

He dismissed her words, uncomfortable with praise. "I'm glad you could make it to one of the sessions."

"Me too. I'm especially glad it was this one. That medal was yours, wasn't it?" He shrugged. It was one of his, but he'd rather Colin enjoy it. Most of his stayed hidden in a box as the accolades and praise embarrassed him. He was doing his job, what he was trained to do. Plus, knowing there'd been far more people he hadn't been able to help, so many failures that haunted him; he felt he didn't deserve them.

"It's not a big deal."

"It is to Colin," she insisted. He followed her gaze. Colin huddled with his family, studying the medal that was grasped in his hand. Okay, so it was a big deal ... to them, he could admit that. As the O'Donnoll's turned to leave, Colin stiffened. Donnie, the bully Colin had fled from, approached them.

"Can I talk to you?" Donnie asked tentatively. By now, everyone knew what had made Colin and Lucy bolt to the woods.

"Umm ... sure," answered Colin stepping slightly away from his family.

"I want to say I'm sorry for the way I acted." There was sincerity in the boy's voice. He wasn't just saying that because a parent was forcing him to apologize. "I've had a lot of time to think, and realized I was an ass ..." He broke off, glancing at the adults still in the room. "What a jerk I've been. I was wondering if we could start over and be friends." He paused before holding out his right hand.

"Umm ... sure. I guess." Colin shook Donnie's hand, and that was it. The two started chatting in the animated way reserved for children.

As they walked toward Graham, Donnie asked, "Did you really do all those things that guy said you did?"

"Kinda," Colin answered with a shoulder shrug.

"Cool!" Donnie said. "Think you can teach me sometime?" Colin's face lit up, obviously thrilled to pass on his knowledge to a friend.

As they walked through the doors, Colin was telling Donnie about how he learned most of it with the scouts, and wouldn't it be cool if Donnie could join too. The forgiveness of children; most adults could learn a lesson from them.

"Wow," whispered Natalie. "I never saw that coming."

"Pretty decent of Colin to forgive him so quickly. I hope the two become fast friends."

Natalie's awe-struck eyes followed the two boys. "They are an inspiration." Graham couldn't agree more.

With Natalie's help, Graham packed up his display while answering some questions she still had about his work. He was happy to oblige her. It was a good feeling that she *wanted* to know more. She picked up his compass, watching as the little arrow spun around till it found north. As she turned it over in her hands, he smiled at the memory of his parents giving it to him.

Not long after the tsunami, he'd been in a bad place with too many dreadful memories of all he'd seen. He had disappeared for a while, afraid he'd taint his family with his moodiness and anger; retreated to their cabin in the Upper Peninsula and spent a few weeks wallowing in his misery. His dad had found him so disheveled that he'd barely recognized his son. During his weeks of self-imposed isolation, Graham hadn't bothered to shave, drank heavily, and had barely bothered to bathe or even eat. His father had cooked him a meal and sat quietly with him until he was ready. He'd been reluctant to share the horrors he had witnessed, but eventually, it poured out of him.

Once he'd told everything, his father gave him the compass; engraved on the back were the words, "So you can always find your way home. Love, Mom, Dad, and David". It had become one of the most precious things he owned. He still struggled to find his way home after the more intense missions, but he managed to connect with his family, even with just a phone call.

Reading the inscription, a sudden sadness crossed Natalie's face. He wanted to lash out at her parents, certain that they had never given her anything as special as that compass was to him. He felt an overwhelming need to make it up to her, to give her the kind of love and attention her family had never bothered to show.

She handed the compass to him to pack away. "Do you have to get back right away, or can you stick around for a while?" she asked.

"I've got nothing on my schedule for the next couple of days unless an emergency comes up." He was thrilled she seemed to want to spend more time with him.

"I still have a few things to finish up here, but I thought we could have dinner together when I'm done."

"Sure, that sounds good. Or better yet," he said as sudden inspiration hit him, "how 'bout I cook for you?"

The sadness in her eyes was suddenly replaced with joy, the emerald irises sparkling. "Nobody's ever cooked for me before."

"Then it's about time, isn't it?" She smiled, handing him more of his gear. "While you finish up here, I'll go shopping for the supplies I'll need. If you don't mind giving me the key to your place, I'll get started cooking."

"That sounds heavenly." He packed the last of the gear and followed her back to her classroom. Kids were racing everywhere in the halls, rushing to grab their coats and backpacks and head to the waiting busses. It was a Friday, and the excitement of the coming weekend was palpable. With the promised snow on the way, the anticipation was elevated tenfold.

Natalie's classroom was slightly messier than it was when he'd first seen it that morning, a sure sign that her students had been busy creating. She took her keys out of her purse, removed the house key from the fob, and handed it to him. "I shouldn't be more than an hour," she said as she looked across the room. Laughing flippantly, she added, "Maybe two."

"Need help cleaning up?" he asked, feeling guilty at the thought of just leaving her here with the mess.

"Nah," she answered. "I've got this down to ... well ... an art." She smiled at her pun.

"Ha! You're so punny," he joked with a wink. "Okay then, I'll see you at home." He leaned toward her and kissed her cheek. Walking out the door, he wondered if she noticed his slip. He'd practically called her home his. Like they were living together. A couple.

Of course, nothing would give him more pleasure. Reuniting with Natalie had been kismet. They'd clicked instantly, just as they'd done twelve years ago at the lake. He had known all these years that something was missing, and he'd tried to find it with the women he'd dated, but they all seemed to fall short. With Natalie, things were different. Things felt different. *Could she possibly be feeling the same way?* The thought that it could possibly be one-sided gave him pause. He knew instinctively that Natalie had the power to break him.

Graham was deep in thought as he got in his truck and drove across town to the local grocery store. There were few recipes in his arsenal, but he knew the exact one he wanted to make for her. And as the first snowflakes fell, he realized it would be perfect.

After letting himself in, Graham got to work, his mood light. She had one of those virtual assistant devices, so he asked it to play classic rock. As the beef stew simmered on the stove, he wandered around her place. The kitchen was spacious but not ostentatious. The cabinets were all white as was the granite counter, but the island that overlooked the living room was painted a slate blue. The contrast between colors was perfect.

He wandered into the living room where picture frames were scattered randomly. Most were of herself and Maddie, though he noticed one of her parents in a not so prominent spot on a high shelf. The furniture was in white and blue tones to match the kitchen, each piece comfortable and inviting. The colors in the throw rug in front of the couch complimented the furniture. Everything was perfect and homey; everything was Natalie.

But it was the framed art on the walls that drew his attention. Natalie had matted and framed some of her exquisite work. There were the birds, of course. Graham guessed that birds still fascinated her, which pleased him. The detailing in the feathers even more precise than he remembered.

The piece that attracted him most held a place of honor over her fireplace. A landscape, it was a view of the lake from the vantage point of the observer standing on the shore overlooking water. Storm clouds gathered on the horizon. Graham was stunned and drew in for a closer look. As more details coalesced in his mind, he recognized the spot. It was his spot. Their spot. It looked as it had that day. The light at the edge of the water was dappled as it shone through a canopy of trees. The water seemed alive, almost audible as it lapped at the shore. In the building storm clouds, he could hear the approaching thunder.

So lost was he in the painting, he didn't hear Natalie enter. She came up beside him and slipped her tiny hand into his. "That day was special for me."

He looked down at her in awe of her talent. "It's exquisite." It was all he could think to say. "I can almost smell the approaching storm."

She smiled at him, pleasure shining in her eyes. "That's exactly what I wanted it to be like. I wanted to go back there so many times. I wanted to go back to that afternoon before the tornado, to freeze time."

Graham turned to face her. Cupping her cheek with his hand, his thumb caressing her skin. "You amaze me," he said simply before leaning over to place his lips gently on hers. He meant it to be just a simple, chaste kiss, but as soon as their lips met and her lavender fragrance enveloped him, it turned into so much more. Before he knew it, his tongue was plundering her mouth. His hands slid around her to draw her closer while hers slid up around his neck. She moaned softly when their bodies met - breast to thigh - he could feel each curve, so different from twelve years ago.

His left hand slid slowly up her spine, drawing the back of her shirt with it. His right hand slipped beneath the edge of her shirt at the small of her back. Then ... skin. Her soft skin was under his palm and he caressed his fingers across her lower back, feeling her body quiver against his.

His other hand moved of its own volition, lower and lower until he was cupping her ass, pushing her heat closer to his. They both moaned.

Slowly coming back to reality, Graham could hear the kitchen timer that had interrupted them. Dinner. He reluctantly withdrew from their shared passion. Resting his forehead against hers, they stared at each other a moment, breathing heavily, neither of them with the strength or motivation to speak coherently. He slid a hand up to caress her cheek again and found his voice, "Let's eat."

She nodded and followed him into the kitchen and together, they set the table. The action intimate, he knew he could get used to this. To have someone like Natalie to come home to and share a meal with every night, was an overwhelmingly enticing thought.

They chatted about mundane things mostly. He thought for sure she would bring up the compass, but she never did, and he was glad of that. He wasn't sure if he was ready to share his darkness with her yet. The darkness *was* still there; he didn't try to fool himself; he knew he could easily lose himself there again and fought hard every day to stay in the light. His family and his work with the Nighthawks helped with that tremendously. He wondered what having Natalie in his life would do to banish the darkness.

The stew was a perfect complement for the weather. Natalie had turned on the floodlights in the backyard, and they watched the falling snow as they ate. A few inches were already on the ground, and they were calling for more. It was a cozy night; Graham couldn't remember the last time he felt so content.

Finished eating, they were cleaning up together when a buzzing in his pocket shattered the serenity. "You've got to be fucking kidding me," he muttered as he read David's text.

"What is it?"

He looked at her in anguish. He didn't want to have to do this to her again. He didn't want to have to leave her. "My team has been mobilized." His voice was heavy with regret.

"Oh," she whispered. "I understand."

"I don't want to leave you again."

Her tiny hand lay against his cheek as she gave him a look of pure understanding. "You are needed, and I realize now how important your work is. I'll always be here."

Would she? Would she always be there for him? Swearing softly under his breath, he kissed her briefly and forced himself to walk away.

Out in his truck, he drove through the snow blanketing the highway with only one thought on his mind, he wanted to go back to her. No, he needed to go back to her. He needed to show her that she was just as important to him as his work.

He knew he was needed, he understood that, but words his brother had told him the previous week passed through his mind. David had said he had a superhero complex. It had always been important for him to be present at each mission, but for the first time since he'd started down the SAR road, he wanted to be a bit selfish. He needed Natalie. Didn't he deserve some happiness?

Besides, there were enough Nighthawks that could do the job just as well as he could.

Having reached a decision, he slammed on his brakes and skidded to the side of the road. No one else was out in this weather, but he didn't want to risk it. Pulling out his cell, he called David. It was time for him to find a life, and the life he wanted included a woman he'd just left alone in a duplex in Lake Haven.

Back on the road, Graham found a spot to turn around, hoping his truck didn't get stuck in the snow. He raced back to Natalie, driving much too fast for the conditions. But all he could think about was getting back to her, holding her, and kissing her. He groaned as his body began to respond to the directions his thoughts were going. *Down boy.*

Before he could knock on Natalie's door, Maddie opened it. "I heard your truck. Didn't think you'd be back tonight."

"Yeah. I wasn't needed after all." He stomped the snow off his boots while shaking the flakes out of his hair. "Is she here?" He didn't see Natalie in her living room.

"She's upstairs in her studio." Graham started for the stairs. "Graham ..." she hesitated. He paused and looked at her questioningly. "Be careful with her," she pleaded.

"Of course," he vowed.

"I know you will. It's just that ... she's got scars, both inside and out. Her ex ..." she broke off.

"She told me it ended badly, but that's all. What happened?" His curiosity peaked, and his worry. He needed to know what Maddie had meant by scars. He remembered the dark look in her eyes when he'd broached the subject of her ex. And the fear.

"It's not my story to tell. If you truly care for her, just be patient."

"Thanks, Maddie, I will," he promised. He gave her a brotherly kiss on her cheek. "I swear I'll treat her right."

Seemingly satisfied by his answer, Maddie nodded toward the stairs. "Third floor. She's got her earbuds in, so she probably won't hear you enter."

He thanked her again as he headed up the stairs taking them two at a time.

Chapter 10

NATALIE LOST HERSELF IN her work after Graham left. Trying *not* to feel like she had been abandoned ... again, she needed something to distract herself. She understood what he did was important, beyond important.

She got that lives were on the line, but it felt like someone was messing with them. Twice now he'd been called away while they were enjoying dinner together.

That kiss. That had been hot! If she had been prone to swooning, she probably would have then. And when he'd pulled her closer, she moaned at all that hardness pressed up against her softer parts.

Maddie used to talk about some men being 'sex on a stick.' Graham was that—pure sex. She'd never experienced such all-encompassing kisses, nor felt such passion in one moment, not even with her ex, and that scared her more than anything. Unwittingly, she touched the small scar on her throat, still able to feel the trickle of blood that slid down her neck, even all these years later.

It was hard to imagine Graham ever treating her like Erik had. Things had started well enough with Erik, then he'd started to change. Drugs had pushed him over the edge, of course, but he had started to become more and more possessive of her even before the drugs. The drugs fueled his paranoia, his only outlet for venting his suspicions was Natalie herself. As his drug use increased, so did the violence. That final night had taken her years to recover from, both physically and mentally.

She'd held Graham in such high esteem for so many years and measured every man against the teenage fantasy. If she took things further with him and he turned on her as Erik had ... she didn't want to even think about what it would be like. She'd loved Graham since she was twelve years old, couldn't imagine that love ever fading. He had the true power to break her.

Maddie would tell her to go for it, that she deserved to be happy.

She turned to grab the blue paint, and there he stood, the manifestation of her fantasies. A thrill erupted inside her; at least until she saw what he was looking at. She had stacked them in the corner of her studio and promptly forgotten about them; the dozen or so paintings she had done after Erik. Her psychologist had called it therapy, and she supposed it had worked, but they were dark. She called that her Hollow Phase; there was no joy, no light in those paintings. She had dumped all her dark feelings on those canvasses until she had felt carved out, hollow inside.

Graham held one canvas that was the most heartbreaking. There were birds in most of her work, and her Hollow Phase was no exception, though most of the birds were unrecognizable. They were grotesque, demonized versions of her birds, dark and shadowy, as she had felt when at her lowest. The background gloomy and bleak, no light in their tiny eyes, no joy in their flight. They were nothing but hollow, just as she was.

The one Graham was studying was the closest representation of Natalie. The background a swirling vortex of dark colors, a void. A chickadee fought the crushing emptiness, its wings broken and disfigured. Feathers shattered, its little body crushed even as it struggled, its beak open, crying out in fear and helplessness, a stark hysteria rampant in its eyes. That was the last painting she had done in that period and it had been a cathartic emptying of her soul. She had drained all her dark, evil feelings onto that canvas. It had cost her much to complete it and she had felt empty afterward. It had taken months to recover but slowly, the light had returned.

She hadn't been able to bring herself to get rid of those canvasses. Gauging by the expression on Graham's face, they'd inspired questions that she wasn't sure she was ready to answer.

She sighed. Now was as good a time as any. She knew it was best that he learn that she was damaged before they went any further. If she wanted to seize whatever happiness she could with him, then she needed to tell him everything.

"Graham," she said softly, removing her earbuds as she approached his side. She laid a hand on his arm, and he looked at her, an expression of pure anguish on his face. Was that sorrow for her or something else? In that moment, he appeared so tormented. Worry swept through her at the thought that he may have demons of his own.

"These ... these are so dark. Is this ... you? What happened? Oh, my little chickadee." He traced one finger over a broken wing. "What did he do to you?" Leave it to Graham to guess the reason behind the painting.

She could only answer honestly as she gazed into eyes filled with sorrow and regret. She sighed deeply, still feeling a twinge of shame. "He almost killed me."

His eyes widened, and his body tensed as if absorbing a blow. He carefully placed the canvas of the broken bird back on the pile and turned to her, hands clenched in fists at his side. "Can you ... will you tell me?" he pleaded.

"Yes, but let's go downstairs." She led him out of her studio and down to the living room. After flipping the switch for the gas fireplace, they settled on the couch, Natalie staring into the flames as she gathered her thoughts.

She knew this was something she had to share with him if they were to progress in this relationship, but it wouldn't be easy.

Knowing that though difficult, this was something she had to share with him if their relationship were to have a chance, she took a breath and launched into her story. "I met Erik Flanders five years ago. He was a lawyer, handsome and successful. It was good for a while and six months into our relationship, he proposed, and I accepted. Everything was perfect ... until it wasn't. Soon after our engagement, he lost a big court case which devastated him. What I didn't know was that he'd turned to drugs to deal with it. He started small, but ..." she trailed off, remembering the day she found the drugs in her house.

"Did he get violent? Many addicts do."

"I didn't notice at first. I know that sounds crazy, but at the time, it seemed they were small accidents. A little nudge into the wall as we passed in the hall. A twist of an arm when he needed me to do something for him. Small things that didn't really hurt, you know what I mean?" She knew she'd been trying to justify his actions, but she hadn't understood at the time what was happening. His harsh words had hurt more. Erik had been under an enormous amount of stress after that lost court battle, it made sense he'd lash out in anger sometimes.

"A few weeks after those seemingly innocent accidents started, I found his stash in my bedroom. I was furious!" Shocked, angry, confused. She'd felt it all in that moment. How dare he taint her home, her *bedroom* with that crap! Then it clicked. They hadn't been accidents but much more dangerous than that. They were the product of a drug-induced rage. And if he kept using, Natalie instinctively knew that it would get worse. She needed to get him help, get him into rehab or something. She ran to flush the drugs down the toilet before he could come home.

"I thought I could ... *should* help him get clean. I researched rehab facilities. I searched the house from top to bottom for more drugs and I flushed it all." She had been proud of herself for that, knowing that the first step in getting clean was to remove the temptation. "He was furious when I confronted him. I tried to reason with him, but that just made him angrier. When he learned I'd flushed it all ..." She broke off. How could she have not seen it coming? Looking back, it seemed like it had happened in slow motion. She had watched his fist slowly come toward her and hadn't done a thing to stop it. It had shocked her, never imagining in all her time with him that he would ever become so violent. Still feeling the shame of being so unaware, she stared at her hands clenched in her lap.

Graham put a finger under her chin and tilted her head up. "What did he do?" He dropped his hand to hers after she met his eyes and squeezed tightly, anchoring her in the here and now. His ice-blue eyes warming her, imploring her to continue.

"He punched me. Here," indicating the left side of her face, she still felt the impact of the punch. Graham briefly closed his eyes, gripping her hands harder.

She'd had a black eye for a while. That had been hard to explain to her students. "That was all it took. One punch and I threw him out. It was over, I hurled his ring at him and forced him to leave."

"Good for you!" he praised. She smiled sadly, a single tear escaping. Graham caught it with a gentle finger before asking, "That wasn't it, was it? Something else happened."

Natalie drew in a shaky breath. She still felt the shame, even knowing it wasn't her shame to carry. That was the problem with memories; they could be a dangerous thing. You watch them play over and over again in your head. Study them. Examine them. Imagine them turning out differently. And those are the edges that will cut you. The second-guessing. The what-ifs. Rewinding the movie in your brain incessantly until finally pressing stop and learning to live with them, but the sharp edges will always be there, ready to gut you, as they were doing now.

He squeezed her hands again, bringing her back to her story. "A few weeks later, Erik sweet-talked my neighbor into letting him in my house. I'd changed the locks after kicking him out. He knew I gave our neighbor, Mrs. Johnson, a spare key. She knew we had broken up, but he'd given her some sob story about leaving an important document at my house. She let him in but stayed with him, wouldn't give him the key. She kept an eye on him."

"Smart of her!"

"Somehow, without her noticing, he had managed to unlock the sliding door to the back deck. After she'd gone back to her place, he snuck around the back and let himself in. He was waiting for me when I got home from work." She shuddered. It'd been so long since she'd talked about it, so long since she'd had to. The last time she'd ever had to tell the whole story was at Erik's trial. She wasn't sure if she could go on.

"Chickadee, look at me." He tipped her chin up until her eyes met his. Those fathomless blue eyes that could promise her security. "You're safe with me. Whatever happened is in the past. You are safe now. Finish it," he urged.

She knew in her heart that she was safe, yet a small part of her was never going to feel completely safe again. "He took me by surprise and knocked me around a bit before I'd completely grasped what was happening."

Natalie choked back a sob. "He blamed me for everything. It was my fault he'd lost that big case, my fault he was so far in debt. I'd flushed thousands of dollars of product and caused all his problems.

"He pinned me to the floor over there." She pointed to the space between the kitchen, living room, and stairs. She still had trouble passing by the spot, never pausing, intent on passing it as quickly as possible. "I fought him at first, I tried everything I knew to get him off me. He wasn't as big or muscular as you, but he was still much larger, much stronger than me. I fought, screamed, bit, kicked, anything to get away. Until ... until he wrapped his hands around my neck."

The fear she'd felt in that moment was unlike anything she'd ever experienced before. She'd known he was determined to kill her, she had to do something, but it had become hard to breathe. His thumbs had pressed unmercifully into her windpipe quickly bringing in darkness. She lost the battle.

"The last thing I felt was his hands squeezing my throat." She broke off as another sob consumed her. She'd tried to put it all behind her, but after one retelling of the story, it had all come rushing back as if it had just happened. Graham wrapped her in his arms, and all she could do was hold on for dear life as she wept.

Graham managed to contain his anger at her ex as he held her tightly. He'd had no idea what she'd gone through, and his heart ached that she'd suffered so much. He'd never have imagined, when she'd said, "it didn't end well," that she'd meant the man had tried to kill her. He'd never understood men like that, and it sickened him; he vowed to find this Erik; he needed to hurt him as he'd hurt Natalie. It was a cliché, but he felt murderous towards Erik. For Natalie ... and he would do anything to protect her. She'd been alone then but she wasn't now. Squeezing her tighter in his embrace, he knew he would always do everything he could to protect her.

As her tears subsided, she sat back and looked up at him in agony, her beautiful eyes swimming. He cupped her face with both hands and gently wiped the tears from her cheeks with his thumbs. "Did he rape you, Chickadee?" He held his breath, waiting for the answer.

Shaking her head, she smiled briefly. "He never got the chance." She paused, taking a deep breath. "Maddie. She heard me scream and called the police right away then came to help me. She found me on the floor and saw him trying to choke me. She "charged at him", as she put it, and swung her cane at him. I came to as he was about to attack Maddie. I grabbed his arm, but I was so weak he managed to get me in a chokehold. He'd moved so fast; I don't know how it happened. That's when I felt the knife against my throat. I felt it cut into my skin. Felt the trickle of blood. That's how the police found us. I felt so much relief seeing the police burst through the front door, but his arm was tightening around my throat and I was fading fast."

"He used me as a shield, his hold around my neck getting stronger as the police tried to talk him into letting me go. He'd moved the knife down to my side just before I passed out again. Maddie told me later that I just dropped. One moment I was standing there, the next, I was on the floor bleeding. I didn't feel the blade enter. He'd stabbed me as I lost consciousness, the knife slicing into me from my kidneys and up my back, as I fell."

He'd never heard anything so horrifying, and it shocked him. His sweet little chickadee had truly been broken, just like the bird in the painting.

"They say I died or was close to it," she continued. "I stopped breathing. Maddie kept me alive until the paramedics arrived. She saved me so many times that day, and in the months that followed, she was always there."

Graham smiled. That's how it was with him and David. "You were there for her after the tornado," he reminded her.

"I hope we're even now. I don't want either one of us going through anything like that ever again."

"You won't. You're not alone anymore, and neither is Maddie." And he meant that with everything that was in his soul. His little chickadee would never be broken again.

They took a break from talking, both needing to let it settle. Together they burrowed further into the couch, Natalie tucked up tight against his side. Both lost in their thoughts as they stared into the flames of the fireplace.

Graham didn't consider himself a hero, but he'd spent all of his adult life rescuing people. It almost broke him to think that he hadn't been there for her. Not only had he not been able to save her, but he also hadn't been aware that she'd needed saving. He regretted his lack of action twelve years ago more than ever. He should have looked for her; it would have been so easy to find her. The question was, why hadn't he?

Something had changed in him that afternoon at the lake. He'd felt things that he'd never felt ... and hadn't since. Those feelings had scared him, and it had been easier to stay away. As a nineteen-year-old, he'd been terrified that she wouldn't feel the same way; he would have been heartbroken.

But he was older and wiser and wouldn't allow his emotions to chase him away from her when he'd been given a second chance. If he'd learned anything in the intervening years, it was that Natalie had no equal.

She was the missing half of himself that he'd been searching for.

They'd been quiet for a while when Graham asked hesitantly, "What happened ... after?"

She remained silent for so long he wasn't sure she was going to answer. She sighed heavily. "I spent a week in the hospital. He'd nicked my kidney, which they were able to repair. I had a couple of dozen stitches up my back. Three stitches on my neck. But it was my throat that took the longest to heal. It was a long time before I could make a sound. Longer still till I was able to talk without pain. It was May, and I wasn't able to go back to my job, so I took a leave of absence for the rest of the school year. It killed me not to be able to work. I had so much time alone, too much. Too much time with only my thoughts. I was in therapy, but that didn't do much to alleviate the doubts and the fears ... the memories and nightmares. That's when I began painting. The ones you were looking at earlier I call my Hollow phase. That's how I felt at the time, a deep, dark, hollowness inside. It felt like I'd ... I'd ..." She trailed off, at a loss for words.

"Like you'd never feel the light again," he supplied. Graham knew that feeling well. That was how he'd felt when his dad had found him in the cabin after the tsunami. It was dark. Hollow, just as she described it. He realized then that he'd been just as broken as she'd been. "What happened to Erik," he asked before she could question him about what he'd meant.

"He got ten years, with a chance of parole after four. He's currently serving out his sentence in central Michigan. He was up for parole last year, but Maddie and I spoke at the parole hearing and his parole was denied."

"I'm glad." They were quiet again for a bit. "Natalie?" She looked up. Those lovely green eyes looked at him with so much trust. He wondered she could trust anybody after what had happened to her. "Thank you for telling me." She smiled the sweet smile that was all her own. Then she pushed herself up so she could put her lips to his, giving him a chaste kiss, but he wasn't quite ready to let her go. He wanted to hold her tightly and safely in his arms, away from the evils of the world. He laid a hand on her cheek and drew her closer to him with the arm that was wrapped around her back. But as he gazed into her tear-filled eyes, he suddenly felt apprehensive.

She'd been through a horrible ordeal. Someone she'd once loved - had once trusted - had hurt her horrendously; yet here she was, letting him hold her. Opening her trust up to him. He worried after hearing her story that he was moving too fast. He started to pull away to give her some space. But she threaded her fingers into the hair at the back of his head and brought him closer. Then her mouth was on his.

Natalie nibbled his lips until he surrendered to the sensation and was plundering her mouth. He would never get enough. Never wanted to have enough. He would never be completely sated, but he wanted to spend the rest of his life trying. With her initiating the kiss, she'd completely obliterated his anxiety.

Never breaking their kiss, Graham turned them slightly, then leaned back against the arm of the couch, pulling her with him until she was sprawled across him. His hands automatically sliding around her, he held her tightly to him, pressing until she squirmed against his erection.

Graham's hand slid beneath her oversized sweatshirt; her smooth skin heated with his touch. He caressed her lower back, but as he moved his hand slowly higher, he felt the texture of her skin change. A scar ... or scars. Like dashes up the left side of her back he traced them, his heart aching for her. For the pain she must have endured. Shaking himself free of his thoughts, he continued to caress her back, his hand moving steadily higher. Higher. Pausing when he reached her bra. He felt her stiffen and pull away from him.

"Graham," she hesitated. "I haven't been ... I mean ... since Erik." She was babbling, and yet she made perfect sense to him. He remembered Maddie's words. *Be careful with her. Be patient.*

"I know, Chickadee," he assured her as she struggled to find the words. "I'm not asking anything more of you than just this right now." He kissed her softly. "Just this," he whispered as he pulled her head down to his shoulder. They lay there together, content to just be with each other. He softly stroked the skin of her lower back, reveling in the feel of her under his fingertips. She was idly circling her finger on his chest.

"Why did you come back so quickly?" she asked suddenly. "I thought you were needed for a rescue or something."

He smiled into her hair before kissing the top of her head. "I realized it was time I grabbed something for myself." He'd spent the last twelve years giving himself to everyone else. Helping everyone. Volunteering everywhere. That had been all that mattered to him, until Natalie had walked into his life again and suddenly, it was time.

Time for him to go after what *he* wanted, what *he* needed. She didn't know it, but she was rescuing him from himself. The Nighthawks were going to have to get used to him not always being there, he would be too busy living his life. They'd be happy for him, especially David, who was always pushing him to find happiness. *Thanks, David; I intend to.*

"They really won't need you?"

"My guys are well trained," he assured her. "They can handle things without me every now and then."

"You ... the work you do ... it's so important. I never want to stand in the way of that. You amaze me," she whispered.

"You are the amazing one." She propped her chin on his chest to look into his eyes; doubt etched in her features. "You've been through so much, but here you are ... with me. Allowing me to touch you. Trusting me."

She smiled sadly. "It's taken a long time to recover from what he did, and I still have days full of anxiety and fear. But I'm determined not to let it rule me, I don't want him to steal my future."

Graham cupped her cheek. She took his breath away. "Your strength astounds me. I hope you'll let me help you in any way I can." Staring into her bright green eyes, he wanted nothing more than to support her, stand beside her. She was so full of light even after the horror she'd lived through, she sparkled as brightly as a star. Her brilliance chased away the darkness that he'd carried around with him since the tsunami. Perhaps, together, they could be each other's guiding stars, each leading the other back into the light.

"Graham?"

"Yeah Chickadee?" He continued to absently stroke her back with one hand as his thumb caressed circles on her cheek.

"Will you ... will you come upstairs with me?"

His hands stilled, stunned by the question. "Are you sure?"

"Yes. But ... I don't know how ... far," she stopped, unable to find the words again.

He tilted her face up so he could look into her eyes. "I understand. We can just hold each other if you want. Just let me hold you," he whispered, wanting nothing more than to keep this woman in his arms.

"Okay."

Together they stood. Graham turned the switch off the fireplace before heading up the stairs to her bedroom. Suddenly nervous, he didn't want to screw this up. He didn't want to take things too far that he scared her. The horror she lived through ... not knowing if she was going to live or die, not knowing if she was going to be raped, that would have left scars. Maddie's warning played in his head. *She's got her scars, both inside and out.* He definitely didn't want to add to them.

The bedspread was a mixture of muted purples and grays and suited her. It wasn't a large room, the king-size bed taking up most of the space, but it was cozy. A large dresser sat to one side; picture frames littering the top, a small armchair beside it. At the foot of the bed a long cedar chest showed off the exquisite scroll pattern carved into the front. A door to the left of the bed led to the closet and bathroom.

The wall the bed was pushed up against was painted a purple color. Plum, he thought it was called. The rest of the walls were gray. It was lovely, and it was her.

"I don't know why I'm so nervous. I've wanted this since I was twelve," she admitted to him as she crossed the room to the dresser to switch on a small lamp.

"You wanted this," he indicated the bed, "at twelve?"

She laughed. "Well, maybe not *that*. But I wanted to be near you. I wanted you to notice me ... just once." He'd had no idea; her confession stunned him. He'd been so completely focused on his sports and which girl he could get next, that he hadn't recognized what he'd been missing. At least, not until that day at the lake. That afternoon was exactly what he'd been lacking, what he'd spent his senior year searching for, though he hadn't known what that was at that time. Talking with her, sharing things he hadn't shared with anyone; she'd been a soothing balm. In that one afternoon, she had centered him.

"I definitely notice you now," he teased. "I'm sorry, I never realized before."

"We were too young."

"But not anymore." Unable to tear his gaze away, he was captured by her intoxicating eyes. He lost himself in the tenderness he saw. So beautiful, yet, with a hint of vulnerability. He needed to remember that and tamp down his needs, to keep them from taking control.

Taking a deep breath, he turned to the picture frames on her dresser, searching for something to distract himself from his longing. "This is a nice picture of you and Maddie, when was it taken?"

She moved to his side, her shoulder brushing against his arm, which did nothing to calm his desire.

"That was just after our college graduation." A huge smile lit her face as she glanced at the photo. "Maddie worked so hard to overcome her injury and still graduate. A year late, but I was so proud of her. We celebrated together." She laughed, reminiscing about that day.

Smiling down at her, he asked, "What is that laugh for?"

"Um ... we celebrated a little too hard. Had a little too much to drink and broke into our neighbor's pool."

He groaned, picturing where this story was going. "You went skinny dipping, didn't you?" The image in his mind went straight to his groin. A naked Natalie ... wet and sleek as she skimmed through the water.

She grinned again. "Yup. Almost got caught too. We thought the neighbors were away, but they came back early." She laughed again. "I'll never forget trying to help a tipsy Maddie back over to our side of the fence while trying to grab our clothes and Maddie's prosthetic at the same time. She was hopping across the yard while I urged her to go faster by waving her leg around like a lunatic. We never laughed so hard."

He chuckled. "Sounds like quite a memory." He turned to face her and pushed a lock of her hair behind her ear to better see the smile he loved to look at so much. "Wish I had been there." He winked.

"I bet." She placed her hands on his chest. "God, these are ... wow!" He grinned and couldn't resist flexing a tad. She threw her head back and laughed, a melodious sound that shot straight to his heart. "Show off."

She then grasped the bottom of his shirt, her pupils turning stormy. "Can I ...?" she whispered. He nodded and helped her pull the shirt up and over his head, then her hands were on his chest again, exploring, feeling the hard texture of his muscles. She moved them slowly downward, examining his abs with her fingers. He sucked in a breath, his muscles twitching as her hands moved over them. "How many of these do you have?"

"Enough," he was luxuriating in the feel of her hands on his skin. He bent his knees slightly —she was so tiny—and kissed her hungrily. Tongue sliding against silken tongue. He wanted to fall into her, drink her in, breathe in her intoxicating scent, commit every moment to memory. He couldn't get enough of his chickadee.

He slid his hands down her back to the hem of her sweatshirt, asking the same question, "Can I?" She nodded. He wasted no time in stripping her of the oversized clothing. He placed his hands on her hips and drew her closer to him. Her breasts covered only in a bit of lace pressed against him. She went up on her tiptoes to resume their kiss, and he met her halfway, their lips meeting, igniting a fire between them, the blaze hot and intense.

Breaking the kiss, he looked at her. He stroked her collarbone, needing to touch her as she had him. Sweeping his fingers across her shoulder, he pushed her bra strap away until it fell down her arm. He leaned forward and placed his lips at the indentation before sliding his lips up her throat to her ear.

"You are so beautiful," he whispered.

Natalie felt as if she had lost her mind. She'd surprised herself in her boldness. She'd never made the first move before, but when she had placed her hands on his chest and felt all those hard muscles, she needed - *desired* to feel them without the cloth barrier. Now she was pressed up against him, shirtless, becoming a mass of goose-bumps when he whispered in her ear. She had started this, not knowing how far she could take it, now, she only wanted more.

His lips left her ear and traveled a path to her mouth. She wanted his kisses ... furiously. Her heart became a wild thing, reckless, leaping and rushing, obliterating her fears.

His stubble rubbed her skin, but she didn't care; it felt wonderful, his taste intoxicating. Sweet, like the wine they'd had with dinner. His large hands were everywhere, spreading his heat, smoothing over her skin, and making her writhe against him for more.

As he explored her mouth, he lifted her slightly higher on her toes until her core was nestled around his erection. She groaned, grasping his biceps, the pleasure over-whelming even through clothing. She moved wantonly grinding herself against him.

More. Needing more, she wrapped her arms around his neck, pressing closer to him, as close as she could. He slid both hands down to her ass and lifted her. She spontaneously wrapped her legs around his hips as he pressed her back up against the wall, his mouth never leaving hers.

She gasped at his hardness, where she most wanted him to be. He trailed his lips down her neck as she distracted herself on his erection, her hips moving of their own accord, grinding against him.

Taking full advantage of her passionate diversion, he pushed the cups of her bra aside, his mouth blazing a path down the slope of her breast. His teeth and lips playful against her nipple, tiny kisses teasing the tight bud. She groaned again and held his head to her breast, her fingers snaking through his thick hair.

Her head back against the wall, she arched her chest closer to the searing heat of his mouth. He pulled a nipple in, teasing it with his tongue, sucking it in deeper. The overwhelming sensation was almost more than she could handle. He kissed a path to her other breast and lavished attention on that nipple as well, nipping gently.

"Oh god, Graham."

"Is this okay?" he asked. It was beyond okay, heavenly, and amazing, it was every fantasy she'd ever had.

"More than ..." she moaned again as his mouth took possession of hers. While her back was anchored against the wall, he reached up and loosened her hair, cradling her head as he devoured her mouth. With her legs still wrapped tightly around his hips, he lowered her to the bed, following her, his weight pressed her to the mattress. As she ran her hands around to his back, she could feel each warm muscle shift as he levered himself up.

His lips explored her, moving to her neck where he found the scar. "Oh, my little chickadee," he groaned as he attempted to heal the scar with kisses filled with so much tenderness, it brought tears to her eyes.

But she wanted so much more. She moved against him, urging him further. As his mouth made its way steadily lower, his hand reached behind her to release her bra. She watched as the lace sailed over his shoulder, then his wonderful mouth was on her breasts again, bathing each with equal attention as his other hand slid down her stomach. She trembled in anticipation as he slipped under the waistband of her leggings, then cupped her, making her squirm, wanting ... needing more.

"Fuck, you are so wet," he breathed into the valley between her breasts. His words only enhancing the wetness.

Graham parted her innermost folds with his fingers even as his mouth devoured hers again. Then he was slowly pushing a finger inside her. She cried out and threw her head back at the sudden rush. He brushed his thumb over her clit and slid another finger inside. She came instantly, crying out in wonder and he drew out her orgasm until she was a puddle of nerves beneath him.

"Beautiful," he murmured as his lips met hers again. He was breathing heavily, his pupils wide and his face flushed. And then he smiled. That sinfully sexy smile that melted her insides.

Wow! She sighed. She had never experienced anything as all-consuming. He slipped slightly to her side, his lips nuzzling her neck as she tried in vain to catch her breath. Sliding one arm underneath her shoulders, he turned her to him, his other hand cupping her ass beneath her leggings. He hugged her tight, allowing her to catch her breath.

"Still okay?" he whispered in her ear.

She chuckled softly. "Not sure if that's the word I would use, it's much beyond that," she replied as the sensations still shuddered through her. She'd been so afraid. For four years, she'd kept herself hidden, afraid she'd never be able to feel again. Afraid Erik had done far more damage than the physical scars he'd left her with. Instead, Graham had awakened something inside her she'd thought was long dead and now she wanted more. She put a hand on his chest and gave a soft push following him as he fell to his back. Feeling more daring than she had ever felt, she captured his mouth, her tongue playing with his. He groaned and kissed her back.

Chapter 11

NATALIE'S HAND ON HIS chest was electrifying. He'd never have imagined that his little chickadee could be so responsive. She'd practically come apart in his arms, it had been breathtaking. Watching Natalie come undone for him had been the most beautiful thing he'd ever witnessed. And if that was as far as she would want to go, he would have been completely content. But then she was pushing him over, rising above him. Sliding her body partially on his, her breasts crushed against his chest, and he knew he wanted more. Needed more.

He took pleasure in her daring, her tongue exploring his mouth. He let her take control. Taking her pleasure wherever she wished, including his chest, as her mouth moved over the muscles. She kissed, licked, and nuzzled her way down, long tresses covering his chest, and he plunged his fingers into her hair as she explored the contours of his stomach muscles. Her tiny hand skimmed slowly across his skin to the button on his jeans which she released with a twist of her fingers. Then her hand was on him and he nearly came, biting back a groan as pleasure swamped him.

Her fingers wrapped him, squeezing gently. She swiped her thumb across the tip, spreading the wetness. A groan escaped from his clenched jaw, and he felt her smile as her mouth moved back up his chest. When she was close enough, he grabbed her face and kissed her, devouring her as her magic touch ignited something intense inside him.

Graham took control as he flipped her over onto her back, kissing his way down her body, his tongue diving into her navel as she writhed beneath him. Grabbing the waistband of her leggings and panties, he stripped her of the garments in one quick motion.

She was gloriously naked, and she didn't try to cover herself as her green gaze boldly met his. The darkness of her pupils nearly eradicated the fascinating color, her face shone with a passionate flush.

"So beautiful," he breathed. He stood to quickly shed his shoes and his pants, and she held her arms out to welcome him back to the warmth of her amazing body. In her arms, it felt like coming home. She was as brilliant as the North Star, steering him home. Maybe, just maybe, the compass had been trying to guide him to her all along.

Graham wanting to go slowly, to give her more pleasure as he gathered her in his arms, he slowed their kisses, drawing them out. He reached a hand down to cup her moist heat again, his fingers quickly finding the little nub that drove her mad. Grinning as she gasped her pleasure, he started to kiss his way down her delectable body. Over her breasts, down over the smoothness of her stomach, dipping his tongue into her navel. His hand tormented her with bliss and as he slipped two fingers inside her, she arched her body, crying out his name.

He moved lower still. His fingers plied deep inside her core until he settled himself between her legs, his mouth finding her soft heat. He flicked his tongue across her clit, curling his fingers to find that elusive spot.

"You taste so good." Like the purest honey. Natalie choked back a near scream as she writhed against his mouth. Graham sucked her clit, flicking his tongue around and around until she lost control. Her hips bucked against him wildly, and he placed his arm across her abdomen to hold her as he continued to strengthen her need. Feasting on her, mouth and fingers working in tandem, he felt her body tense until she erupted. She cried out his name again as she came; the sound giving him more satisfaction than he could ever have imagined.

He kissed his way back up her body as he drew out her pleasure. He wanted to be inside her. Needed to be inside her like he needed his next breath. "Tell me you still want this. Tell me you want more," he breathed, straining to hold off the longing that threatened to overcome him.

"Please," she whispered. "I need ..."

"What do you need, chickadee?"

You. I need you."

He kissed her briefly on the lips before withdrawing. At her moan of displeasure, he assured her, "I need a condom."

She opened her eyes in shock as if the idea of protection never occurred to her. "I'm on the pill," she informed him.

He moaned. He'd never gone without a condom before. "Are you sure? I'm clean. We get tested all the time for the job. But I need to make sure this is what you want." He needed to be absolutely sure. She nodded.

"Please," she moaned, reaching for him. "I need you inside me. Now!" She didn't need to ask him twice. In an instant, he lifted himself over her, his erection probing her moist folds. With one agonizingly slow thrust, he was deep inside. The sensation was all-consuming, and he was afraid he'd come right then. Her heat, her wetness ... he felt it all; without a condom, he felt *everything*.

Fuck! She was incredibly tight. He gritted his teeth as he began to move. Slowly, Graham withdrew and thrust again, her inner muscles clenching while simultaneously stretching around him. She was so wet that he slid easily in and out.

"Incredible. My chickadee feels incredible," he breathed. Graham watched her. Her head thrown back, revealing that long, delectable neck where he couldn't resist placing his mouth. Her dark hair spread over the pale sheets, and her eyes were squeezed shut.

Plunging a hand into her hair, he tilted her head up, "Look at me, Natalie." Her eyes flew open, and in them he saw everything he'd ever wanted. She gazed up at him, an enchanting mix of vulnerability and hunger in the green depths. Her expression was raw and loaded with unfiltered emotions, and desire – a heat so intense it threatened to burn his own icy orbs.

"I can feel every inch of you. Your heat surrounding my cock is intense."

"Faster. Harder," she moaned, spurring him on. He leaned in to capture her mouth with his, thrusting his tongue to match his movements. She was incredibly responsive as he moved within her.

"I need ..." she groaned. "More. Please." Reaching down between their bodies, Graham flicked her clit as he thrust harder. Once. Twice. Three times and Natalie shattered. Her orgasm all-consuming as she arched against him. He continued to pump into her as he rode her orgasm, her inner walls tightening around him until he was overcome by his own orgasm, her name bursting from his lips.

She held him tight, wrapping her legs around his hips as he emptied himself inside her.

Graham collapsed on her, breathing heavily. She ran her hand up and down his back as she held him to her breast as he attempted to calm his racing heart.

Nothing he'd experienced had prepared him for this, he felt as if he had been knocked over, everything flipped upside down.

Graham gathered her close, grounding himself with the feeling of her in his arms. He kissed the top of her head as she sighed. "Wow!" she whispered, as overwhelmed as he was. "I ... wow!"

He chuckled. "I know," was all his brain was capable of saying. They lay there for a while, basking in the afterglow until the chill in the room cooled their heated skin. Returning from the bedroom after freshening up, he found a naked Natalie peeking out the curtains. His heart leapt; he had just had her, yet he wanted her again already.

She was magnificent standing in the snowy glow entering through the curtains and highlighting her curves. "There are at least six inches out there."

He looked past her to see for himself. "Doesn't look like it's going to slow down anytime soon." He wrapped his arms around her and placed his chin on the top of her head as they watched the snow. If he could freeze time, this would be the moment. He wanted to hold on to this time forever. It was perfect. She leaned back into him, and he sighed. *She* was perfect. How could he, with all his internal darkness, measure up. He was suddenly seized with fear and doubt.

Natalie turned around in his arms to face him; she was so little standing in front of him. Smiling up at him, she whispered, "Do you know how perfect you are? How absolutely wonderful this moment is?"

"I have an inkling," he winked down at her. The tenseness he had felt a moment ago dissolving upon seeing her smile. She placed her cheek against his chest and wrapped her arms around his waist, and he was content to just hold her.

She shivered as he breathed her in. "Cold?" he asked as he tightened his arms around her.

"Maybe a little." He kissed her head, reluctant to release her. He didn't want this interlude to end, didn't want to leave.

"Let's get under the covers."

Her eyes widened. "You'll stay?"

He tilted her chin up. "I'm not going anywhere," he assured her. He steered her to the bed, and together they crawled under the covers. One arm under her head, the other wrapped around her stomach, they faced the window. He relished having her in his arms as he listened to her breathing while sleep claimed her, and the still falling snowflakes blanketed the world outside.

Chapter 12

NATALIE WOKE THE NEXT morning, her body wonderfully sore. Graham was sitting on the edge of the bed, talking softly to someone on his cell. "I think you can handle things for one weekend without me." Wait, did that mean he planned to spend the whole weekend with her? She hoped it did. "Come on, David, give me a break," he continued pausing to listen to whatever David was saying on the other end. He ran his fingers through his hair, causing some of it to stand on end. "When have I ever asked for anything before? Fuck, give me a break!" He laughed then. "I'll remember this the next time you ask for time off ... I plead the fifth ... no comment ... I'm hanging up now." And he did, placing his phone on the nightstand.

He turned towards Natalie, still smiling. "Siblings."

She laughed. "Is David giving you the third degree?"

"And then some."

"I'll probably get the same from Maddie."

"Ugh. Before you know it, the whole town will know our business."

"Oh, I don't know," she teased, sitting up to kiss his shoulder. "It may take a whole week to reach the *entire* town."

"Ha ha. Very funny," he said lightheartedly as he lunged for her. She let him wrestle her back onto the bed, laughing as they fell into each other. Then he was kissing her again, and all she could manage was a sigh. But way too soon, he lifted his head and looked down at her.

"I'm starving."

"Aww, does the poor growing boy need sustenance?" She reached down and wrapped her hand around his erection. He moaned.

"Fuck, Natalie! What you do to me." Before she knew it, he was inside her again. She met him thrust for thrust, reveling in the feeling of him moving within her. All too soon, she was climaxing, Graham soon following.

When their pounding hearts slowed, Graham suggested they hop in the shower before making breakfast. Natalie had always wanted to try shower sex and before long their hearts were racing again as the water sprayed them.

Thoroughly sated, they threw on some clothes and headed for the kitchen where they prepared a quick repast of eggs and bacon for their required sustenance.

The snow had tapered off as they slept but had left a foot covering the ground and it was enchanting, trees, still with their colorful canopy, draped in white. While it was beautiful, Natalie wasn't looking forward to digging out. Maddie sometimes had trouble in the snow with her prosthetic, so Natalie often cleared both the driveways while Maddie did the porch and sidewalk.

As they sat to eat, Graham asked, "So, what do you want to do today?"

She didn't know why but it surprised her he wanted to spend the day with her. "You don't have to go to work?"

"Nope. I'm all yours."

She grinned, pleased she would have some more time with him.

She grinned at the notion of having more time with him and pondered what she wanted to do with him today; most of her ideas involved the bed ... the couch ... the floor; or the kitchen table where they were currently enjoying their meal. She blushed at the direction her thoughts were taking. She answered quickly so he wouldn't guess where her mind had gone. "The whole town is probably shut down today, there won't be much we can do."

"I'm sure we can think of a few things," he winked at her. Obviously, his thoughts were on the same track as hers.

She blushed again. "I ... I should probably clear the driveways before it freezes too much."

"Sounds like fun!"

"Oh, I'm not asking you to help. ..." she broke off when he placed a finger on her lips.

"I want to help."

Together, they cleaned up the breakfast dishes then bundled up to face the snow, Graham thankful that he'd remembered to grab his go bag before joining Natalie in her studio since it held clothes for any kind of weather.

Natalie trudged through the knee-high snow to her garage to get the shovels. By the time she reached the garage, Graham was already there waiting for her, laughing. What had been challenging for her to trudge through had been nothing for his six-foot-two frame. "Laugh it up, fuzzball!" she taunted.

"What took you so long?"

"Very funny," she groaned as she unlocked the door. "I can't help it that I'm short."

He grabbed her up against him, lifting her slightly out of the snow. "Short and sweet, just the way I like you." He gave her a full-on smack on the lips before releasing her. "Whoa," he blurted as he glanced in her garage.

Not the most organized garage, it held what she needed it to hold; her gardening equipment in one corner, a small workbench with the tools she used to make her canvasses of all sizes and the supplies – lengths of 1 x 2-inch boards and rolls of canvas material to assemble the canvasses. In here she could make any size of canvas she required. "Guess you really do need your own studio," he mused.

"Oh, shut up. It works for me."

"But what if you need some of your art supplies and your tiny little legs can't get through all the snow?"

"Oh, ha ha. Are you done teasing me?"

"Hmm," he mused. "Not sure. Can I let you know later?"

Natalie shoved a shovel at him. "Get to work, slave."

"Yes, ma'am," he saluted, then started in on the snow. Together they made short work of the two driveways and sidewalk. With the shovels back in the garage, Graham locked the door, and Natalie hit him dead in the chest with a snowball.

"Oh, it's like that, is it?" Graham threatened while he bent down to make his own weapon. But before he could launch it, he was hit in the face, snow sliding down inside his coat. He glared at her a moment as the snow dripped off his face. One gloved hand flew to her mouth, and her eyes widened with shock.

"I ... I'm sorry. I didn't mean for it to hit you in the face." She felt horrible, knowing how bad snowballs in the face could feel.

He grabbed up more snow, pressing it into a ball as he stomped toward her. "I'll get you for that," he promised with a gleam in his eye.

Natalie shrieked and turned to run away. Due to her short legs, she didn't get far before he'd grabbed her from behind and lifted her out of the snow while the one hand dumped snow on the top of her head. She squealed as the snow slid under her shirt and down her chest. *Cold! God, that's cold.* She shivered even while laughing. Somehow, she managed to wriggle free of his hold, and with two hands, she scooped up as much snow as she could launching it at him before dashing away again, laughing.

Graham covered in snow was the funniest thing she'd seen in a while. From a safe distance, she doubled over with laughter. His hair was white with snow, and it stuck to his unshaven face. Even his eyelashes had snow dotting them. He attempted to shake off the worst of it while she laughed. Then he was chasing her again but when she slipped and would have landed flat on her butt, Graham caught her. He snatched her up and threw her over his shoulder as she flailed and kicked, trying to free herself, laughing uncontrollably.

Face down over his shoulder, she couldn't see where he was headed and was soon flying through the air as Graham threw her into the largest snow pile. Snow covered her as she landed in the heap. He helped the snow along by pushing more of it on her legs and stomach, burying her in the white mass. He stood back to examine his work; taking his phone out of his pocket, he took several pictures of her efforts to free herself. He was the one who was laughing this time as he watched her struggle to get to her feet. She must have looked like a turtle stuck on its back, arms and legs flailing, trying desperately to gain traction.

"All right. All right. You've had your fun. Now can you help me get up?" She shivered as more snow slipped under her clothes. The back of her coat had ridden up leaving her bare back against the snow, some of which was starting to creep down inside her pants. It was cold and unpleasant, but she still had a wide smile on her face.

"Do you give up?" he asked.

"Does it look like I can continue the fight?" He hesitated a moment before he reached out a hand to help her up. Natalie grabbed the proffered hand and pulled hard instead bringing him down into the pile beside her.

"You did that on purpose," he accused as she giggled hysterically.

"No, no ... I would never," she managed between giggles.

"Why you ..." he threatened as he rolled over on top of her. The giggles died instantly, replaced with need. She may have had snow in some very uncomfortable places, but that did nothing to suppress the sudden fire that burned through her as his lips claimed hers. She wrapped her arms around him as their tongues wrestled. Damn, they had on too many layers of clothing.

"Hey!" Natalie vaguely heard her sister call out. "You guys done wrestling in the snow yet? I've got hot chocolate!" Graham broke their kiss and grinned down at her. She smiled back; sure he could see the desire burning in her eyes.

"Come on, Yeti," he said, tweaking her nose. "Let's get warmed up." He stood with just a little bit of difficulty as the pile of snow they were on shifted. He easily pulled her to her feet before she could tumble off the mound of snow into the driveway. Once upright, she attempted to straighten her clothes, managing to get more of the cold, wet snow down her shirt and pants. She heard him stifle a laugh.

She glared up at him. "What?"

"You really do look like a Yeti," he teased as he reached out to her hair. There were big clumps of snow stuck to the strands since she'd lost her hat somewhere. She shook her head in an attempt at dislodging the worst of it. Graham helped her with the rest and as wetness trickled down her back, she met his gaze and shivered. Whether from the cold or the intimate look in his eyes, she couldn't say.

He grabbed her hand and turned to walk toward the house, calling, "Did I hear something about hot chocolate?"

"Absolutely," Maddie called back. She had managed to clear the deck and turn on the gas fire pit table. They stamped off the snow as they joined Maddie for the promised hot chocolate. "You two looked like you were having fun," Maddie remarked with a wink as they sat down to enjoy their drinks. Taking a sip, Natalie tried to hide her blush behind her mug.

She nearly choked as the liquid burned a path down to her stomach. "Jeez Louise, Maddie. What did you put in this?"

Maddie smiled a serene smile that could charm even Sheriff Dodd, "Just a little something extra to heat your blood."

"A little. Tastes like you poured the whole bottle in."

"Well, I had put in the proper amount, but there was only a tiny bit left in the bottle. Figured I might as well finish off the bottle."

"Define 'a tiny bit,'" Natalie insisted. Maddie held her hand up, thumb and finger about two inches apart. "You call that a tiny bit. Some people would say that was enough for three more drinks."

Maddie shrugged and sipped her potent hot chocolate. "To each their own."

Graham snorted. "Don't encourage her," Natalie told him. "She'll be spiking all your drinks."

"Thanks for the warning. I'll have my food tester taste every drink she makes for me from now on."

"Oh, very funny. So, I may have gone a little overboard," Maddie admitted. "I just got off the phone with mom."

Natalie groaned. That woman could drive even the most pious to drink. "Completely understandable then. And what did mother dearest have to say?"

"They're coming to visit for Thanksgiving."

Natalie nearly spit out the sip she had just taken. "What? Why?"

"Dunno. She just said she wanted to see what her girls were up to."

"What did she mean by that?" Natalie wondered. There was always an ulterior motive to everything their mother did when it came to her children. Usually, in a futile effort to push them to be somebody they weren't. "Guess that means we have to cook then."

"Ugh, you're right. I hadn't thought of that," Maddie groaned. "And if it's not perfect, we'll definitely hear about it."

"Then she'll start in on how we are not living up to our full potential, wasting ourselves in our current jobs."

"Won't that be fun," Maddie lamented. "God, Natalie. I don't know how you could stand her constant criticism growing up."

Natalie shrugged. "I learned to tune it out."

"Yeah, but I'm sure some of it still leaked through ... like toxic waste," mused Maddie.

"Therapy helped." They both knew that wasn't completely true, but neither argued the point.

"God, Natalie. How are we going to get through this?" Maddie whined.

"I have an idea," Graham said. Both sisters turned toward him. "How bout we throw Thanksgiving for both our families. My parents will be here too. David and I can help with the cooking and stuff. My parents could act as a buffer."

"You'd want to subject your parents to ours?"

"Might be fun."

Natalie snorted. "I don't think fun has ever been used to describe Debra Ghannon before." Maddie laughed. They both knew that somehow over the years, all the joy had been sucked out of their mother. They'd never understood why, though. She seemed happy enough with her marriage. With her daughters ... well, they told themselves she just wanted what was best for them. William, their dad, went along with whatever Debra told him. He never argued with her. He'd learned long ago, just like his daughters had, that it wasn't worth the aggravation of arguing. Maddie called it whipped. It was an accurate description. William was like a broken mustang.

"They might be useful to deflect her, at least for a little while," Maddie admitted, and Natalie agreed.

"Well, we've got a whole month. We'd better start cleaning now." The sisters laughed. It was nice to finally be able to share with Maddie her frustration with their mother. Growing up, she'd wished she'd had an ally when it came to facing her mother's disappointment. She'd long ago stopped letting it get to her, but it still would have been nice to have someone who understood. It seemed weird being thankful to a tornado for allowing Maddie to see their mother's true nature, But Natalie finally had her ally in her sister.

Chapter 13

NATALIE LAY ON HER stomach on her bed, completely spent from the incredible lovemaking she'd just experienced. Earlier, after sharing a quick lunch, they'd settled on the couch to watch a movie. She'd picked a Marcus Rayne film, laughing when Graham groaned his displeasure, but after arguing how hot the actor was and that his Titan superhero movie was thrilling, he begrudgingly relented.

About halfway through the movie, Natalie found another thrill when she straddled Graham's lap, though she had no idea where her brazenness had come from.

"I can't believe that just happened," she stated. "Why can't I control myself around you?"

"Who's asking you to?" he teased as he stroked her back.

"That was one of the most erotic things I've ever done," she whispered in wonder.

"Really ... well ..." She could hear the pleasure in his voice.

She lightly slapped him on the shoulder. "Oh, stop being so pleased with yourself."

"Can't be helped," he said, threading his fingers through her hair. "You have that effect on me." She smiled shyly then placed her cheek against his chest.

"Your heart is beating so fast."

"That's the effect you have on me."

She sighed as he lightly ran his fingers across her back. *God, that felt good.* He certainly knew how to make her come apart. She sighed again as an image of the two of them in the shower flashed. What he'd done to her had been mind-blowing. Her past sexual experiences could only be described as conservative at best. But with Graham—it was sensual, freeing. She found she craved more and more.

"You sound relaxed," he whispered near her ear.

"Mmm," was all she could manage. She felt his smile as he kissed her shoulder. His hand stopped suddenly over her scars. He pushed himself up on one elbow to look at them, his body tensed up. "It's okay, you know. I'm okay."

He shook his head as his fingers gently traced the long scar. "No, Chickadee. It's not okay. I wish I could go back and put some serious hurt on him." His anger was palpable.

Natalie turned on her side to face him. She reached up to stroke his jaw as she saw the agony reflected in his eyes. "Just the fact that you care enough to want to hurt the one who hurt me means more to me than you'll ever know."

He grabbed her hand and kissed her palm. "I do care. I've always cared. Through all these years, I've never forgotten you. I was just too stupid to realize how important you were to me."

His confession shocked her. She knew she'd carried a torch for him, but she never imagined he would have the same feelings. She hadn't considered he gave her a single thought since. Having watched the interview and hearing his confession just now, she knew she'd been wrong. He wasn't the only one who'd been an idiot, though.

"I watched the video of the interview," she admitted. "What you said about me ..."

"Figured that out, did you." He flopped onto his back, an arm thrown over his eyes.

"I had no idea. I wish I had seen that video months ago."

"I wish I'd looked you up years ago. Maybe I could have spared you all the hurt." He traced her scar again.

"No, Graham. You can't think like that. You are not to blame for what happened to me. Besides, I could have tried to look for you too."

"We were both stupid," he muttered.

"True. But that day at the lake—it was barely a few hours spent together. How were we supposed to know then how important that time would become for us? We were young, too young to truly understand anything."

"Young and stupid."

"Exactly."

"I just wish ..."

She placed a finger over his mouth to stop him. "I know. But we're together now. And I, for one, am not feeling stupid at all." She knew what she was feeling but was terrified to say it out loud. Her feelings were too new, too fragile. She'd thought her heart was too broken to ever love again, but each moment spent with Graham was a balm on her shattered heart, mending it bit by bit. Was she ready to risk her heart again? For the man beside her, she might be, especially when he looked at her like he was right now, a devilish tilt in his lips.

"You're not feeling stupid? Apparently, I didn't do a good enough job in the shower then." He pushed her back as his mouth captured hers.

"Couch sex and shower sex all in one day. This certainly has been a weekend of firsts for me. What's next? Sex on the kitchen table?" she joked.

"If you're lucky," he said, kissing her nose.

Much later, they were cooking dinner together. Spaghetti with sauce from a jar, and a salad that Natalie tossed together – fast and easy and just what they needed. They needed sustenance, especially if the night proved as entertaining as the previous one.

They talked about nothing in particular as they ate. She shared a few fun stories about some of her students, showing him some pictures on her phone of their projects. The pictures she'd shown him of Lucy's paintings had him in awe of the little girl's talent.

"I know, right?" she said after seeing his jaw drop. "Her talent is unmatched. She's a wonder."

"I can't believe someone so young could make something this incredible. It's so realistic." Lucy had drawn her dog managing to capture the joyful expression on the dog's face as he panted. "It's amazing."

He described some of his memorable rescues. As she listened, she remembered something he'd said the previous night in her studio.

"Can I ask you a question?"

"Of course." He rinsed off their dishes and placed them in the dishwasher. When she hadn't asked her question for a moment, he paused while drying his hands. She was suddenly nervous though unsure why. She didn't want to pry. If he wasn't ready to talk about himself, she didn't want to push him away. "Natalie?" he asked, concern etched into his face. "What is it?"

"I ... I need to know about something you said last night," she continued hesitantly. She began to pace. "You don't have to tell me if you'd rather not."

"Natalie." He caught her wrist as she paced past him, bringing her to a halt in front of him. "Why don't you ask me and let me decide if I want to answer or not."

She took a deep breath. "Last night, when you were looking at my Hollow phase canvasses, you mentioned something about light. I've been wondering about it ever since. It seemed like ... like you'd had an experience like mine. Depression ... living in a dark place, like I had."

She watched his body stiffen as if her question took him somewhere he didn't want to go. A shutter slammed over his expression. "I'm sorry. You don't—"

"There was a time when I thought I'd never see the light in anything again," he said softly. He turned his back to her lost in thought, his posture slumped; her heart broke for him.

She stood beside him at the island. Placing her hand over his where it rested on the counter, she willed him to share with her.

"It was after the tsunami," he began. "It ... that place ... it changed me."

When he didn't say more, Natalie asked gently, "How so?"

Graham sighed heavily. "Seven years ago, I was confident, arrogant even, in my abilities to help." His chin fell to his chest as he bowed his head. "I was an idiot."

Natalie took his hand and led him to the table, encouraging him to sit and continue. "I was deployed to Sumatra in Indonesia. An area called Banda Aceh. We didn't know it at the time, but that area had been hit the hardest. Fifty-foot waves struck with the force of a two-megawatt bomb. Everything was gone. Remember the tornado, when it seemed like my house had just disappeared. Imagine that times thousands. Every house, every building, everything that wasn't made of concrete was wiped away."

Natalie placed her hand on his, and he linked their fingers. She squeezed in sympathy. "In all, there were over two hundred thousand who perished. But in the area I was working, one hundred twenty thousand souls lost their lives. Men, women, old and young. Those waves didn't discriminate.

"They had no warning," he continued. "At least they didn't understand the warning at the time. It was exciting to them when the water started to recede as the wave built. Kids flocked to the beach to look for shells, fish, whatever they could find in an area that was usually covered in water. They didn't realize they were in danger. All those children," he broke off on a shuddering breath.

"Oh god, Graham! I had no idea. She struggled to contain her tears, needing to hold it together till he was done.

"My group ... we were tasked with finding and burying the bodies. They were worried about disease so there was a sense of urgency. No time for funerals, We did our best to identify the dead, but most often, we were burying people in a mass grave. As the days went on, the hope of finding people still alive in the wreckage dwindled. The occasional cheer could be heard as someone was found, but those became fewer and fewer. The damage to the bodies was one of the things I remember most. That and the smell. Fuck. That smell. Some days, it's still with me, still tainting everything." He scrunched up his nose as if the memory were assaulting his senses.

"The images of all the bodies still hit me." Graham continued squeezing his eyes closed, trying unsuccessfully to block out the images. "Some bloated beyond recognition in places where the water never receded. Others crushed under mounds of debris. I had been to many disaster scenes before, but nothing that prepared me for what we saw there. We blocked it out as best as we could, just to get the job done.

"The ones who were still alive wandered around the area like the walking dead, in shock. Searching for their loved ones. The stories they told ...

"One man told me he was searching for his wife. They had been sitting on a bench, sharing in the beauty of the day. She had been in his arms, and then she was gone, ripped away from him. We did our best to help him find her, but it was an impossible task. He had cuts all over from the debris in the water, so we treated his wounds as best we could and sent him to where the command center was being set up. Told him he needed to add his wife's name to the list of those lost, trying to give him as much hope as we could even though we knew hope was futile." He stopped for a moment as the image of that man wandering off played through his mind, still searching for his love, still hopeful deep inside that he would find her. But outwardly, he was dejected, his shoulders slumped, and his head bowed as he shuffled down the path through the debris to the command tent.

"The children," he continued quietly as he stared blankly at their clasped hands. "The children were the worst. Both alive and dead. The ones that were still alive … most of them were alone. Their entire families had been wiped out. They hung onto us, desperate for comfort. We tried … but we were there to do a job. And we had to do it quickly before those little ones caught diseases from all the rotting corpses." His ice-blue eyes met hers, radiating anguish.

"I'm sure you did all you could for them, and for a brief time, you *did* give them exactly what they needed," Natalie assured him.

"The little bodies, though," he choked out. "All the dead children, their bodies were so broken, like the bird you painted. I had to shut down. Shut it out. Do the job. Don't think. Don't look too hard at the faces. But it was impossible. The faces seeped in and settled deep inside me. Somedays, they are still there," he ended on a whisper.

Natalie let him be for a bit as he struggled with his emotions. A few tears ran silently down her cheeks, but she stayed quiet, just squeezing his hand. Anchoring him to the here and now with her touch.

Graham took a deep breath, letting it out slowly before continuing. "When I returned home, it stayed with me. The smell, the faces, the sense of hopelessness. The darkness swallowed me, and I let it. My family … they tried. But I felt … wrong. Tainted somehow. I didn't want it to spread to them, so I went to our cabin in the UP. I just stopped living. I barely ate, drank heavily, and hardly slept. I couldn't get away from that place. All those faces." The memories of those faces still inundated him. He went there full of passion, confident in his skills. Skills that it soon became glaringly obvious were useless. He'd felt impotent. There was no saving the hundreds of thousands of people who'd perished. The most he could do was try to offer closure to the surviving family members, most days, even that had been impossible.

Even as he sat in Natalie's dining room, the anxiety of the hopelessness he'd felt swamped him. His shoulders tightened, and he gritted his teeth, struggling to stem the flood of despair. The bleakness he'd felt during those days was a dichotomy to the beauty of the area. When the waters had receded, the ocean had returned to its quiet splendor. The magnificent shades of blue and green that the ocean manifested once calm, juxtaposed against the grays and browns that had brought destruction with them. The hope on the faces of the families still missing loved ones contrasted with the futility of the situation.

"My family let me be for over two weeks," he continued, his voice gritty. "Then one day, my father was at the door. He'd decided I'd had enough of facing the darkness alone, dumped the remaining alcohol and sat with me, giving me time to sober up. For days he sat next to me, not saying a word. Somehow it worked, and I opened up to him. We exorcised the darkness. That's when he gave me that compass." Graham still struggled when the memories were triggered, but his family and his teammates kept him grounded. Soon afterward, he'd started Nighthawk, knowing in his heart that he would never be able to participate in a large-scale search and rescue again.

Natalie went to him. Lowering herself onto his lap, she wrapped her arms around him. He buried his face in her hair and breathed deeply, the hint of lavender a solace to his shattered soul. They sat like that, drawing comfort from each other. A strange peace surrounding him.

"The darkness is still there. It always will be."

"I know. Believe me, I know," she whispered against his throat.

"The thing is, though," he continued, "when I'm here, with you - there's light." He leaned back slightly so he could look into her eyes. "So much light that it chases away the darkness. I've only ever felt that with my family. But with you it's so much more … intense. Your light warms me from the inside out. That sounds so cheesy, but it's true."

"It's not cheesy." He shot her a doubtful look. "Okay," she chuckled. "It may be a little cheesy, but I happen to like cheese. Almost as much as I like you. And for the record, I feel the same way. You chase away my darkness too."

He cupped her face with both hands and kissed her deeply. Passionately. Natalie kissed him back with everything she had, communicating the depths of her feelings. He moved his hands to her hips and stood, lifting her to sit at the edge of the table. His irises turned stormy as he stared down at her, the pupils dilating, overtaking the icy hue.

She leaned back on her elbows as he loomed over her, trembling at the intensity in his eyes. "Did you say something earlier about sex on the table?" he whispered, his hushed voice sending delicious sensations curling through her stomach. He was wreaking havoc with her senses, firing up her imagination.

"I seem to recall a conversation like that … I think." The breathlessness surprised her. When did she become this sensual being? He made her feel … everything. His hands made her feel beautiful, his eyes made her feel extraordinary, his mouth made her feel sexy.

"What do you say. Wanna give it a try?" His mouth moving over her throat was scrambling her ability to put together a coherent thought.

"Abs … Absolutely!" She grasped his biceps, the muscles flexing under her fingers.

Graham ripped her shirt up over her head before his mouth took hers, his shirt soon following hers to the floor. He gently pushed her to lie on her back. She gasped; the difference between the cold of the table under her and the warmth of the body on top was shocking. She arched her back, a squeal escaping from her lips, making him chuckle. His mouth moved to her breast, his tongue reaching out to tease her nipple through the lace of her bra. As she lost herself in that sensation, he opened the clasp, then pulled it off and in one swift motion threw it over his shoulder. It disappeared into the kitchen while Natalie giggled.

Her pants followed the bra and her giggles ceased. Left with just her panties, she lay wantonly on her kitchen table. "Now there's an image I want to remember forever," His eyes flared with heat and she blushed, her whole body heating. "I love how expressive you are. How you turn that wonderful shade of pink all over. Even here," he said as he lifted her leg and kissed her ankle. "And here." His lips slid to her calf. "And here." He nuzzled the inside of her thigh. She ached in anticipation, craving his mouth on her.

"And most definitely here," he whispered as he placed his mouth over her mound. He kissed her through her panties, the warm heat of his breath on her most intimate of places.

He sat in the chair between her parted legs, ready to feast on her. She bit her bottom lip when she looked down to see his head between her legs. His eyes slowly moved up her body until they met hers, burning with intensity. The corners of his lips lifted, giving her the sexy smile that made her want to do naughty things.

Placing her legs on his shoulders, he pulled her closer to him, her ass just at the edge of the table. He pushed her panties to the side, and his mouth was on her again. He used his tongue to part her before dipping inside. Her body bucked as her hands clenched around the edges of the table. He placed an arm across her to hold her in place. He alternated licking and dipping, his tongue driving her out of her mind.

Plunging two fingers in, he curled them toward that deliciously elusive spot. A sound escaped her lips as she tossed her head from side to side, the pleasure almost too much. Her inner walls clamped around him as he worked over her until she was grinding herself on his face. Wanting more. Needing more. Needing to …

She came so suddenly, the force of it washing over her, that she cried out; but he was there, swallowing her cry with his kiss as he drove himself deep inside her. The jolt of his cock entering her was glorious. The fullness sent a wave of sparks throughout her body, prolonging her orgasm.

Her legs were still propped up on his shoulders and allowed him to slip deep. Deeper than she'd ever felt, ever imagined he could be. He set a relentless rhythm that was nothing short of amazing.

"Fuck, I can feel you stretching around me," he moaned as he moved his hips grinding against her clit with each thrust.

She was building towards another spectacular orgasm as he continued to drive inside her. He grasped her hips, his fingers squeezing as he moved, harder and faster. Every muscle in her body tightened until she felt herself flying, overcome by her second orgasm. His fingers tightened on her hips as he pulled her to him for one final thrust. With a grunt and a moan, he emptied himself, caught in orgasmic bliss.

They both stayed like that, breathing hard. Natalie let her legs slip from his shoulders as he folded over her and lay his head on her chest. She couldn't tell whose heartbeat she was currently feeling. Could be hers. Could be his. As long as there was one, then she was assured that they were alive and hadn't died from the pleasure. Although, being in his arms like this certainly felt like heaven.

"Was table sex everything you imagined it to be?" he asked as he kissed the side of her breast.

"And then some," she sighed. He chuckled and stood. Hitching his pants back up to his hips, he helped her sit up. He sat in the chair in front of her again and she placed her feet on the seat on either side of him. He leaned over and kissed her inner thigh, her skin tingled, and she nearly jumped him again.

But then she remembered all they had discussed. She slipped off the table and straddled his lap. Lifting herself to be eye to eye with him, she placed her arms on his shoulders, her fingers running through his hair. "Thank you for sharing your darkness with me. I hope you'll let me try to be a light for you for as long as you need it."

"Oh, Chickadee. I would love nothing more," he declared as he kissed her softly.

"What a pair we are," Natalie lamented. "I wish ... well; we both have regrets. I guess it doesn't do any good to dwell on them."

"Probably not. That is where the darkness hides." They both had worked too hard to live in regret.

Chapter 14

AFTER ANOTHER FABULOUS NIGHT together, Natalie and Graham had enjoyed a quiet Sunday morning. Eventually, real life intruded. Graham had to take several business calls for groups who wanted to book training at Nighthawk and Natalie retreated to her studio while he worked.

She was working on adding the finer details of her latest bird's wing when Graham joined her. He wrapped his arms around her and placed his chin on her head. "Now, this bird I like a lot more than the broken one," he remarked after studying the canvas for a moment. She had painted another chickadee, but instead of being broken and bloody, this one was soaring in flight. Light radiated all around it, its eyes bright and alive. The feathers wispy and strong; the image was pure joy. "I am always fascinated that you can paint light like that. And the eyes ... amazing."

"I spent quite a bit of time when I was younger working on eyes. They are the windows to the soul."

"I remember. You had pages and pages of eyes in your sketchbook."

"You mean the sketchbook you stole," she teased.

"Borrowed."

"Semantics," she countered. She stepped out of his arms to start the brush cleaning process. She wiped them with a rag, dipped them in paint thinner then wiped them again. She repeated this process until they were clean of paint. "Did you get everything arranged for that group?

"Yup. They are all set."

"That's good." She hung her painting apron on a hook on the easel.

"You don't have to stop working just because I'm here," he told her.

"No. It's okay. I need a break and the paint needs to dry before the next step."

"In that case, Maddie stopped by when I was finishing up my call. She said to tell you that the band you like is playing tonight at Jolene's. She'll be at the usual table if we want to join her."

"Great! I love listening to them. Maddie and I usually go and have some dinner there before the band starts, does that work for you?" The all-female band mostly did covers of some of the better classic pop and rock songs, but occasionally, they'd play an original piece, written by the keyboard player.

As they left Natalie's house for Jolene's, she noticed footprints in the snow wrapping around the side of her house. "That's strange."

"What is?"

"Those." She pointed then followed the footprints to the side of her house, Graham right behind her. "That's weird."

Maddie joined them, having seen them leave. "Did you walk around out here?" Natalie asked Maddie.

"No," she had her phone out. Natalie knew who she was calling. "Ian, yeah, it's Maddie. We've got a situation at our place." Ian McClintock, the deputy with the sheriff's department, had been first on the scene when Natalie had been attacked. Ever since then, he'd watched over the sisters, always making himself available if they need- ed help. And, of course, this situation was no different. It wasn't long before he was pulling up in front of the duplex.

He studied the footprints, following them to the side of the house, then to the back. Even though Maddie had cleaned off the deck, they could still see where someone had stood near the sliding glass door.

"I checked on the way over," Ian was saying. "He's still locked up." He was referring to Erik, of course. There was always the outside chance of him getting out and coming after Natalie again.

"Okay," Ian continued studying the prints. "Looks like someone walked from the front of the house. Stopped at the side. Peering in windows maybe? Then continued to the back where bold as can be they walked up onto the deck. Small feet perhaps, but hard to tell with all the snowmelt from today."

"Why would someone want to look in my windows?" Natalie wondered. "Is there some sort of peeping Tom going around town?"

"Not that I know of," Ian said as he took a closer look at the windows on the side of the house. "I'll dust for prints on the window and sliding door. Maybe we'll get lucky."

"Though probably not," Graham remarked dryly.

"Yeah, probably not." Ian walked to his cruiser to get his kit. "You headed to Jolene's?" he asked them.

"Yeah. You gonna be able to stop by too?" Maddie asked.

"I'll be there when I'm done here."

Natalie gave him a quick hug. "Thanks so much for this, Ian."

"You'll let us know what you find?" Graham asked.

"Absolutely."

As the trio walked down the block, the lake breeze hitting them in the face, they discussed the situation. Who would want to peek in Natalie's windows and why? She remembered the things she and Graham had done within sight of those windows. A shiver chased through her body at the thought of someone spying on them. Graham, of course, guessed where her thoughts had gone and reached for her hand.

"It was probably just someone who was lost," Graham tried to reassure her.

"Yeah, maybe," she replied, not entirely convinced.

The three of them joined David at Jolene's. At David's mention of food, the others in the team had been only too anxious to join. They had pushed a couple of tables together and were all talking animatedly with each other. Finch and Jude were the loudest. Evan was quietly talking with Lauren and Logan.

It wasn't long before the ribbing started. Since Graham had opted to get a life instead of going on their last SAR mission, he was fair game. He took it good-naturedly. And Natalie managed to give as good as she got even though she didn't know the men all that well. Graham could tell beneath all the teasing; his men were happy for him. Most of them knew about his struggles after the tsunami. And they could see that Natalie was going to be good for him. But still, they couldn't resist knocking their stoic boss down a peg or two.

"I know that Maddie's your sister, but she seems to be a little occupied with David at the moment." Tin Man shouted across the table to Natalie. "Do you happen to have any other sisters hidden anywhere?"

"Sorry, Tin Man, just the one sister." "Cousin? Aunt? Mother? I'm not picky." he appealed to her. "Nope. Sorry. And believe me, you do not want my mother."

"There's a story there," he remarked.

"Not one we have time for," Maddie muttered. She shared a knowing look with her sister, and Natalie laughed.

Graham loved seeing Natalie so relaxed. Her laugh was magical and lit up her whole face. He promised himself he would try to keep her laughing as often as possible. Natalie was pure light, and he never wanted it to dim.

Jolene joined them just as they were finishing up their meals. Finch, of course, rose instantly to his feet, nearly knocking his chair over backward in the process. The guys were used to Finch's old-fashioned manners, but this somehow seemed different. Instead of the suave, confidant Finch that usually made a show of his impeccable etiquette, this Finch behaved awkwardly and seemed unsure. Graham studied Jolene more closely. She was pretty in her own way. Her auburn hair was pulled back at the sides and held with a fancy clip at the back of her head. She had pale skin, like Natalie's, but hers was more covered with freckles. That was redheads for you. And ... Was she blushing? She chatted with Natalie and Maddie, but Graham noticed she kept stealing glances at Finch. Mutual attraction? He certainly hoped so for Finch's sake.

"You remember everyone, don't you?" Natalie was asking Jolene.

She nodded, waving hello to the group. "Are you all staying for the band?" Jolene asked the group as a whole.

"Wouldn't miss it," Finch rushed to answer, earning a smile from the redhead. Surprisingly, he blushed and lowered his head, a curl of hair flopping into his eyes.

"Well, bless your heart," she said with a wink in her deepest southern drawl. Jolene told him she had grown up in Georgia but went to college in Michigan and had liked it so much that she'd stayed. For the most part, he hardly heard her southern twang, but now and then, she brought it out. But now and then, she brought it out. 'Bless your heart' in Jolene's world could mean either 'you're sweet' or 'you're an idiot.'

"The band starts in five. Hope you enjoy it." She gave a wink to Finch as she walked to the stage to the right of the bar, to check in with the band, already plugging in instruments and arranging things to their liking.

The guys noticed Finch's preoccupation with the bar owner, and the ribbing started up once again with him as the target causing him to blush even more. Once the band started playing, everyone grew quiet to listen.

"You know, at the rate you Nighthawks are going, we'll have you all paired off in no time. I do have a few other single girlfriends," Natalie teased when the band took their first break.

"See, I knew I should have looked you up long ago. We could have all been married with kids by now and have gotten into far less trouble over the years." He leaned closer to Natalie to give her a quick kiss. "Not that I wouldn't love to get into a bit of trouble with you right now," he whispered in her ear suggestively. Natalie blushed. Graham then felt eyes on him, and he looked across the table to see Lauren watching them. He sent her a wink.

"Did you have a good weekend, Phillips?" he called across the table to Lauren. He always called her by her last name. He wasn't entirely sure why. It had just become habit over the years.

"Yes. You?"

He glanced briefly towards Natalie, chatting with Maddie and David, and replied, "The best." A strange look passed over Lauren's features which she masked quickly. He was momentarily curious about it but shrugged it off. "Were you able to dig out from the snow?"

"Yes. It was nothing. It will probably mostly be gone by tomorrow."

"If the temperatures stay this mild, it will be gone in no time," he agreed. "Did you get my email about that group from Ohio?" Their conversation turned briefly to business until the band went back on stage. When the band finished their last set of the night, Jolene took the mic to announce she was running a special the next day for Halloween.

Natalie groaned. "Oh crap. I forgot tomorrow is Halloween."

"What's wrong with Halloween?" David wondered.

"She's a teacher," Maddie supplied. "All teachers hate Halloween."

"Kids are hyper enough without the added sugar. Every class tomorrow will have a party that will involve way too much sugar," she groaned. Everyone laughed.

"But at least you get to send the little ones home at the end of the day for their parents to deal with the sugar crash," Jolene said.

"But then they go trick-or-treating and start the sugar high all over again," Maddie remarked.

"Tuesday will be even worse," Natalie informed them. "They will have had an epic crash from the amounts of sugar consumed and be useless."

"They really should make the day after Halloween a holiday," Finch added.

Evan joined in with, "Or always put Halloween on a weekend."

"Yes, an equally good idea," Finch agreed.

Conversations started up around them again as Natalie leaned over to Graham to say, "I really should get home. I still need to dig out my costume for tomorrow."

"You're going to wear a costume?"

"Most of the teachers do. It's kind of a requirement when you teach elementary school." He grinned at her. He'd like to see her in a costume. But the ones he had in mind were not very kid-friendly. If she was a sci-fi geek like him, maybe someday he could talk her into a certain costume from a certain Sci-Fi film. The thought had possibilities.

"What's that expression?" Natalie asked him curiously.

"Oh nothing," he smiled slyly at her. "Just imagining you in a certain costume." He draped his arm around her shoulders and pulled her closer to him to whisper in her ear. "Two words ... Star Wars." She blushed, and he laughed. He could have teased her some more, made her blush deepen, but he decided to let her off the hook in front of everyone. They were being watched too intently.

He thought for sure Lauren knew exactly the direction his mind had gone and now *he* was blushing.

"Come on, let's go home."

"You're staying again?" she asked, trying and failing to hide the joy in her voice.

"If you'll have me."

"Well, sure. But I thought you'd want to get back to Nighthawk tonight."

"I'll get up early." He pulled her into his arms as they rose to their feet and gave her a loud kiss catching everybody's attention. Most of the expressions around the table were ones of happiness, but Lauren had that weird look again. He tried to place what it might be but failed. Before he could study it more closely, she had turned to say something to Logan. He shrugged, said his goodnights, and ushered Natalie out the door.

As they were getting ready to go upstairs to bed, a flicker of light caught Graham's attention outside. "Fuck," he shouted, and rushed to the door.

"What is it?" Natalie gasped spotting what had grabbed his attention as he ran out onto the porch. The pumpkins that had been decorating the steps were now directly in front of the door and burning. Someone had set them on fire.

While Natalie stood in shock, Graham had raced to the side of the house, grabbed the hose, and doused the mess. Once the last flicker of flames had been put out, Graham was on the phone with Ian.

"Are you okay?" His voice slowly pulled her out of her shocked stupor, and she nodded.

"What the hell happened?"

"I don't know, Chickadee. I don't know." Graham wrapped his arms around her as they stood staring at the remains of the fire. If he hadn't noticed the fire...if they had gone to bed...the whole house could have burned down, a thought that filled him with a sense of dread.

Ian arrived with the Fire Chief who after careful in-spection identified the mess as arson. The Chief, assuming it was a bunch of kids doing stupid shit for an early Halloween prank, didn't garner much hope that the culprits would be found.

Graham laid awake in bed long after Natalie had dropped off, his worry about the fire consuming his thoughts. He wasn't convinced the culprits were kids as the Fire Chief alluded.

Remembering the footprints they'd found earlier and now this intentional act of arson, his senses were tingling. It was going to be a long week, knowing he wouldn't be able to return to see Natalie because of work.

Chapter 15

FRIDAY EVENING, GRAHAM RACED to Lake Haven, an unfamiliar fear clogging his throat. He'd been on countless rescues, some more dangerous than others, but he'd never before felt such an all-consuming fear.

Natalie had called him from the back of an ambulance. Some drunk asshole had jumped the curb and nearly hit her as she walked home; almost taking his precious chickadee from him. Anger warred with fear in his mind. And until he could lay eyes on Natalie, the fear was winning.

She was in her studio when he found her, standing in front of the painting she'd been working on. She didn't notice he was there, so he took advantage of her distraction to study her carefully. She looked none the worse for wear from her battle with the sidewalk; she'd been able to leap out of the way of the car. He knew, though, that her clothes were hiding the worst of her scrapes and bruises. He took a step forward, needing to touch her, when a floorboard squeaked under his foot. She turned to face him, and the look of relief in her eyes nearly undid him. She vaulted into his arms. He caught her and kissed her thoroughly.

"Fuck, Natalie. Fuck," he moaned. He felt out of control, murderous.

"I'm okay," she whispered between kisses. "I'm okay." He didn't know if she was trying to reassure him or herself, but he needed confirmation she was indeed all right.

He grasped her hands in his noticing her wince. Turning them over, he saw the raw, redness of her palms. Fury burned in his gut. Someone had dared to hurt his chickadee; he needed to see the rest.

He reached for the bottom of her shirt, carefully pulling it up over her head. Worked his way up from her palms, he saw more scrapes on her elbows though the rest of her torso was unmarred.

Kneeling in front of her, he gently tugged her pants off and leaned closer to place soft kisses on her bandaged knees before deftly pealing the tape back on one side of each bandage to see the damage for himself. The broken skin was nasty, but the paramedics had done a good job cleaning the gravel and grit of the sidewalk out of her wounds. The remnants of blood left on the pristine white of the bandages knotted his gut and made him grind his teeth. From his position on his knees, he looked up to find her eyes blazing with trust and love. He wrapped his arms around her, his cheek against her stomach. Her hands dove into his hair, and he squeezed her tighter, never wanting to let her go.

He rose to his feet and moved her to the small love seat as he removed her bra. Natalie lowered herself to the couch, and he made short work of his clothes. In their rush to be naked, he heard a rip as he removed her panties. Neither of them cared. Then, in one long thrust, he entered her. They both groaned in pleasure. It *had* felt like an eternity since he'd been inside of her. But in reality, it had only been four days.

With a few thrusts, she was quaking with release, her inner muscles gripping him. He continued to pound into her, desperate to be part of her, to be as deep as he could get. He no longer recognized anything but pure carnal pleasure as he lost himself in her.

Her orgasm tore through her. Tremors vibrated as the tight grasp of her pussy strangled his cock. He slammed into her one last time, his release deep within her, her name a desperate groan against her skin.

They lay there, his cock still pulsing inside her, locked together in ripples of aftershock. When they had both returned to earth, Graham lay on the couch beside her, his legs dangling off the edge as they spooned. Clearly, this thing wasn't made for him. But he wasn't going to complain, not with Natalie laying naked in his arms.

"I guess it's true," she sighed.

"What is?"

"You *did* miss me."

He moved her hair aside and kissed her neck. "Those guys I work with just aren't as good company as you are."

She snorted. "I bet."

He sighed, his arms tightening around her. "Are you sure you're okay?"

She turned her head to kiss him. "I am now."

After a mostly sleepless night, Graham had some work to do at the Nighthawk complex. Even though her body was achy and sore, Natalie went with him, which pleased him enormously. The separation the last few days had been more difficult than he'd thought. He'd missed holding her in his arms as they slept, her smile in the mornings was enough to chase away the darkest night.

He hurried through the work waiting in his office, hoping he and Natalie could find something fun to do for the rest of the day. He had a few ideas of the kind of fun he'd most enjoy, and none of them involved leaving the house. A sound from his phone alerted him of a text. He looked at the display to see David asking him to join him in the gym. He needed to discuss something.

Graham finished up what he was working on and left to search for Natalie. He found her in the reception area, reading through some of their advertising materials. Lauren sat behind her desk; lips tight as she watched Natalie.

"Everything good?" he asked, wondering what was annoying her.

"Hunky-dory," she replied tersely, sending a glare across the room in Natalie's direction. Did the two women have some sort of fight? There seemed to be animosity from Lauren toward Natalie. It would be a shame if the two couldn't be friends. He'd have to ask Lauren what was going on the next time he was alone with her.

Natalie turned, spotting him, and smiled, her eyes shining. He crossed to her and kissed her lips briefly. He'd never get enough of kissing her. She tasted like pure light.

"David needs to talk to me at the gym. Wanna join me?"

"Sure, sounds good." He took her hand to walk out of the office building.

"See ya, Phillips," he threw over his shoulder as he went to the door.

"Bye, Lauren. It was nice chatting with you," Natalie said, giving his receptionist a shy smile. At least Natalie didn't look like she had a problem with the other woman.

Lauren grunted a response as he opened the door and ushered Natalie outside. The sun had done its job melting most of the snow that had fallen a week ago. Since it was a nice day, they opted to walk to the gym instead of riding one of the ATVs.

David was working his way up one of the more challenging routes on the climbing wall with Logan on belay. Natalie stared in awe. "Amazing. How does he make it look so easy?" she wondered.

"Years of practice," Graham answered.

"Come on up, Natalie," David called from the top. "The air up here is fine!"

"Really? Can I?"

"Absolutely!" Graham grabbed a harness and more ropes. Together with David's help, he taught Natalie the basics while fitting her into the harness. After indicating she understood the concepts, David went back to the wall to act as a guide while Graham stayed on belay for her. David remained by her side and instructed her on grabbing each hold, be it a crimp, a jug, or a pinch. Natalie handled each one as they came with steady ease. She slipped only once, a squeal escaping her lips. She caught herself before he could tighten his hold on her ropes, and within no time, she had reached the top.

Graham smiled from ear to ear, and David dubbed her a natural. After he lowered her to the ground, David guided her back up using a slightly more challenging course, with more difficult holds, forcing her to reach higher and wider. He was impressed with her flexibility.

After reaching the top for a third time, she declared her arms to be jelly. Graham grounded her once more before grabbing her up in his arms in a big congratulatory hug. She was very pleased with her accomplishment, he could tell. And he was more than happy that she had shown such an interest in every aspect of his work.

"How are you feeling, Natalie," Logan asked as they were putting the equipment away. The Nighthawks all knew what had happened to her and had been just as worried as he.

"I'm good. That climb worked wonders in loosening the achy muscles."

"Do they have any idea who was behind the wheel yet?" asked David.

Graham shook his head. "There are no cameras in that area. Ian said he was going to check some of the doorbell cameras of the nearby houses. But he didn't have much hope he'd find anything."

He discussed his business with David, and they left the climbing gym with Natalie still flying high from her accomplishment. "Thought I nearly had you with that one hold," David was teasing.

"Not a chance. I didn't spend the last ten years practicing yoga not to balance properly on one leg. Easy peasy."

"Listen to her," David quipped. "Full of confidence! I'll have to give you a more challenging route next time."

"Bring it," she challenged. The two of them chatted on, Logan adding his two cents occasionally, leaving Graham to tag along behind. He might have been a little put out at being ignored by the three of them, but he was beyond thrilled at how easily she fit in with his family, both blood and Nighthawk. The fact that she and David could joke and tease each other so easily made Graham extremely happy. He couldn't wait for her to get reacquainted with his parents. He remembered that Natalie had spent lots of time at his house when they were young. She had loved helping his mother out in the kitchen. And his mother had loved her like a daughter. He had been convinced that she wouldn't wait for Thanksgiving to visit after Graham had told her they had been reunited. She had been so thrilled for him that she shrieked, a sound he'd never heard from his mother before.

His thoughts turned to Natalie's mother and the differences between the two women. The more he learned about Mrs. Ghannon, the more he wondered how Natalie had grown to be such a loving and caring woman. It was no wonder she had spent so much time over at his house when they were young. She was desperate to feel a mother's love, even if it came from someone else's mother.

"What are you thinking about?" Natalie asked as they entered the dining hall.

"Just thinking about how incredibly proud I am of you." He put an arm across her shoulders and hugged her to his side. She flushed a brilliant shade of pink, of course, she always did when he complimented her. He'd have to make sure to do that more often.

"Thanks for today," she said. "I learned so much. And had fun doing it. I'm the one who should be proud. What the two of you have accomplished is nothing short of amazing. I see great things for the future of Nighthawk." Graham couldn't resist. He spun her to face him and gave her a long kiss. He could hear the guys hooting and hollering behind him, which made Natalie turn that lovely shade of pink again.

Chef Layla had made another one of her special meals for Natalie. The guys all complained, having requested

Layla's unique dinners more than once, but she reserved them for special occasions. She promised her "Boys," that the next time they brought an important girl to dinner, she'd make something special for them too.

Dinner with the Boys had been a lot of fun. There was an easy closeness among them, and Natalie was happy Graham had such a solid group of friends, and that they had included her in their little family so readily. After spending the first eighteen years of her life with virtually no family, it was nice to be accepted without having to change who she was to fit in.

After dinner, Graham took her to his riverside cabin. He and David each had built cabins on the property, having grown tired of dorm life. But as they were passing the parking lot, they both noticed that Natalie's car had a flat tire. Graham promised to have it fixed before Natalie had to head back to Lake Haven the next day and called Tin Man to request that he see to it.

After arriving at the cabin, Natalie stood stunned. She wouldn't call Graham's place a cabin, far from it. It was large and luxurious, at least as far as cabins go. He gave her the grand tour leading her through the kitchen with its granite counters and modern appliances to the living room with a cathedral ceiling transected with large wood beams and a large woodburning fireplace surrounded by stone. A flat screen tv was in place above the mantel. The home boasted three bedrooms, one of which he'd turned into a home gym.

It was his bedroom that fascinated her the most. It was woodsy, just like him. He'd managed to bring the outdoors in without being too ostentatious. The wall at the head of the bed was made from reclaimed wood, floor to ceiling. The large window at the foot of the bed overlooked the river. The bathroom was bigger than her bedroom, with double sinks and a shower large enough to fit ten people with a wall full of spray nozzles. Natalie was looking forward to experiencing that.

Back in the bedroom, Natalie took a closer look at the picture frames decorating the top of a long dresser. There were pictures of his family and teammates, of course, but there was one frame that caught her eye and she picked it up for a closer look. Another of her chickadee sketches from the infamous book. It was interesting that he'd framed that particular piece and kept it in such an intimate place.

Graham came up behind her. "I know what you're thinking," he said when he saw what she held in her hands. "But technically, I didn't steal it."

She smiled at his attempt at a joke, but she had to know. "Why?" was all she could choke out as emotion overcame her.

"It reminded me of you. My little chickadee," he whispered as he wrapped his arms around her. "It's always been with me, just like you've always been with me."

"I always thought ..." she started but broke off when the emotions swamped her. She felt the burn as tears threatened. Graham took the frame from her hands and placed it back on the dresser, then took her hand and led her to the seat at the foot of the bed. When they both sat, he threaded his fingers through hers, waiting for her to finish her thoughts.

"I always thought it was me," she confessed. "That I'd done something wrong ... or I wasn't worth it ... or good enough."

"I don't understand. Good enough for what?"

"For you," she murmured. "You left and never came back. Never called, texted, messaged, or emailed. Nothing. Not a word. I thought it was your way of saying you weren't interested in continuing our friendship." She remembered those weeks and months after the tornado, filled with confusion and sadness. The worry she felt constantly threatened to drown her. Worry for her sister. Worry for her community. But most of all, the worry that her mother was correct; she truly wasn't good enough or worth anyone's time.

Left alone most of the time, her insecure thoughts took control. As the months passed with no word from him, Natalie convinced herself she just wasn't worth it and never would be. Her mother was correct; she was unlovable.

She mourned then. Mourned for the sister who would never be the same again. Mourned the actions of her unfeeling parents. And most especially, mourned the loss of what could have been. For one afternoon, she'd been happy. She had liked who she was with him. Had been confident to be herself with him. She'd shared more with him than even her family knew about her. And for one brief afternoon, she'd thought he'd been truly interested. Throughout those lonely months, she realized how stupid she had been. How could anybody be interested in her when her own parents weren't?

Natalie sniffed back her tears. "I figured it was me. If my parents didn't like who I was, how could anybody." It had taken her a long time to get over her self-pity and longer still to trust her heart to anyone. In a way, she had Maddie to thank. After their parents left, she and Maddie had become truly close. Natalie opened herself up to Maddie and vice versa. And when her sister didn't reject her, she was finally able to let go of the old hurts.

"Oh, Chickadee." Graham placed a finger under her chin to lift it up 'till she looked him in the eyes. "Nothing could have been further from the truth."

"I know that now but didn't at the time." she sighed.

"I'm so sorry, Chickadee. I didn't realize how you would have interpreted it. If I could go back ..." he broke off, they both knew how useless it was to dwell on past mistakes. He drew her into his arms to sit across his lap. "That little chickadee drawing has gone with me everywhere. I've always kept it close. Kept you close. Even in my isolation after the tsunami, that little bird was a light for me in a very dark time."

Natalie placed a hand on his cheek and gave him a slightly watery smile. "I'm glad my drawing could do that for you." He kissed her then. Kissed away all the past mistakes. Kissed her until past regrets were forgotten, replaced with forgiveness and love.

Chapter 16

T HANKSGIVING WAS UPON THEM. The Ghannons had opted to stay in a bed and breakfast in nearby South Haven instead of with their daughters. Natalie didn't care, but she could tell Maddie was a little hurt.

Natalie's head was swimming with everything that had happened the last few weeks and the added stress of her parents was not helping her anxiety. After Natalie's first night at Graham's cabin, Tin Man had informed them that it appeared Natalie's tire had been slashed. Graham had been furious. He was kicking himself for not having security cameras installed in the parking lot leaving them no way to discover who had done it.

The following week, Natalie's driver's side window had been smashed. Several other cars on the street also had damaged windows so authorities assumed it was unrelated to the arson incident, but Graham remained unconvinced. And after yesterday, Natalie would have to agree with him.

After an exhausting day at school, Natalie had been looking forward to the next four days off even though her parents would probably make those days hell, but she would still be able to spend them with Graham, so ... bright side. She had been driving to school since her near hit and run, instead of walking, worried that it could happen again. Reaching her car in the school parking lot, a piece of paper fluttered in the breeze trapped under her windshield wiper. Thinking it was an advertisement,

Natalie glanced at the other cars, not seeing any under anyone else's wipers. Smiling, imagining that perhaps it was a note from Graham, Natalie pulled it out and unfolded it. The large, typed letters didn't register at first, but when they did, her hands trembled.

You're not good enough. Nobody will ever want you.
A worthless waste of space.
Go Away
Or you will regret it!

It seemed that whoever had written the note had listened in on her conversation with Graham in his cabin. All her insecurities typed in boldface on that unassuming piece of paper. Hands shaking, convinced that the note had also contained a thinly veiled death threat, Natalie placed a call to Deputy Ian, who agreed to meet her at the parking lot. Calling Graham, her voice trembled as she spoke. It was only in that moment that she wondered if all the incidents had been intentionally directed at her. But who would wish her harm?

The footprints outside her house. The arson, slashed tire, smashed windows, the hit and run, and now this. She was an elementary school teacher, not someone who made enemies. Ian bagged the note to take to the crime lab and was going to check security cameras in the area, but he wasn't hopeful he'd find anything. And with the holiday weekend, answers would not be had for a while.

Meanwhile, she had the added drama of her parents' visit to surmount. They had agreed to hold dinner at Natalie's place since she had the larger dining table. Graham, David, and his parents were expected at any moment. Maddie was attempting to entertain their parents in the living room as Natalie put the final touches on dinner. The kitchen was overly warm since the two ovens had been working all day, so Natalie cracked the window over the sink relishing the cool air that rushed in. She leaned her elbows on the counter, letting the autumn air refresh her overheated skin and calm her nerves as thoughts of the note crowded her mind.

Her mother chose that moment to enter the kitchen. Her dark hair pinned up in a classic chignon, Debra wore an ivory cashmere sweater and black silk pencil skirt, perfectly appointed in every way, as always. No matter how Natalie dressed, she always felt frumpy next to her flawless mother.

"Since you have all the time in the world to relax, Natalie, be a dear and make me another drink." Natalie rolled her eyes before turning to face her mother. Of course, Debra would think she wasn't doing a single thing in here. Their meal would just magically appear; Natalie had nothing to do with it.

"Yes, mother," Natalie, ever the dutiful daughter, took the vermouth off the shelf where she stored her alcohol. She mixed her mother's martini as Debra poked around the kitchen, inspecting Natalie's work. Seemingly satisfied that everything was up to her standards, she took her martini from Natalie and went back to the living room without another word.

Natalie sighed; it was nothing new where Debra was concerned. She'd never understand what made her mother so cold and distant. In twenty-nine years, she'd learned that it was useless to even try to break through to Debra.

The doorbell rang, announcing the arrival of the boisterous Whitakers. They were the polar opposites of her parents. Mrs. Whitaker was giving Maddie a warm hug as Mr. Whitaker shook hands with Natalie's father, William. Graham joined her in the kitchen, his arms loaded with platters and bags of assorted food. Whatever Mrs. Whitaker had made in that covered platter smelled heavenly. She reached over to take a peek, but Graham slapped her hand away.

"You'll have to wait, just like the rest of us. And believe me, that was no easy feat in the car ride here. That wonderful smell filled the whole car. David and I threatened mutiny just to get a bit of mom's peach cobbler."

Natalie giggled. "I can't wait to try it. If it tastes half as good as it smells, I'd mutiny too."

"Aww, aren't you just the sweetest?" Graham's mother said as she joined them in the kitchen. Natalie suddenly found herself enveloped in Mrs. Whitaker's arms. Never had she been hugged that tightly by a mother before. Soft, that was the word to describe Graham's mother. Her lovely gray hair lay loose on her shoulders. Her make-up understated. Even her clothes were soft, a cotton sweater in harvest orange and dark brown leggings. She looked so much more comfortable than Debra could ever be.

"Let me look at you." She grabbed her hands and held them in her own. "Aren't you a looker? You are even more beautiful now than you were in high school."

This surprised Natalie. She had never considered her-self beautiful. Not now and certainly not in high school. Maddie had been the beautiful one. She still was, but it didn't intimidate Natalie as much anymore. "Thank you, Mrs. Whitaker. You are very kind."

"Please, sweetie, call me Mary. And of course, you re-member Tim," she indicated her husband, who was still chatting with Natalie's father. Interestingly, the contrast between the two fathers wasn't as severe as the mothers. Both wore a button-down shirt and slacks as if they were headed for the office, and both on the verge of having a full head of gray hair. The only difference was that Natalie's father was wearing a tie, while Tim's neck was bare.

"All right, Mary. Welcome to my home. I'm so glad you could join us. Can I get you something to drink?"

"You just relax now. Graham will get me what I like," she said.

"One glass of white wine coming right up, Mom." Gra-ham reached into the fridge and pulled out the bottle of wine Natalie had placed there earlier to chill. He also grabbed a beer, she assumed for his father.

"So, what can I do to help?" Mary asked.

Before she could answer, Graham told his mother to go sit down. "I'll help Natalie."

Mary patted Graham's cheek before she left the room. "Does my heart good to see you so happy." He grabbed her hand and gave it a quick kiss before shooing her out of the kitchen.

"I forgot how incredibly nice she was," Natalie confessed, the sudden sting of tears tingling. "I always looked forward to spending time in her kitchen when we were young. She was just so different from my own mother. I don't know why I've forgotten all that."

"You know, I've never heard my mom squeal before," Graham told her. "That is until I told her about us a few weeks ago on the phone. She was so excited she actually shrieked like a little girl. I've never heard anything like it. I had to hold the phone away from my ear, she was so loud." Natalie laughed at his retelling of Mary's reaction. It warmed her heart that he had told his mother about them.

Graham waved a hand in front of her face. "Hey, where did you go?"

"What? Oh, sorry. Just lost in thought."

"Anything wrong?" His voice was full of concern.

"Not a thing. Just trying to think if I remembered everything." It was a slight lie. But it wasn't like they could have that 'where is this going?' conversation in front of everybody. "Would you mind carving the turkey for me?"

He grabbed the electric knife she had plugged in. "Lead me to that bird."

The two families were enjoying the food and the company, or at least most of them were. The Ghannon parents were not really investing themselves in the conversation, which was normal for Maddie and Natalie. But for Mary, who was sitting directly across the table from Debra, it was uncomfortable. She kept trying to draw Debra into a conversation but would only get one-word answers.

Natalie sat between Graham and his mother. The fathers had the heads of the table. Maddie was across from Natalie between David and Debra. *Sorry, Maddie.* Graham was currently telling Mary about the day that Natalie had asked for his help in searching for the O'Donnoll kids. She was hanging on every word, fascinated with the story of the two of them reuniting after all these years.

"So, you just walked into his office," Mary was clarifying, "And as soon as my boys saw you, they agreed to help you immediately?"

"Yup," Natalie grinned at Mary. "I only had to say the words 'missing kids', and the two of them were printing out maps and grabbing supplies."

"That's my boys," Tim said, obviously very proud of all his sons had accomplished.

This conversation seemed to pique William's interest. He began to ask all kinds of questions about the Nighthawks and their SAR missions. Graham went into great detail to describe the intricacies of a rescue.

"Each rescue is unique." Graham was telling William. "We never know what we are going to face when we get there. That's why we train so hard."

"You're the group who saved that actor a while back!" William excitedly remarked. "What was his name?"

"Marcus Rayne," Maddie supplied.

"That's right. Wasn't he trapped on some sort of cliff or something? How did you get him down?"

"We had to climb down to him," Graham began to explain.

William's eyes went wide. "You mean like mountain climbing. That stuff people do with just the tips of their fingers and their toes?"

Graham smiled at the description and nodded his head. William was in awe.

Debra finally chimed in to the conversation, her tone icy. "That sounds awfully dangerous."

"That's why we train. David and I built several climbing walls at Nighthawk to keep our skills current. And of course, we train our clients on the walls as well."

"Your lifestyle doesn't sound very steady," Debra said baldly. "You do dangerous work. Gone all the time on these so-called missions. How could you ever provide a steady future for anybody? For my daughter?"

"Mother!" Natalie gasped. How could she say something so rude? Natalie was outraged. She could feel her face flushing as her anger built.

But Debra wasn't finished. "Don't get me wrong, Graham, what you do is," she paused, "nice." *Nice?* Everybody stared at Debra in shock. Natalie wanted to crawl in a hole. Or better yet, push her mother into that hole to shut her up.

Maddie was outraged as well. "*Nice?* Do you even understand what they do?"

"I understand perfectly," Debra replied in that 'don't sass me" tone. "I just don't think *my* daughters should be subjected to that type of ... lifestyle." Natalie hadn't any idea that her mother still had the power to hurt her, she'd thought that had died out years ago, but she was wrong. Debra wasn't finished though, as she asked the one question they had avoided for four and a half years. "Whatever happened to that other man you were dating, Natalie? The lawyer?"

Everybody around the table was quiet. Equally incensed at her outrageous opinions and confused by her current line of interrogation. "Umm ..." Natalie stammered. "We broke up. A long time ago." Her parents didn't know the whole story of what happened to her. She and Maddie had agreed it would be better not to tell them. Especially their mother who would have found a way to blame Natalie for it.

"That's a shame. He was very successful. He would have provided a suitable home for you." Natalie was mortified. How could her mother be so harsh? Her heart pounded as her embarrassment threatened to drown her. She felt sixteen again, waiting for her parents to show up to the first art show her teacher had set up for her. They never came.

Debra had met Erik only once. He must have put the charm on for her. Erik was good at that. He hid his flaws well. "Why did you break up? What did you do to chase that man away?"

"What did I do?" she asked, incredulous. "Why would you assume I did something."

"That's just your usual way. You've always been an ... unusual girl. That can be off-putting for some. You have a habit of chasing people away."

Natalie's jaw dropped. *Tell me what you really think of me, Mother.* Suddenly, she'd had enough of her mother's bullshit. "You're right, Mother. I did chase him away. But that was after I found the drugs he'd been hiding in my house!"

"And you kicked him out for that?" Debra gasped. "A better person would have tried to help him. Would have *wanted* to help him get clean. He needed that support from you, and you turned your back on him," she admonished.

"Mother, you don't know what you are saying," Maddie tried to intervene.

"I know exactly what I'm saying. You were engaged. Your job was to take care of him. Not abandon him in his time of need!"

The sisters were shocked. It was exactly what she had done to them, to Maddie after her injury. The doctors, at their mother's insistence, tried to save Maddie's leg. She lived in agony for nearly a year as her leg practically rotted from the inside out. They'd had no choice but to amputate it before it killed her. It wasn't long after that that their parents had moved to Florida, leaving Natalie to deal with helping in her sister's recovery alone. They'd paid the bills, paid for anything they required, but it was their parents they had needed.

"I think you need to stop, Mother, before you say something you might regret," Maddie said quietly. It took everything they both had not to lash out at their mother for her insensitive words.

"He would have been perfect for you, Natalie," Debra went on. "Handsome, successful, wealthy."

"He lost all that to the drugs," Natalie said simply. Hating what her mother was saying. She felt like she was close to hyperventilating. She didn't want to have this conversation. Not now, not with an audience. She closed her eyes to concentrate on steadying her breathing. Graham's warm hand covered hers, and she latched on, needing the lifeline he provided.

"Only because you abandoned him," Debra insisted. *Oh, God! Just keep breathing.* She said it over and over again to herself. She would not let her mother push her over the edge.

That's when Maddie had had enough. "He tried to *kill* her!" That shut her up. She gaped at Maddie, then at Natalie.

It was their father who spoke first. "What do you mean, Madison?"

"I mean exactly that!" she yelled. "He was angry she had flushed all his drugs. Tens of thousands of dollars worth of drugs. He was deep in debt to his dealers. They convinced him to sell for them. He had it hidden all over the house. Natalie flushed it all. When he found out, he hit her. She threw his ass out in the street, and I, for one, had never been prouder of her!"

"Hear! Hear!" Graham cheered under his breath as he squeezed her hand under the table.

Natalie hoped Maddie would stop there, but she was too angry. It was time their parents knew everything. She met Maddie's eyes across the table, her sister's gaze fierce. Ready to do battle on her behalf. "But he wasn't done with her. The suppliers were threatening him. He had to replace all the money lost, or they'd most likely kill him, but at that point, he had no money. He blamed Natalie for his downfall. Which was complete bullshit!"

"Watch your language, young lady," Debra admonished.

"Seriously, Mother?" Maddie rolled her eyes.

"Debra," William said slowly. "Let her talk." He turned back to Maddie. "What happened?"

"We had the locks changed and took out a restraining order. We took every precaution, but he succeeded in talking our neighbor into letting him into the house. When Natalie came home, he was here. He jumped her, beat the shit out of her. I ... could hear her screaming," Maddie broke off for a minute, her voice thick with emotion. Natalie noticed David had reached over to cover her hand in comfort and support.

Maddie took a sip of water with a trembling hand. "I called the police then ran to see what was wrong. I found her on the floor. He was on top of her. Strangling her. Killing her." You could hear a pin drop. Everybody was quiet listening to Maddie tell the horrific story. Even Debra was silent.

Maddie told them the whole story. The strangulation, the knife, the fear. Natalie listened quietly, staring at her plate. She couldn't tell her parents any of it, leaving Maddie to tell it all. The shame was there again too; she really hadn't wanted Graham's family to know.

But Maddie finished it. "I ... I was losing her. She collapsed, dropped like a rock. In all the chaos, no one noticed the blood at first. He'd stabbed her. In the side, just as she fell."

She turned to William. "God, Dad! She wasn't breathing. I thought ... I thought she was dead," Maddie started crying, still very upset at what they had gone through. It was then Natalie noticed that not only was Graham holding her hand, but so was his mother. Both offering solace.

To his credit, William had gone to Maddie and was patting her on the back as she sobbed. "She saved my life, attempting to slow the bleeding until the paramedics arrived. I owe her everything," Natalie finished quietly, meeting her sister's eyes across the table.

"Me too," Graham stated, squeezing her hand.

"Where is that man now?" William asked, eyes wide in shock and fear for his daughter's safety.

"Jail. Maddie and I testified at his trial."

"Thank God," William intoned.

Debra gasped. "There was a trial? That means media coverage." Debra was irritated. Her horror wasn't for the fact that Natalie had been attacked. She was only outraged that her daughters had been connected with a story like that in the media. "Couldn't you have figured out a way to send him to jail without involving yourselves?"

Maddie erupted again. "He *killed* her! Natalie was dead for nearly five minutes!"

"I understand that. But people will talk. What will my friends think when they find out about this?"

"Debra," William admonished.

"That's it, Mother. Get out!" Maddie yelled.

"You can't kick me out! I'm your mother!"

"She's right, Maddie," Natalie interjected, her voice surprisingly steady. "You can't kick her out." Then she straightened her spine and looked her mother directly in the eye. "But I can." Debra gasped, her hand flying to her throat, aghast that her daughter was speaking to her in such a manner. "This is my home. You are no longer welcome. Please leave," she finished bravely, and it felt good. She'd finally stood up to her wretched mother.

"After all we've done for you over the years, this is how you treat us?" Debra was outraged, but the floodgates were open now, and there was no closing them.

"What have you done for us?" Maddie joined in.

"Paid for your education, your medical bills, your living expenses. See if either one of you gets another penny from us after this!" she admonished them.

"We haven't needed your money in years. We are both doing quite comfortably in our jobs without you."

Debra snorted. "Hmpf. You," she pointed at Natalie with a sneer, "with your pitiful *art*. And you," she turned to Maddie. "You could have been so much more. What are you now? Some crippled 'gal Friday'? You could have been so much better! Now ... now you are nothing! Just like your sister has always been!" Both sisters paled at her harsh words. Graham's hand clenched on hers, making her heart skip a beat knowing he cared enough to be angry on her behalf.

"That is enough, Debra!" William shouted at her. Both Maddie and Natalie stared at their father. They had never heard him stand up to her before. "Grab your stuff. I'm taking you back to the bed and breakfast. And not another word."

Much to the sisters' surprise, Debra stood, back ramrod straight as she walked to the hall closet, grabbed her coat, and walked out the front door without a backward glance, the door slamming behind her.

"I'm sorry for all of this," William was telling Mary and Tim, who assured him none of it was his doing. He thanked his daughters for the meal; then he was gone too.

Both sisters collapsed back into their chairs, completely done in. No one said a word. Mary stood and took charge, allowing the girls some time to come to grips with what had just happened. "Okay, Whitaker boys. Time to clear this table and wash the dishes." She hustled the three men into the kitchen like a bunch of toddlers. Graham stood and kissed Natalie on the head before grabbing dishes and heading into the kitchen.

Natalie and Maddie sat across from each other. Staring into each other's eyes as the men worked around them. The emotions too raw, too overwhelming. They'd always known their mother was a cold woman. They just hadn't realized the extent of her callous attitude. Now they knew.

Suddenly, they both burst into laughter. "God, that felt good," Natalie gasped, trying to catch her breath from her laughter.

Maddie wiped tears from her eyes. "I'll say! Did you see her face when we told her to get out?"

"And when Dad told her to shut up!" They burst into another round of hysterics.

When they had calmed down enough, Natalie reached for Maddie's hands across the table. "Thanks for having my back. It means more to me than you'll ever know."

Maddie smiled, tears threatening again. "Should have happened a long time ago, we're in this together."

"Always," Natalie promised, quickly wiping a tear away.

Mary plunked down a tray carrying glasses and a pitcher of … was that margaritas? "Who wants a margarita?" she asked, pouring the first glass. Both sisters seized on the chance to get tipsy.

After the margaritas were poured, Mary sat at the head of the table, a deck of cards in her hands. "Okay," she started shuffling the cards. "Do you want to talk about it, or do you want to play a game?"

They glanced at each other briefly before they turned to Mary, saying, "Game!"

They played gin for several hours, the boys eventually joining in with the cobbler and another pitcher of margaritas. Natalie couldn't remember having a more enjoyable night. The Whitaker's were unlike any family she'd ever experienced. The love between them was obvious; they enjoyed each other's company. They had fun together. That was … different. And incredible.

"Natalie," Mary said, dealing the cards for what seemed like the hundredth time. "I just have to tell you that I love that painting over your fireplace."

"Natalie painted it," Graham informed her, pride in his voice.

"That's one of yours? It's wonderful," she said wistfully. "Tim, does that view look familiar to you?"

He glanced at the painting again, "Is that ...?"

"Certainly looks like it, doesn't it?" She shared a private smile with her husband. Graham and Natalie had their own private smile. Apparently, they shared a wonderful memory of a special spot with his parents.

David and Maddie looked between the two couples in confusion. "What is it?" David asked.

"It's a hidden spot that overlooks the lake off of Lakeside Drive back home in Indiana." The older couple looked at Graham, the shocked expression on their faces that someone else would know about that spot made Graham laugh out loud. "Come on, guys," Graham said to his parents. "You don't honestly think you were the only ones in town that knew about that spot."

"I didn't." David remarked.

"Me either," Maddie concurred. "How do you know about it?" she asked Natalie.

Natalie smiled; the memory precious to her. "Graham took me there the day of the tornado."

"Yeah, you remember," Graham teased Maddie. "You abandoned your sister on the side of the road." Maddie winced, reminded of what a bitch she had been in high school.

"Graham rescued me."

Mary sighed. "Aww, isn't that sweet?" She turned to her husband then. "Imagine that, Dear. At least one of our sons had manners back then."

"Hey!" David cried.

"Don't worry, Kid," Graham told his brother. "I'll give you some pointers." Everyone laughed until the sound of the doorbell interrupted them. Natalie and Maddie met each other's eyes, wondering who that could be at this hour.

Natalie opened the door to find her father standing there, suitcase at his feet. "I ... I was hoping I could talk to the two of you," he said nervously.

Mary stood then, "That's our cue to leave, boys." They packed up their belongings as William wandered the living room, going from painting to painting, studying each one. David left with his parents, and Graham stayed behind but went upstairs to give them privacy.

"Why didn't you ever tell us?"

"We didn't want to worry you. We didn't tell you because ..."

Natalie had had enough tiptoeing around. "You abandoned us," she told William flat out. "It seemed to us that you didn't want to have anything to do with us anymore. Me? I was used to it. You and mom hadn't wanted me around for years. But Maddie, she didn't deserve any of it. It wasn't her fault the tornado hit. It wasn't her fault she was hurt. It wasn't her fault she lost her leg. It was like she was suddenly damaged goods to our mother."

William took a moment to mull that over before responding, his lips pressed together in a tight line. "You're right. We did abandon you. I see that now."

"Why did you always take her side? Why did you always blindly follow her lead?" Natalie wanted to know the answer to Maddie's question herself.

"I guess I was tired. I'd spent so many years early in our marriage fighting her, it was easier to do as she wanted than to continue to fight her; I gave up.

"What you've both been through and survived," he shook his head. "It's nothing short of a miracle. And look at you both now. You're thriving. Such strong women. Now that I know everything, and don't think I'm not just a little peeved that you didn't tell me what happened, but now that I know ... I've missed so much. All this time, I could have been getting to know the amazing women you have become. I've made mistakes, I'm only human, but I hope you can forgive me. I regret ..." he broke off, unable to finish as emotion overwhelmed him. Natalie was shocked to see tears swimming in his eyes.

William gathered both his girls in his arms, and they accepted his hug. "You should know, I'm done. Saturday, I will escort Debra back to Florida. But that's it."

"If that's what you want, Dad, we'll support you. We want you to be happy." Maddie assured him.

"I don't want to stay in Florida. I hate it there. Too hot. And don't get me started on the mosquitos!" The girls laughed. "I was hoping one of you would let me stay a while, until I can find my own place."

"You can stay with me," Maddie said. "I have the guest room. We turned Natalie's guest room into our gym."

As William hugged them again, Natalie mused on all that had happened that day. She'd lost a parent. She'd have to grieve for that later. But at least they were beginning to mend things with the other parent. That was beyond what she had expected from this weekend.

Chapter 17

A s Graham waited while Natalie talked to her father, his mind raced. Not only was he worried about how Natalie was feeling about the fight with her mother, but he also couldn't get the words from that simple sheet of paper found on Natalie's car out of his mind. Somebody had threatened his woman. The question was ... who? After tonight's conversation about her ex, Graham had to wonder if he was behind everything. Perhaps orchestrating a plan from prison to terrorize Natalie for his downfall.

And then there were the dealers Erik had worked for. What if they were behind the threat? After the trial, they had to know it was Natalie who had flushed their product. He made a note to ask Deputy Ian about that avenue of investigation. Did they ever find the dealers Erik was working with?

All the unknowns had his stomach seizing with fear. He'd just found Natalie again and discovered his feelings for her ran deep. He couldn't lose her now.

After holding an exhausted Natalie in his arms all night, Graham had agreed to take William on a tour of Nighthawk. Natalie was thrilled her father had shown an interest. The two sisters and his own parents had joined them. It was an unusually warm day for late November as they had watched David go through the paces on the outdoor climbing wall while Graham was on belay. William showed particular interest in the climbing facilities and asked to try it out for himself. Just as they had with Natalie, they had given William a quick lesson.

He took to it immediately and quickly reached the top; the elation on his face at having accomplished his first climb was evident, and unless Graham was mistaken, Will was hooked.

Later, the Ghannons, the Whitakers, the Nighthawks, and Lauren were all at what had become their usual table at Jolene's. Will and Tim had just declared the place to have the best burgers in the northern hemisphere, for which they received Jolene's deeply southern 'bless your heart.' They were all enjoying Jolene's latest brew, developed for the holidays. This time the beer had a tart cranberry flavor to it. It was excellent, as were the tunes playing from the old-fashioned jukebox in the corner. Jolene's was quickly becoming his new favorite place to hang out.

Natalie was sitting next to Lauren, trying to engage her in conversation. He'd known Lauren a long time; they'd spent many hours together at the various disasters they'd both been assigned. Their close friendship had grown in the past couple of years when Graham had talked her into leaving the Red Cross and coming to work with him. She'd become a valuable asset to the Nighthawks. It was natural for him to want his best friend and his girlfriend to develop a friendly relationship.

Girlfriend. The word hit him suddenly. He guessed there was no getting around that. Natalie was most definitely his girlfriend.

Of course, he and Natalie hadn't had *that* discussion yet. The one where they clarify what they were to each other. Graham was more than ready to commit, but he wasn't sure if she was. He thought she might, but there was always that bit of doubt that lived with the darkness inside of him.

Then there was the worry that had plagued him recently about his ability to juggle his job and a girlfriend. He didn't want one to suffer because of the other. He would have to find a balance. Having Natalie in his life made everything that much better. Nighthawk was important to him, but so was Natalie. He wanted more than anything to keep them both.

"Graham has told me you've known each other for a long time," Natalie was saying to Lauren when he refocused on the conversation. "How did you meet?"

Lauren sighed, answering slowly. "We were both assisting at a flood in Ohio."

"You were with the Red Cross, right."

"Right," Lauren answered simply.

Graham leaned closer to Natalie to join the conversation, his arm across the back of her chair. "Phillips is amazing when it comes to handling people who are having the worst day in their life."

"It's not that hard to care," Lauren admitted blushing slightly at his praise.

"It is for some people," Natalie mused. Graham figured she was thinking of her mother.

"I just did my job." Lauren wasn't acting like her normal cheerful self, instead she was somewhat cold and distant. Graham wondered if there was something wrong with her and made a note to remind himself to have a chat with her.

In the meantime, he would keep singing her praises. "Phillips has been amazing with the Nighthawks team. She keeps us all organized and often assists us if we get called out on a SAR. She helps to keep the family and friends of the victims occupied so that we can do our jobs. She has a special way with people."

"That is such a rare talent to have," Natalie said. "Do you teach any of the seminars? You know, something that teaches about dealing with victims and their loved ones during a crisis?"

"That's a good idea. Most counties have some sort of victim services unit, but they often don't have extensive training. Learning how to comfort someone who is going through shock at a catastrophe, crisis intervention can be an enormous job for the untrained. What do you think, Phillips?" Graham asked. "Would you be interested in teaching something along those lines?"

"I don't know, maybe."

"I bet you'd be good at it," Natalie declared.

"It's a good idea, chickadee," Graham said after giving Natalie a quick kiss. "Think about it, won't you, Phillips?"

"Sure." Her lips were pressed together tightly; her expression closed up. Graham shot her a concerned look. She seemed so unhappy, angry even, and that was so unlike the Lauren he knew. Something must be wrong. Graham was surprised he didn't know what; she usually shared everything with him. They had that kind of close friendship where they could talk about anything and everything. She was like a sister to him. He didn't want to see her hurting.

Just then, Miss Letty walked up to their table. "This looks like a fun party!" Natalie introduced her to the group. And Letty being Letty, walked around and met each person individually. Shaking each hand.

"Won't you join us, Miss Letty?" Graham offered.

"I don't want to interrupt."

Will stood then, offering her his chair, "Nonsense. We'd love for you to grace us with your presence, pretty lady."

Natalie and Maddie stared at their father in shock, jaws dropped. Graham chuckled at the expressions on their faces. Their dad was flirting and though it was unexpected, it was charming. Miss Letty waved her hand at Will. "You flatterer."

Will grabbed an empty chair and placed it next to hers. Graham leaned closer to Natalie and whispered, "Look! They are wearing the same sneakers." Natalie snorted and glanced down at their shoes. Both Will and Letty wore flat canvas sneakers; Miss Letty's were red while Will's were blue. The two of them continued their banter as other conversations started back up around them. Seemed to Graham that Jolene's was becoming a great place to meet people. And maybe, just maybe, fall in love? He looked from Finch and Jolene - who were deep in conversation - to Will and Miss Letty. Then he turned his gaze to the amazing woman beside him, an overwhelming feeling of love filling him. Yup. No two bones about it. He had fallen in love with his little chickadee.

He must not have been able to mask the flurry of his thoughts because Natalie looked at him, concern in her emerald eyes. "You okay?"

He smiled at her, sure that his eyes reflected his love for her. "Yeah, chickadee. I'm good." He grabbed her hand and brought it to his lips.

Miss Letty overheard them. "What did you just call her?"

Natalie blushed as Graham answered. "Chickadee."

"That's such a unique nickname. Wherever did it come from?" Suddenly the table was quiet, all equally curious about the nickname.

"We shared a nice afternoon together in high school, full of ice cream and conversation."

"And Tornados," Natalie interrupted with a smile.

"Right, but before that, I asked to see some of her artwork. The chickadee was one of the first drawings I saw. It suited her with her cap of dark hair. Not to mention the fact that she's just so tiny," he teased. Graham could practically hear the women around the table sigh as the men chuckled.

"I hadn't realized you two had known each other for that long," Miss Letty mused.

"We grew up together as neighbors," Graham answered. "We lost touch after I graduated, though."

"When Natalie asked for his help to find Colin and Lucy, that was the first time they'd seen each other in ... what was it again?" Maddie asked of Natalie.

"Twelve years."

"And then you just clicked, I'm guessing," pondered Miss Letty.

"Never thought I'd be grateful a couple of kids went missing," Graham joked kissing Natalie's hand again. The table erupted in laughter.

An alert tone sounded, and both Graham and David reached for their phones. The other Nighthawks went quiet. Graham looked up at his men after reading the message and nodded. They all stood, well-practiced in the routine of being called out. Graham apologized to Natalie for having to leave, and after ensuring that her father would see her safely home, he kissed her a little too hard and a little too long and begrudgingly followed the rest of his Nighthawks out the door. He'd never felt so reluctant to go out on a mission.

Chapter 18

IVE DAYS. IT HAD been five days since Graham and his Nighthawks had been called out from Jolene's. Five days and not a word from Graham, which was unusual. He always called and texted numerous times a day if they couldn't see each other. She couldn't go to him because it was a busy time at school getting ready for all the holiday celebrations.

And still, no word from Graham. Her own texts and voice mail messages went unanswered. *He'd ghosted her.*

Yet she knew that Graham wasn't the type to play those games, even with his reputation from high school preceding him. But that scene with her family on Thanksgiving had been ugly. Maybe he decided she wasn't worth the drama.

Weatherwise, the last few days had been just as miserable as Natalie had felt. An unceasing deluge of rain had blanketed the region. It could have either been sunrise or sunset with the low clouds and curtain of rain draping the area in dreary darkness.

Graham's radio silence was odd. Of course, it was. *Stop second guessing yourself.* Besides, they had made plans for this weekend. Since she had Friday off from school, Graham was taking her to his cabin in the UP for skiing. A long romantic weekend, just the two of them. It was sensible of her to find out if they were still on for the trip. So, with her skis and an overnight bag packed in the trunk, she'd made the decision to go to him.

The drive was taking longer than ever, the torrent of rain forcing her to drive slower as the windshield wipers fought furiously to clear the water away. The trip giving her more time to get lost in her head and allow her misgivings to take root.

The sincerity of his feelings towards her had seemed real enough. The look in his eyes just before he kissed her—the heat and desire she saw there surely couldn't be faked. She needed answers. So here she was, in her car on a Thursday afternoon, driving to the Nighthawk complex to get them. White knuckling the steering wheel while trying to see the road through the sheet of rain, she second-guessed every moment, every decision.

Natalie hated that her past insecurities were making her question everything. Including this trip to find Graham. A weird shiver of foreboding made her spine tingle. Maybe this wasn't a good idea. But five days was a long time. Especially since they hadn't gone a single night without talking to each other for the last month.

Finally, she wove her way through the Nighthawk grounds to Graham's cabin. Pulling up in front, she turned off the engine and eyed the cabin. There was a dull light shining through the front window, which she took as a sign he was home.

Taking a deep breath and praying she was making the right decision, Natalie climbed out of the car, the deluge instantly soaking her to the skin. She slammed the door behind her and raced up the porch steps to the front door. She hesitated a moment before knocking. Shivering, she waited for Graham to answer.

After a minute of waiting, he still hadn't come to the door. Maybe he was at the main part of the complex teaching classes. But she thought they were usually done by this time of the day.

Maybe he was sleeping. That was probably it. She raised her hand again, knocking louder this time. She cupped her hands together, blowing warm air into them to warm herself as she rocked back and forth. Waiting.

When there was still no answer, she tried the door handle.

Feeling like an idiot when it turned. Instant warmth greeted her, and she sighed in gratification. The room was shadowed, only a small lamp shone next to an armchair. Embers glowed in the fireplace from a recent fire. And it was quiet. Unnervingly quiet.

Stepping further into the great room, she was startled to see the shape of someone sitting on the couch. Sighing in relief after recognizing him, she moved closer. "Graham," she said softly. His stillness was eerie.

She stood in front of him, and still, he did not move, only stared into the embers. Natalie glanced around the room; several surfaces held empty beer bottles. On the coffee table in front of him, she spied two bottles of whiskey. One was empty, laying on its side, the other nearly empty. Something was very wrong with the scene in front of her.

She turned back to Graham and knelt down in front of him, placing a hand on his knee. "Graham."

Slowly, he blinked his bloodshot eyes and directed his gaze on her. Natalie had a feeling he wasn't really seeing her though. His once-bright blue eyes were now dull and lifeless. "Graham, are you okay?"

He answered. One terse word. "Fine." Then focused back on the fireplace. His voice was gravelly, like he'd been chewing on glass. After staring at him for another minute without seeing a spark of recognition, she stood and headed toward the kitchen. Grabbing a glass from the cabinet, she filled it with water and went back to Graham.

She held the glass out to him. "Here. Drink this." He didn't move. She held it in front of his face willing him to take it. Sighing deeply, she gave up and placed it on the coffee table.

Kneeling back down between his legs again, she tried to garner his attention. "Graham? What's going on?"

"Nothing." His answer was slurred.

"Are you drunk?" Shocked to see him in this condition, she searched the room again, appalled at the sheer number of empty bottles. She knew he enjoyed the occasional drink, but never to this extent. His hair was greasy and unkempt, as if he'd run his fingers through it repeatedly. The stubble on his jaw almost a full beard. His clothes were wrinkled and had numerous spills dotting the front. He looked absolutely awful.

"Yup," he finally answered popping the p sound.

"Why? Did something happen?"

He didn't answer.

"Graham, talk to me, this is so unlike you." She placed her hands on his knees and felt him tense.

"Go away," he grumbled.

"I don't understand, Graham. Where have you been all week? You haven't returned any of my texts or messages. I was worried."

He remained silent. But Natalie could sense the tension building in his body. Something was very wrong. She had to find a way to get him to open up to her.

"Please, talk to me. Maybe I can help."

Suddenly he rocketed to his feet pushing her backward. "I said, go away!" he roared. She landed on her butt, her back crashing against the coffee table. Hard. The glass of water fell over, drenching the back of her already damp shirt. She winced and reached a hand around to rub the soreness on her back, her eyes watering. She stared up at him as he moved away, shocked. He'd never raised his voice to her like that.

She watched him stalk over to the fireplace; a tiny trickle of fear slithered through her. Erik had erupted at her like that too. She shook that thought out of her head. This was Graham. He'd never hurt her. She wanted to believe that. But try as she might, the residual fear from Erik leached in.

Graham was in hell. Again. The alcohol had managed to numb it somewhat over the last few days, but Natalie's presence was exacerbating it. He grabbed the nearly empty whiskey bottle and staggered over to the fireplace. He took a swig and dropped his forehead to the arm that was resting on the mantel. Staring into the dying embers, he struggled to block the feelings raging through him.

He'd failed. Again. Involuntarily, his mind flashed back to Saturday's rescue. Needless to say, it hadn't gone well; and it brought on the feelings of failure and the need to drink till he forgot.

He'd lost two of the five family members. Their van had tumbled down an embankment by the river and was starting to sink. When the Nighthawks had arrived, three of the family members had managed to free themselves from the car and were standing on the bank of the river. The Nighthawks got immediately to work. Reaching the van, Graham could tell the driver was already gone. He concentrated his efforts on the passenger who was trapped by the crumpled dashboard – a young boy, around twelve years old.

Logan and Jude got to work cutting up the mangled mess with the jaws of life while Graham tried to reassure the kid. He'd climbed into the back of the van, trudging through knee-high water to reach the passenger. Falling back on his paramedic skills, he tended the boy's wounds.

The boy steadily became paler and weaker the longer they took to cut him out. His lower lip quivered as his eyes filled with fear, and pain was etched into the lines of his face. The kid was old enough to know something was seriously wrong with him. His eyes pleaded with Graham, and the most he could do was hold the kid's hand and reassure him that everything would be all right.

It was bullshit. Graham knew it. The kid knew it. The same helpless feeling he had while working in Indonesia inundated him, threatening to drown him in guilt and anger.

Despite all of Graham's best efforts, the child ultimately closed his eyes and drifted away.

Remaining professional and detached, he'd pushed it all deep down. Blocked out the sound of the family member's grief. Finished the job. Rescued the surviving victims. Helped the coroner retrieve the bodies. Even helped the wrecker crew salvage the van. All while drifting through a cloud of numbness.

The drinking began as soon as he'd gotten home in the early hours, deadening the emotions. In his mind, the faces of the two who died morphed into the bloated visages of the hundreds he'd been unable to help in the wake of the tsunami. Becoming one and the same. Finding the alcohol anesthetizing his brain, he drank until he could no longer see all the faces. When the beer was gone, he'd turned to the harder stuff.

The last thing he remembered was opening the second whiskey bottle until Natalie crouched in front of him. Then everything came flooding back. And all he felt now was impotent anger.

Logically, he knew there was nothing he could have done. Internal bleeding. Those words had been bandied around that night by everyone. especially by David, who could spot the tenuous grip he had on his anxiety.

Fuck them. What do they know? If he had been faster. Forgone that last goodbye kiss with Natalie. Driven faster. Grabbed his gear sooner. Climbed down quicker, sacrificed his own safety. Accelerated his actions. Been better and more focused. The outcome may have been different.

What a load of crock. His brother's voice bellowed in his head. He winced and took another sip from the bottle. He knew ... *knew* ... it was a crock. But he'd lost himself so deeply in the darkness he couldn't escape.

That's just the alcohol talking. This time his father voiced his two cents from inside his head. Whatever. Booze good. Emotions bad.

Don't be an idiot. Great. Now his mother had invaded his thoughts. Why wouldn't they all just leave him alone?

A delicate touch on his back made him flinch. "Graham?" Her voice quivered. "What can I do to help you?"

He shook his head. Right now, the last thing he needed—the last thing he wanted—was Natalie to witness his failure. He didn't want her here.

Anger fired through his veins. And in his drunken state, she was as good a target as any. If he hadn't been so distracted by her—preoccupied by his need to be with her, to fuck her every chance he got—maybe that kid would still be alive.

Yup. Too stupid to live. All three of his immediate family screamed at him. But he couldn't hear them over the roar of irrational resentment in his ears.

The whiskey bottle slipped from his fingertips as Natalie grabbed it away from him. She placed it out of reach on the mantel. He aimed a piercing glare at her.

"What'd you do that for?"

"We need to get you sober so we can talk."

"No." He stepped around her, grabbing up the bottle again and draining the rest of it. He tried to place the empty bottle back on the mantel but misjudged his aim. The bottle cracked off the wood and shattered. He watched as the glass shards dropped to the hearth and floor like shiny scraps of confetti.

Natalie squatted down in front of him and began picking up the larger pieces of glass. In his inebriated state, he couldn't comprehend the hiss of pain that slipped from her lips, let alone notice the drops of blood that seeped from the slice in her hand. "What do you mean, no?"

"Juss what I said," he slurred, stumbling to the kitchen. Halfway there, he forgot where he was going and stood swaying for a moment until it came back to him. Booze. Need more booze. He staggered into the kitchen, opening random cabinets.

Natalie followed him into the kitchen dumping the glass into the trash. She grabbed a paper towel, wrapping it around her hand before turning to the coffee maker. "I'll make some coffee. Maybe that will help sober you up."

He growled at her. He didn't want coffee. He wanted more mind-numbing alcohol. He pushed his way past her, she grunted as her stomach hit the counter. Ignoring the annoying woman in his kitchen, he stalked to the hutch behind his dining table. He was pretty sure he kept some alcohol in there.

"Come on, Graham," the tiny bird twittered at him. She grabbed his arm and pulled him away from his quest. He wrenched his arm out of her grasp hard, causing her to lose her balance. She stumbled before catching herself with the hand wrapped in paper towels on the table, her barely discernable whimper not registering. He growled at her to go away before returning to his search.

"Graham," she admonished. "I only want to help."

He turned on her so fast he was momentarily dizzy. "Help?" he shouted. "Help? How can you possibly help? You're too much of a distraction, a hindrance. I don't need your kind of help. I need you gone!" Each word out of his mouth had grown progressively louder until even the sound of his own voice made his head pound.

Ignoring the tears that were building in her eyes, he gripped her arm tightly and dragged her towards the front door.

"Graham, please," she cried. "You're hurting me." Even in his inebriated state, he knew that was wrong. He dropped her arm instantly.

"Just leave, Natalie," he growled.

"Why are you doing this?"

He looked down at her, the emerald color in her eyes swimming in tears. He needed to remain impassive to her waterworks. "Because if it wasn't for you ..." he hesitated, knowing somewhere deep down inside there wouldn't be any coming back from his next words. They flew from his mouth anyway. "If it weren't for you, I wouldn't have failed. You distracted me and muddled everything. I need to be completely focused on the job, or people die. And when my brain is preoccupied with constant thoughts of when I can get inside of you again, I can't do the job."

He thrust his hands into his hair, pulling on the strands, allowing the twinges of pain to pacify him. "I knew getting involved with you was a bad idea. But fuck if I could stay away. And now ..." He turned away from her. He didn't want to face his failure to save that kid again.

"I got sidetracked. It shouldn't have happened. And it can't happen again. I can't have you distracting me from what's important. Christ. You're no better than those sluts in high school who used to flutter around me hoping for a good lay." He heard her shocked gasp but blocked it out.

The words were harsh, but they were loose, flying through the air like daggers. They'd spilled from him in his drunken haze, and he couldn't erase them. He glared at her. Willing her to just leave. He needed her to leave. His rage was uncontrollable, needing an outlet. Like nothing he'd ever experienced before. He had a tenuous hold on it, even as his subconscious screamed at him to stop.

"I ... I need to focus to be able to do my job."

"How's the alcohol helping with that focus?" she scoffed.

"A lot better than just painting through my emotions," he mocked. He sneered down at her, unwilling to allow the tear-filled emerald eyes to move him even as a tenacious voice begged him to shut the fuck up. Shit, his head hurt.

But at least he was feeling something besides failure and helplessness. The rage overpowered all the other messy emotions. Graham needed to get Natalie out of here before it tainted her too.

"Just get the fuck out of here, Natalie. I don't fucking need you here."

He shot his hand out, intending to reach for the door behind her. She flinched. He saw it. Saw the color leach from her face. Saw the fear flash through her eyes. He froze. His inebriated brain, trying to tell him something. But he ignored it, opening the door behind her instead.

David stood on his porch. He took in the scene before him. Saw Natalie's fearful posture with Graham a towering rage looming over her. His eyes narrowed on Graham. "What the fuck, Graham?" David shouted at him. The words slicing like daggers through the pain in his head.

David's anger on Natalie's behalf created a crack in his irrational rage. He suddenly saw everything a little more clearly. Natalie's tears and protective posture, her body vibrating with fear began to coalesce through the alcohol-induced haze. For the first time since she'd arrived, he centered his focus on her. She was soaked through to the skin. Her hair was plastered to her head and dripping down her shoulders. Her shirt was damp and clinging to her curves. Her arms wrapped around herself as she shivered. Shielding herself from his barbs. Some of which were so sharp he knew they'd pierced her soul. Shame besieged him.

But the worst was seeing the tears streaming down her face. Tears that he'd caused. Tears falling from the emerald eyes he loved so much. Their vividness deadened. *Fuck. What had I done?*

"Natalie," he whispered. She turned and ran out the door into the rain before he could say more, before he could take every hurtful word and action back. Belatedly, he stumbled after her, but she had already reached her car and was tearing down his drive, away from him.

"Fuck," he yelled into the rain.

He didn't know how long he stood there. He was soaked and half-frozen but more sober than he'd been all week. Now, the only emotion he felt was shame.

He trudged his way back inside his cabin where his brother stood. "I could hear you yelling at her from outside. The things you said to her ..." he broke off, shaking his head. Graham's chin dropped to his chest. He couldn't meet his brother's eye; he knew he'd fucked up royally.

David sighed. "Your superhero complex sure fucked up this time. When are you going to learn you can't save them all? You can't stand on every street preventing every accident. You can't control the weather. You can't stop people from doing dangerous and idiotic things. You are only human, and you're entitled to have a life which you just chased away. You're my brother, and I've always looked up to you. Always been proud of you. Even when you were a horndog in high school and chasing after every girl in a forty-mile radius." He paused before taking a deep breath.

Looking Graham straight in the eyes, he said the words that tore him up with guilt so sharp he felt gutted, even as he acknowledged their truth.

"But I've never been ashamed of you. Until tonight." With those words, he walked out the door, leaving Graham alone with his misery, shame, and remorse.

On the floor at his feet lay a blood-soaked paper towel. He bent to pick it up but lost his balance and ended up on his ass. He leaned against the door, his arms resting on his raised knees, the bloody rag hanging from his fingers. Banging his head against the door behind him repeatedly, he released the hot tears allowing them to flow freely.

Chapter 19

NATALIE LOCKED HERSELF IN her studio, intending to lose herself in the painting that was giving her such a hard time. She still couldn't figure out what was bothering her about it. What was missing from it? Now she had all the time in the world—alone—to figure it out.

She'd been working on it since arriving home the night before, feeling numb and empty. She'd managed to change out of her wet clothes into an oversized hoodie and leggings. She was as warm as she could physically be, but still felt frozen inside.

Dark thoughts and insecurities inundated her. She still wasn't entirely sure what had happened last night. When she'd seen how much Graham was hurting, she thought for sure she could help him. They'd seen each other through the retelling of their darkest moments. How could this be any different?

The anger made it different. Graham had exhibited so much rage it scared her. Deep down, she knew he would never hurt her. But when his hand had shot out towards her, the memories of Erik's assault filled her. She couldn't help the flinch and couldn't stop the fear that engulfed her. She did what she needed to do to shield herself. She ran.

David had called her a few hours ago. He'd tried to explain his brother's behavior. If he'd only talked to her, if he'd explained the situation to her, she would have listened. She would have comforted him, given him the light to pierce the darkness, then told him he was an idiot, and it wasn't his fault.

She understood the need to lash out at someone in anger when feeling your lowest. She'd been there. Had spoken harshly to Maddie too many times to count and had been immediately contrite. She'd apologize; they'd hug and talk it out, then move on.

She didn't know if she could move on from the hurt Graham had caused. The words had been ugly. Words she'd never heard him use. The viciousness shocked her. Her gentle blue-eyed hesitant hero morphed into a cruel tyrant spewing malice.

She wanted to blame the alcohol, but those feelings had to have come from somewhere. Some deep-seated unresolved issues. The darkness he'd warned was still there had erupted. The volcanic ash of rage smothering everything. Suffocating anyone within range. And unfortunately, Natalie had been an available target.

She wanted her kindhearted Graham back. The man who called her chickadee with such sweet reverence. Who held her all night as she grieved for the loss of a mother she never actually had. She wanted to be in his warm embrace again as they purged the darkness that threatened to annihilate them.

And now she didn't know when she would get the opportunity to hug and talk it out. David had informed her the Nighthawks had been called out to help with water rescues due to the flooding in Wisconsin. But still, she couldn't bring herself to answer the dozens of calls he'd made throughout the night. The type of conversation she needed to have with Graham couldn't be done over the phone.

He'd called several times, but she hadn't been ready to talk to him. As if on cue, her phone rang. She pulled it from the charger and checked the display. It was him again. She still couldn't bring herself to answer it. So instead, she rejected the call and slipped it into her back pocket.

Natalie played around with colors and shapes on her painting as the hours passed. Nothing was working. Exhaustion and frustration overwhelmed her. She was seriously considering trashing the canvas and starting over when the doorbell rang. Natalie quickly wiped her hands on her apron as she took it off and hung it on its hook. She was running down the stairs when the bell rang again.

"I'm coming," she muttered. She reached the door before the visitor could ring it again. "Lauren!" She opened the door, surprised to find Graham's friend standing on her porch.

"Can I come in?"

"Of course," Natalie stood back to let her inside. "I thought you'd be with the team."

"They didn't need me for this one. I thought maybe you and I could spend some time together. Get to know each other better." Lauren stood just inside her door. Her blonde hair covered, in a stocking cap. The puffy gray coat she wore swathed her slight frame. It was so long it fell to just below her jean-clad knees.

Natalie felt hope fill her, temporarily trouncing the pain and grief. She'd been trying so hard to get this woman to warm up to her, knowing it was important to Graham. "I'd like that. Do you want something to drink? Coffee, tea?" Lauren fretfully shook her head. With her hands shoved deep in her coat pockets, her eyes darted all around, never landing on anything for too long. Natalie wondered if there was something wrong with her.

"Actually," she answered, distress underlying the tone in her voice. "It's such a nice day I thought we could go for a walk together." The rain had finally stopped, and the clouds parted, allowing the sun to make an appearance.

"Um ... Sure. Let me get my coat." Natalie opened the closet and chose her slightly lighter parka. It was still chilly out even though the sun was shining. "Lead on," she offered as she held the front door open for Lauren.

Together, they walked down the porch steps and turned in the direction of the school, away from the lake and the biting winds. They spent several minutes quietly walking. Natalie racked her brain to think of something to talk about to no avail. If Lauren wanted to become better acquainted, she was going about it the wrong way, staying so silent.

When they approached the path that led into the woods where Colin and Lucy got lost, Lauren walked in that direction with a confidence that said she had a destination in mind. Natalie shrugged. It'd be colder in the woods with the canopy of trees blocking out the sun, but if that's where Lauren wanted to walk, she wouldn't argue.

"I'm glad some of the trees still have their leaves," Natalie remarked. "It makes it look so beautiful in here."

Lauren responded with a twitchy nod. For some reason, she looked nervous, periodically glancing behind her. Her shoulders were hunched, nearly touching her ears, hands still ensconced deep into her pockets. Leading her deeper into the woods, Lauren's behavior grew more and more erratic, making Natalie nervous. Why wasn't she saying anything?

When Natalie saw her glance behind them for what seemed like the hundredth time, she finally said, "Is something wrong?"

"Yes, Natalie. Something is very wrong." A hand finally came out of her pocket. Natalie stared in shock at the gun she held, gripped in her palm. A gun that was pointed directly at her. "You are what's wrong."

Natalie's breath caught in her throat. That familiar fear that she'd unfortunately experienced before surrounded her. "Lauren! What is this? What are you doing?" Natalie spoke quickly, stumbling back a few paces and raising her hands up in front of her. "I ... I don't understand."

"That's right," Lauren hissed, her eyes narrowing with hatred. Her nervous twitches were gone. A stone-cold conviction dominated. "You don't understand. Things were going so well before you came along. Stay right there," she ordered as Natalie attempted to slowly back away. Her hand trembled faintly as she trained the gun higher at Natalie, her confidence wavering a fraction.

"I don't understand. What are you talking about? What's changed?"

"He did!" she yelled, spittle flying from her mouth. Another crack in her self-assured armor. "He was supposed to be *mine*! Mine! I've invested so many years of my life. Followed him everywhere. Done everything for *him*. He's mine. And you are in the way." *Well, crap on a cracker.* Had she been in love with Graham all these years?

"He never knew?" Natalie asked.

"Of course not. He was so focused on building Nighthawk. I waited patiently. Worked side by side with him to build his dream. Our dream. I was so close. He was nearly ready. Nearly mine!" she hissed. She punctuated each word by stabbing the gun at her. Natalie was afraid it would accidentally go off. "Then you came in with the sob story about those kids. You ruined it. All my hard work. Ruined in one afternoon when a stupid girl came begging for help." Lauren was growing more and more hysterical. Losing her grip on reality. Shock had Natalie standing as still as possible, letting the woman berate her.

Lauren stopped and took a deep breath. "Okay. Keep walking," she demanded, waving the gun in the direction she wanted her to walk. Natalie hated turning her back on the woman with the gun, but she did, moving slowly, keeping her hands out where Lauren could see, dragging her feet as they left the path. Lauren followed closely behind and slightly to the left of Natalie. The gun pointed at her side. She felt a hysterical laugh bubbling up in her chest.

This could *not* be happening. She had survived and she certainly could survive this. She had to. She had so much to live for now. And she desperately wanted to have that talk with Graham so that she could forgive him and be in his arms again.

The issues she'd been having the last few weeks were starting to make sense. Coalescing in her mind. The footprints at her house ... Lauren had been spying on them. The pumpkins smashed in anger. The near hit and run. The car keyed. The tire slashed. All a manifestation of Lauren's anger. Even the note made sense now. She had wanted Natalie out of Graham's life. For good, it would seem.

Her thoughts inevitably turned to Graham. He'd be frantic with worry if she disappeared. He would search. Her heart thudded painfully at that thought. He would search, and he would lose.

He *would* search. And he had a particular skill at tracking. She saw him use them when they were looking for Colin and Lucy. He could find her. She spent the next few minutes surreptitiously leaving a trail. She stumbled over sticks, kicking them aside, dragging her feet through the decaying layer of leaves. Graham had shown her how a broken branch shows a brighter, newer color under the bark. She did everything she could think of to lead Graham to her. It remained to be seen whether he would find her alive or dead.

As she walked deeper and deeper into the woods, Natalie kept her eyes out for any movement; any sign someone else was in these woods. Someone who could help. Or get help. But the farther they walked, the more that hope waned. It would be up to her. But how does one disarm a crazy person without getting shot? She felt sick with fear.

In the distance, the clearing became visible. They were close to the crumbling cabin she and Graham had found that first day. Maybe there was a means of getting away from Lauren there. Perhaps she could get her hands on one of the stones from the chimney. There had to be a way.

Entering the clearing, Natalie searched frantically for something, anything that could possibly save her. The anxiety preventing her brain from developing a viable plan.

Lauren prodded Natalie with the gun. "Over there." It was then Natalie knew. The well. Lauren was leading her to the well. She was going to shoot her and drop her body in that deep pit. If they searched, following her trail, they'd find her dead body.

Lauren ordered her to remove the old plywood that covered the well. Natalie refused to look down into the darkness. Instead, she turned to Lauren after pushing the wood aside. Hands still half-raised; fear sweat sliding down her back. "You don't have to do this," she reasoned.

"Yes, I do!" Lauren said harshly. "I want Graham. You are in the way. Therefore ..." she let the sentence go unfinished.

"But maybe we could work something out. I could leave. Go away. Then Graham could be yours," she tried, desperate to talk Lauren back to reason.

"No, that wouldn't work. He would only go after you. This way, he'll grieve for a bit. Maybe turn to his best friend for comfort. Eventually, he will be mine. I've been patient this long. I can wait."

Her heart squeezed painfully. She loved Graham and had never gotten the chance to tell him. He would never know.

"You don't want to be a killer, Lauren. It's not in your nature. You are a giver. A helper. A nurturer. Think of all those years you've spent helping people. All the good you've done. You don't want to throw all that away. Not like this," Natalie reasoned. Made sense, didn't it? How does one person who's devoted her life to helping other people suddenly turn to murder.

But she was too far gone to listen. Something had short-circuited in her brain. "Turn around." When Natalie hesitated, she yelled, "Now!"

As Natalie slowly turned her back to Graham's crazy-assed friend, she tried to reason with her again. She wasn't beneath begging. "Please, Lauren. Don't do this. You are a good person. You are not a murderer!"

"Oh, I know I'm not!" she said. Natalie felt a moment of confusion, then nothing.

Graham was in hell. This time of his own making. Natalie still hadn't answered his calls. He was desperate to talk to her. He still couldn't believe how he'd acted. He hadn't been that bad after the tsunami. And he especially hadn't lashed out at his loved ones. He didn't know what had come over him. He'd had time over the past twenty-four hours to think. The fear of failure had been palpable. He'd been worried he couldn't juggle his job and a relationship without one of them suffering. The death of that boy had seemed to prove that theory.

There was some deep-seated desire to be perfect at his job, his superhero complex as David would call it. Even while despising the term hero and hating the notoriety, succeeding at his job made him feel virtuous. But if people saw him as a hero, his failures become more prominent, twisting things in his mind until his failures became all-consuming.

This time the darkness had been much worse. And he'd taken it out on the one person who could have helped him the most.

As the day wore on, he recalled the events of the previous night, the images flashing through his mind.

Natalie falling over, crashing into the coffee table. Because he'd pushed her over.

Natalie's grimace when she bumped her stomach into the kitchen counter. Again, because he'd pushed her.

Natalie's cry that he was hurting her because he'd grasped her arm too tightly. He was a right solid bastard.

Natalie's whimper of pain as the glass from the broken bottle sliced her hand. And he hadn't done a damn thing to help her treat it. He slipped his hand into his pocket fingering the paper towel with Natalie's blood-soaked into it. For some perverse reason, he couldn't throw it away.

But the worst image he recalled was seeing her cringe in fear. Of him. That was the image that was now burned into his brain. He couldn't unsee the fear in her eyes.

He scowled at the water, resenting the fact he was stuck here when he should be camped out in front of Natalie's place, begging her forgiveness. And yet, with the cruel words and actions he'd used last night, he knew he didn't deserve her forgiveness.

He steered the RIB with the latest group of evacuees and their assorted pets and belongings aboard around the debris floating in the floodwater. He should have had David and the others handle this one instead of freezing his butt off in the frigid water and heavy rain as he carried people from their flooded-out homes in southwest Wisconsin. But he was still firmly rooted by his damn superhero complex.

He needed to be home. Needed to figure out what to do about Natalie. All the years he'd been doing search and rescue, he'd never felt pulled to be somewhere else.

Distracted by his thoughts, he nearly missed the turn that would lead to the closest Red Cross station. *Get your head back in the game!* If he was going to keep doing this job that he loved, he was going to have to find a way to do it without missing Natalie so much. He was going to have to find a way to have a relationship and continue to be effective at the job. But most importantly, he needed to find a way to deal with the losses.

Counseling immediately came to mind and as the thought took root, he knew it was time. Getting help for his issues could be the jump-start the entire team needed to heal their own hurts. And maybe then he could be the man Natalie deserved.

It never occurred to him that these longer missions would be so difficult. It'd been a little over twenty-four hours, but he ached to see her again. He'd tried calling her repeatedly. She still didn't answer.

Steering the RIB as close to the edge of the flooded road as he could, he waited for this latest group to disembark. He pulled out his cell ... again. Nothing from Natalie. He made a quick call that still went unanswered. Then he sent off another text hoping—praying—he'd get through to her. He debated contacting Maddie to check on her. His brow furrowed as he tried to figure out what move would be acceptable. He knew Maddie would do it for him, but would that piss Natalie off more?

David shot him a concerned glance as he handed Graham a bottle of water. "Still nothing?"

"Nope," he replied, his worry and frustration evident. He uncapped the bottle and nearly chugged the whole thing, the plastic crackling in his hand.

"Want me to ask Maddie to look in on her?"

"I was just debating that. She probably just needs time. I don't want to intrude too much." He ran a frustrated hand through his hair. "Shit! I don't know. I know how royally I fucked up and she's probably still mad, but I need to know she's safe." He ran a hand through his damp hair. He'd never felt so uneasy before. "Maybe I'm overthinking everything. But with that note she found last week ..."

"I'm calling Maddie," David said, pulling out his own cell. "If nothing else, it will ease your mind so you can concentrate on the job."

"Yeah, okay," he agreed.

"Maddie, yeah, it's David," he said into the phone. "Listen, Graham can't reach Natalie. Can you check on her? Yeah, I'll wait." He put the phone on speaker.

"That's weird," he could hear Maddie say through the phone. "David? There's a note on the table here. She says she's decided to head to the cabin anyway. She wanted to do some skiing."

Graham breathed a sigh of relief. It was a little strange of her, but if she needed to get away, he was glad she didn't allow her anger at him keep her from enjoying his cabin. He'd told Natalie where they kept the spare key if she ever wanted to use the place. And he certainly knew how spotty reception was up there. That's why they kept a sat phone there for when they needed it.

"Okay, thanks, Maddie," David was saying.

"I'm surprised she didn't tell me in person. That's so unlike her."

"I wouldn't worry about it too much. Maybe she was just in a hurry," David reasoned.

"Yeah, maybe," replied Maddie not sounding entirely convinced. "Any idea when you'll be back?"

David looked at Graham for confirmation. "Monday, maybe." He nodded, then shrugged his shoulders. Jobs like this could be unpredictable. It could last another day or another week. They were never sure.

"Okay. Stay safe," she told them.

"Will do," David responded before hanging up the phone. "There, does that make you feel any better?"

Graham shrugged. "I guess." Although, Maddie was right. It did seem kind of odd for Natalie to take off like that. Maybe she was so upset and hurt, she hadn't wanted to face anyone. But even that seemed out of character.

Graham finished off his water and pitched it into the nearby recycling bin. He needed to get his mind off his worries and back to the job at hand. "Ready to go back out?" he asked David. They both climbed back into the RIB and took off, passing another boat carrying Finch and Logan and their load of evacuees.

Natalie came to, slowly. Painfully. Everything hurt. She opened her eyes or at least she thought she did. She couldn't see anything. Darkness pervaded. Where was she? She turned her head, pain radiating. Gingerly she touched the place where the pain thumped steadily on the back of her head, her fingers coming away sticky. She groaned and attempted to open her eyes again. There was some light. Faint and far away above her. Was that the sky? She tried to focus through the pain radiating through her body.

Then she remembered. Lauren! The well! Was she in the well? She put her hand down in an effort to push herself up and screamed, her wrist erupting with pain. Broken? She could hardly think through the agony. She tried breathing through the worst of it, keeping her wrist cradled in front of her. If she didn't move it, it didn't hurt so badly.

When the worst of the pain subsided to a throbbing ache, Natalie looked up again. Spots of sunlight peeked through ... yes! The plywood. Lauren must have covered the well again with the plywood. But parts of the wood had rotted with age, allowing at least some light to reach her. Despite that, it was still intensely dark. Uncomfortably dark. She never thought she'd ever be afraid of the dark, until now.

Natalie got slowly, unsteadily, to her feet. The pulsating ache in her head making itself known. Had she hit it as she fell? Wait, no. She remembered. Lauren had hit her. Hard. Probably with the gun.

Lauren's last words rang in her head. "I'm not." What did she mean by that? She wasn't what? She wasn't going to kill her. Natalie was still alive. So that made sense. Lauren wasn't going to kill her herself. No, her plan had been much more devious. She was going to let the elements, starvation, dehydration, hypothermia ... whatever ... do it for her. Natalie hadn't been shot, but she was as good as dead trapped down here.

Unless she could think of a way to get herself out. She had climbed with Graham a few more times since that first time, slowly building up her arm strength. But could she climb out of this? One-handed? That remained to be seen. She had to at least try.

With her uninjured hand, she reached out and felt for the walls. What were they made of? Dirt? Stone? Whatever it was, it felt damp. Circling the pit, she heard sloshing in one spot. There was still water in here. If she wanted to survive, she had to make sure to stay away from that water or she'd freeze to death. Back on the dry side, she felt the walls again. Okay, she could do this. She just needed to find some handholds. Or dig some out.

Keeping her injured arm out of the way, Natalie reached up as high as she could with her uninjured hand. She dug her fingers into the damp earth. Trying to dig as much of a handhold out without the rest of the earth around it crumbling away. The dampness of the dirt was helping. When she was satisfied, she reached lower. She lifted her left leg as high as she could, measuring where to dig out a toehold. She dug two, shoulder-width apart from each other.

She held her breath as she placed her toes in the first hole while reaching up for the handhold. Okay, so far, so good. She balanced her weight on her toes and proceeded to dig out another hole where her foot could reach. Then another one slightly higher. She gingerly moved one foot to the next hold and pushed herself higher, grabbing the handhold she'd already made. Head throbbing, she paused to breathe. Damn the pain. It was so hard to concentrate.

She kept at it. Dig, pull, dig, pull. She thought she got about halfway up when the dirt turned drier. Each hold crumbling as soon as she put any weight on it. She attempted to dig one more, refusing to admit defeat. But the wall she was clinging to gave way. She fell with a scream as dirt and rocks collapsed on top of her.

Dazed, Natalie lay still. Her hair and injured arm in the water. Tears threatened. Hopelessness seeped in. *Stop it!*

Get up! Okay, she could do that. She put her hand down in the water to push herself up, momentarily forgetting the injury as pain swamped her. *Fuck. Fuck. Fuckity Fuck.* She gasped, hugging her arm to her chest, willing the pain to ease as tears threatened. She looked up, resolutely compelling the tears to dry up.

Okay. Do not *do that again!* She had to remember her injury or things were only going to get worse for her.

She nearly laughed out loud. How could things get worse? Things were already bad. As bad as bad can get. She took stock of her situation. Again.

Natalie tried standing, but the pain pulsing in her head made her dizzy. She plopped her butt in the newly fallen earth, her back against the wall, injured arm cradled in her lap. Thankfully, the dirt she'd knocked down made a nice little pile. Which meant she was slightly higher, away from the water.

She shifted slightly to dislodge the rock that was digging into her ass, but the damn thing followed her. *Wait!* That wasn't a rock. Cell phone! How could she be such an idiot? She hurriedly dug it out and looked at the display and her heart sank. No service. She held it higher, thinking that would help. Nope. She struggled to her feet and held the phone as high as she could. No use. She dropped back down in defeat. The tears that had threatened finally spilling over.

Chapter 20

NATALIE LAY ON HER side; her injured right hand cradled between her breasts. She shivered, kicking herself for not grabbing her heavier parka.

She hurt. Everywhere. She'd tried climbing again this morning, only to fall. Hard. She may have bruised her ribs this time. Or maybe broken one or two. The cold was making things worse. Her body tensing as she shivered, triggering muscle aches.

She wondered vaguely what day it was. Saturday, she thought. Saturday night. Or maybe it was Sunday morning by now. She was too tired to take her phone out to look. No matter what, she'd been in here for over twenty-four hours now. Surely, Maddie knew she was missing. She had to have gotten people out searching for her. Natalie thought a few of the Nighthawks had stayed behind. Finch, perhaps. Or maybe Jude. Maddie would certainly have gotten their help.

The problem was they didn't know where to start the search. She hadn't left a note or a text to anyone to let them know where she was going. She imagined Graham would have been trying to reach her too, if the number of calls he'd made the other morning was any indication. He might know something was wrong when she didn't answer any of his texts or calls. He'd mobilize the team. All she had to do was hold on a little longer.

Or he'd think she was still angry with him. In that case, he would give her space.

Her stomach growled, tearing her from her morose thoughts. She moaned. *I get it already! You're hungry!* Well, too damn bad. She hadn't thought to pack a meal. It was just going to be a simple walk with a friend. How wrong she'd been. She certainly was glad now that she had eaten the cheese and crackers before this little adventure.

Natalie started humming to distract herself from her misery. That only worked for so long, though. She pulled her phone out instead. If she was going to die, she wanted to leave her loved ones a message. She pulled up the messaging app and started to record. Her first message was to Maddie and her dad. She let them know she loved them, and she was sorry to leave them.

Next, she began a message to Graham. It was harder than she thought it would be. She wanted more time. Time with him. A future with him. She wanted to make a home with him. Have his children. Grow old together.

She told him she understood his anger the other night and that she forgave him. Then she told him how much she loved him and how happy he made her. As she spoke, she started to cry again. She sniffed back her tears as best she could to finish her goodbye to Graham. She didn't know if anyone would ever get those messages. Maybe someday someone would find her skeleton and her cell. Maybe they could even retrieve the messages. She doubted it would ever happen, but she'd had to do it anyway.

Natalie put her phone back in her pocket. It was nearly dead anyway. She lay still, letting the tears slide down her face. Regrets overwhelming her again. So much wasted time. Twelve years of wasted time. A month of wasted time.

Had it only been one month since that day in his office? Natalie tried to think back. It'd been late October. A day that was so dynamically different than the one twelve years ago. One day held a chill in the air. The other day's heat stole your breath. And yet those two days were also similar. The easy camaraderie. The instant attraction, at least for her. She wasn't sure if he'd been as attracted to her as she was to him all those years ago. But that kiss he gave her...The way he'd grabbed her back and deepened it. The way he'd held her, could he have felt what she did back then? She liked to think he did.

And since that attraction had had twelve years to simmer, when they finally were together again, it boiled over. Exploded. Their passion was intense. He made her feel things beyond her wildest imaginings. He was beyond good in bed. An Adonis. And she, his Aphrodite. She could hardly believe he had been all hers. At least for a little while.

She wondered morbidly how long it would take him to move on after her. She hoped to hell he wouldn't move on with Lauren. She kicked herself for not telling Graham about Lauren in her message. Pulling out her phone again, she attempted to record another message. The damn device died before she could finish.

She had to get out of here. But how? She'd tried everything she could think of, injuring herself further. The well was too deep. Too dark. She had nothing to help her. *You still have your brain!* Yeah, but she couldn't think of anything else to do. She was so tired. So cold. She fell asleep even as she yelled at herself to think.

Graham held her in his arms. He was so warm. So soothing. She felt so content. She loved laying in his arms. Loved the attention he showered on her. Loved to feel his fingers stroke her back. Her hair. A moan of gratification escaped her lips. She reached up her right hand to touch his face. Jeez Louise, that hurt. She let it fall limply as the pain radiated up to her shoulder. Frowning, she looked at the

offending hand. Had she injured it somehow? Maybe it had just fallen asleep. She'd feel the pins and needles of it waking up soon. Her mind drifted. Away from the pain.

So tired. She struggled to keep her eyes open. She wanted to gaze at Graham for a while longer. Memorize every feature. But her eyes wouldn't obey. They were so heavy. "Chickadee." She could hear him call. She wanted to wake but couldn't. "Chickadee." He was louder this time. She felt herself recoil. His voice exploded harshly. Urgently. Something was not right. She fought to wake up, but she was so tired. "Chickadee! Wake Up!"

Natalie awoke with a start. Convinced she'd heard Graham. She looked up at the roof of her prison. It might be daytime. But it was darker than it had been previously. Slowly, her sluggish brain registered the rain. It was raining. Hard. Falling through the holes in the plywood that had been her lifeline to the light. Filling her prison with water. Water creeping steadily toward her. She scrambled back away from the growing puddle knowing instinctively that with these temperatures if she got too wet, it would be game over. But she'd get wet anyway. The rain would see to that.

Natalie struggled to her knees and began to dig into the dirt wall. She needed protection from the rain. Why hadn't she thought of that earlier. Weakness seized her body. Her strength waning. Still so tired. *Keep digging!* She could hear Graham yell.

"I am!" she yelled back out loud.

Faster!

"I'm going as fast as I can with only one hand," she told him. Her exasperation towards him growing. He wasn't hurt. He wasn't chilled down to his bones. He wasn't in constant pain. He wasn't even here! God! She was losing her mind. Arguing with *no one!*

Get a grip, Natalie. Her own chastising voice pealed through her head as she continued to dig. Her fingers ached. The nails had been torn away long ago. She could barely feel the tips anymore; they were scratched up so bad. And so cold. Numb with the cold. Not for the first time, she wished she'd kept gloves in the pockets of this coat.

She tried using her injured hand to dig, but the pain was excruciating, nearly causing her to pass out. After dislodging a large rock, she used that to dig and was able to move the dirt much faster.

Finally! *Finally*, she thought she had a space big enough for her to climb into. She had to lay on her side in the fetal position, but at least it was helping to keep the rain off her. She lay there, exhausted, cold seeping deep in her bones. Hopelessness swamped her again. No! She wasn't going to give in to it. How does one combat hopelessness?

She remembered Colin and Lucy then. Thinking of them all alone in their own prison gave her a tiny bit of courage. If they could survive at their ages, then so could she.

But they had food. "Shut up!" She told the voice.

It wasn't as cold then too! "Can you just stop!" Now, back to Colin and Lucy. What did they do? How did they cope when all hope seemed lost?

Sing! The kids were singing when they found them. She could do that, couldn't she? "Frosty the snowman. Was a jolly happy soul," Natalie sang. Soon exhausting her repertoire of Christmas songs. She moved on to nursery rhymes. Sometime during her rendition of "Oh Suzanna," she drifted off to sleep again.

Halfway through the morning on Monday, Graham and his team were packing up to go home. They had done all they could for the victims of the flood. There would be a lot of clean-up once the waters receded, but that was for somebody else to worry about. He had enough on his mind. He still couldn't get ahold of Natalie. He'd tried the sat phone at the cabin a few times, but there had been no answer. He figured she was out skiing or something, and he kept missing her. But this morning, he'd tried texting her again. He thought for sure he'd get her before school started. Had been hopeful she'd answer his desperate text begging her to just let him know she was safe, but still nothing. Where was she? He was itching to get out of here. To get home. To wrap Natalie up in his arms, apologize, and gather up the courage to tell her how he felt about her.

David called to him, interrupting his thoughts. He held out his phone a strange expression on his face. "It's Maddie," David said in explanation. Graham's heart clenched. Natalie.

"Graham, can you hear me?" Maddie called.

"Yeah, Maddie. What is it? What's the matter?" At this point, Finch and Logan had stopped packing to listen, the fear in Graham's voice alerting them.

"I'm not exactly sure. Lucy is here." Lucy? "She said Natalie wasn't in school today. She was worried. She's been babbling about seeing Natalie in the woods or something. I'm worried, Graham. If she went to your cabin, could she be hurt or something? Hold on a sec," she broke off as a small voice tried to get her attention. He could hear her muttering assurances to somebody. "Lucy insists Natalie is in the woods," Maddie told them. "Are you guys coming home soon?"

"We're packing up now," David told her. The worry in Maddie's voice was scaring him. He was convinced now more than ever that something had happened to Natalie. He had to get to her now! It was still going to take them hours to drive. That was too long.

"I need a helicopter," Graham said to no one in particular.

Finch, the Nighthawk's helicopter pilot, said, "On it!" He dashed away, phone already to his ear.

Logan spoke up then. "I'll continue to pack up here and drive back. You guys go with Finch."

"Right," Graham said, already trying to think five steps ahead. He paused briefly to place a hand on Logan's shoulder. "Thanks," he said sincerely, squeezing his shoulder. Logan nodded.

David hung up with Maddie after assuring her they were on their way. Finch was back in no time. "Made a deal with a buddy. He's got a helicopter he's willing to let me borrow. He's getting it ready now. If we're done here, let's go." They all hopped into the truck to make the short drive to Finch's friend's landing pad.

In no time, they were in the air. But still, it wasn't fast enough. He willed it to go faster. His sole thought—getting to Natalie. "Should we go to your cabin first?" Finch asked him through the headset.

Operating on pure instinct, Graham replied, "No. Go to Lake Haven." He couldn't explain why, but he knew she wasn't at the cabin. David, meanwhile, was calling in as many Nighthawks as he could. Telling them all to meet at Natalie's place.

"I've got Jude, Evan, and Tin Man coming. Lauren's not answering." David told him.

"Just leave her a message."

"I did."

"Good," he replied distractedly. He was trying to figure out what Lucy meant. She said woods. What woods? Was Lucy talking about the same woods she and Colin had gotten lost in? And if so, why would Natalie go in those woods by herself? Especially after seeing what had happened to Colin and Lucy. She must have gone in with somebody to help them with something. Or maybe ... he shook his head, denying the direction his thoughts were heading. But the theory slipped out and took root. Did someone force her? Fear gripped him. The note.

Was Erik still locked up? Graham took out his phone, searching for the number for Lakeland Correctional. He wasn't above using his credentials to get the information he needed. When he finally reached the right person, he breathed a little easier. Erik was still locked up tight.

"What are you thinking?" David asked.

"I'm thinking Natalie wouldn't go into those woods, any woods, alone."

"You think she was forced?"

"Seems crazy, I know. But it's the logical conclusion. Especially after the threatening note." But who? How? And more importantly, where? He needed to talk to Lucy.

Finch landed at the local airfield where Tin Man was waiting for them in his truck. It was decided that Finch would fly up to the cabin just to double-check she wasn't, in fact, there. Then he would join them. As the helicopter lifted into the air, the truck was already careening down the road toward Lake Haven.

Arriving at Natalie's fifteen minutes later, Graham jumped out before the truck came to a complete stop. Maddie met him at the door. "I need to talk to Lucy."

"She's still here. She's with her parents in the living room."

When Lucy spotted him, she jumped up and ran to him. He scooped her up, and she squeezed his neck with her tiny arms. "She's lost. I know it. I saw her. She's lost like me and Colin were."

He sat down at the dining table, placing her on the edge of the table. An image of Natalie sitting in the same spot the day they made love here flashed through his brain. His heart clenched. He shoved the thought away for the moment. "Okay. Tell me from the beginning," he coaxed. "When did you see her?"

"Friday. After school."

"Where were you?"

"I was playing in the front yard. I saw her walk up the sidewalk that Colin and I take to school. I wanted to go to her," she broke off.

"Why didn't you?" Graham said more calmly than he felt. He needed to stay calm. Slow his panic if he was going to get the answers he needed from the frightened girl.

"She wasn't alone."

"Do you know who she was with?" His suspicions had been correct. She hadn't gone alone. Now the question was, did she go willingly?

"It was that lady. The one who gave me the cookie after I got out of the hole." Lauren?

"Do you remember her name? When she gave you the cookie, did she tell you her name?"

Lucy thought hard. "Sharon. Karen. No, that's not it."

"What did she look like?" he asked. He needed to make sure.

"Blonde hair. Taller than Miss Ghannon." Graham took out his cell and scanned through his pictures. Finding one of Lauren, he held it out for Lucy to see.

"Could this be her?"

Her little face lit up. "Yeah, that's her. She looked mad. Not as nice as she did when she gave me the cookie," she whispered.

"Why do you say that?"

Her little shoulders shrugged. "I don't know. I guess it was the way she was walking. Kind of like marching. My mommy does that when she gets mad. And her face looked mean."

"Okay. Do you remember where they went?"

Her face crumpled. "I know I shouldn't have done it. I just wanted to be with Miss Ghannon. Mommy's going to be so mad."

Graham rushed to reassure her before he lost her to hysterics. "It's okay, Lucy. You're not going to get into trouble. Especially if what you tell me helps me find Miss Ghannon."

"R ... really?"

"Yup."

She still fought to hold back tears. Then she leaned closer to whisper to him, "I followed them."

"Good!" he praised, bolstering her courage. "Where did they go?"

"Into the woods. They were on the path. I followed for a while. They didn't know I was there. I hid behind the trees every time that lady looked over her shoulder. She was yelling stuff to Miss Ghannon."

"Do you know what? What was she yelling?"

"I guess Miss Ghannon had something that was hers. I kept hearing her say 'mine.' A lot. I don't know what Miss Ghannon had of hers. I saw Miss Ghannon's hands. She had them raised up like this." She bent her elbows slightly, her arms in front of her, palms up. Natalie had been holding up her hands? For what? To fend off Lauren? But why? It didn't make any sense. "Miss Ghannon's hands were empty. She didn't have anything of the cookie lady's."

"Okay. What happened next? Did they stay there, or did they keep walking?"

Her face crumpled again; this time, the tears fell freely. "I don't know," she wailed. "I didn't see. I was afraid I'd get in trouble for being so far in the woods. I didn't want to get into trouble. I ... I ran back home," she broke off, overcome by her tears. He hugged the girl tight to him and stood.

Handing the sobbing girl off to her mother, he turned to David. "Find Lauren."

"On it!" he took off, Maddie following.

He then turned to Evan. "I need a pack. Med pack. Got a spare?" Evan ran to his truck to get it as Maddie joined them again.

"I gave David my car. And Ian's number. They'll find her," she assured him. "What now?"

Evan handed him the pack as he walked out Natalie's front door. "Now I find her." He ran up the sidewalk, stopping briefly at the entrance to the path to confer with his Nighthawks. "Same search pattern as last time," he ordered, referring to Colin and Lucy's search. "Maddie, can you handle the terrain?"

"Absolutely. You're not leaving me behind."

"Then you're with me. Try to keep up as best you can."

"Don't worry about me."

He raced down the path, eyes searching. Always searching. He cursed; it had rained again recently. That would make finding a trail slightly more difficult. But not impossible. Have to hurry. Have to find her. Those words ran through his head over and over again with each step. Have to find her before it was too late.

Fuck, what if it was already too late? His steps faltered. This is now *the* most important search and rescue of his career. He *would not* fail. He refused to entertain the possibility that he had already failed her. She was alive. She *had* to be. They weren't done. *He* wasn't done. He wanted more time. Time with her. The rest of his life with her. He loved her so much.

He stopped. His heart twisted. He rubbed his chest over his heart and continued on the path.

Not too far in, he noticed a disturbance in the leaves on the ground. As if someone had shuffled through them, leaving a path. He followed it off the trail. Maddie, for her part, kept up pretty well.

He spotted more signs. More disturbances in the layer of leaves on the ground. A few broken branches. She was leaving him a trail. *That's my girl.*

Suddenly, he knew where they went. He turned north. The same direction he and Natalie had gone when they were looking for that clearing with the ruins. She was there. He knew it. He picked up his pace, Maddie huffing along behind him.

Chapter 21

"CHICKADEE, SING ME A song," he pleaded.

"No," she whined. "Too tired."

"But I love hearing your voice. Please sing."

Natalie opened her mouth to sing, but she couldn't remember the words.

"Come on, Chickadee. You know the words. Remember? Silent night. Holy night."

She tried to join, but her mouth wouldn't form the words. Her tongue was too dry. Her body exhausted. Her brain muddy.

He started to get angry with her. "Leave me alone!" she pleaded. She just wanted to sleep. Just a little bit longer.

"No, Chickadee! Sing! Now!" he was screaming at her.

Natalie started to sing again. "Silent night. Holy night. All is calm. All is bright." Wait. It was bright. Why was it so bright? It hadn't been this light for days. Did it finally stop raining?

She continued to sing. "Round yon virgin. Mother and child."

"Chickadee?" Graham's voice again.

"I'm singing, okay. Leave me alone. I'm singing. Quit bossing me around."

"Chickadee? Can you open your eyes?"

"No. Too tired," she slurred weakly. The exhaustion was overwhelming, she could hardly think of the words. "I ... I've forgotten the words again," she whispered as she felt something pinch her on her good arm, and warmth seeped in.

"That's okay. You can stop singing now," he told her.

She smiled, or at least she thought she smiled. But she didn't feel her lips move. "Good," she said, drifting off again.

Warmth. She felt so much heat. How was that possible? She tried to open her eyes. They wouldn't obey. She could still smell the musty earth of her prison, so where was the warmth coming from. She tried to roll onto her back. Something was preventing her.

"Chickadee? Are you with me?" Natalie felt something wet at her lips. Water. She let it trickle into her mouth. God, that was good. She swallowed and let more drip in. And more. She desperately wanted more. "Easy," he cautioned. "Just a little at a time."

Something was trying to penetrate the brain fog. There was warmth and water. But she knew she was still at the bottom of the well. How could there be warmth and water? She hadn't had any of that in ... days. She felt something move against her. Enveloping her in more heat. A lone thought filtered through her confusion. She wasn't alone.

She commanded her eyes to open. She had to see. Had to know for sure. "Graham?" she croaked.

"I'm here, Chickadee." Natalie felt arms squeeze her tight.

"Wha ... what took you so long?" She didn't know why she said that. It just popped into her head. She felt his chuckle against her body. His lips on her forehead.

Little things. She started to notice little things. She could feel skin against her skin. She glanced down. He'd lifted both their shirts and was laying torso to tor-so against her. Warming her with his own body heat. He'd also draped something shiny over them. There was something in her hands. What were those called? Hand warmers? She raised her uninjured hand to look. It was covered with a glove, but she could definitely feel something warm in her palm. And there was a tube coming out of the crook in her elbow, but her addled brain couldn't decipher what it was.

"Here, try some more water." He poured the warmish liquid into her mouth. Natalie heard something crackle, then another voice.

"Boss, we're lowering the basket now."

"Copy," Graham answered. She mourned the sudden loss of heat. Graham was leaving her. She tried to protest but couldn't get the words out. He lowered her shirt and wrapped the shiny thing tightly around her. He was talking with someone, but she couldn't make out the words. Then he was kneeling down near her again. He placed something over her head. A hat? Maybe.

"We're gonna get you out of here now." She couldn't respond. Only stare at him. His ice-blue eyes had her mesmerized. She felt an arm slide behind her shoulders and another under her knees. Then she was lifted. Finally, off the cold hard ground. She must have passed out again because the next thing she knew, she was leaning against something that felt like part metal. Graham was placing straps around her. Tying her into the metal thing. She tried to search her mind for the proper words but failed. It was beyond her right now.

Flying. She was flying. A bird. She'd turned into a bird. "I'm flying," she rasped past her parched lips.

Graham chuckled. "That's right, Chickadee. You can finally fly."

"Cool."

There was light. Everywhere. So much light it hurt her eyes. She squeezed them shut to block out the worst of the brightness. She was lying on the ground again. Still strapped to that ... thing. Why couldn't she think of the word for it? More warmth was being piled on top of her. Then a woman's voice.

"God, Natalie. You gotta stop scaring me like this." Maddie. Her sister was here. But where was Graham? She opened her mouth to ask but could only croak out the slightest sound. "Shh," Maddie said. "Don't try to talk. The boys will get you to the hospital, and you'll be warm again in no time." That sounded nice.

"Love you," she heard Maddie tell her. Love you too, Natalie tried to say. Love Graham. Must tell him, but where was he? She tried to look for him, but the muscles in her neck wouldn't obey. Must tell him. It was like a mantra in her head as she drifted off again.

Graham paced the hospital corridor waiting for them to bring Natalie back. She was in x-ray getting her arm and ribs looked at. It was late now. They had waited to do the x-rays until her body heat rose. She was so frail. So pale. She looked like she was dead. If she hadn't been singing, and yelling at him, he'd have been sure she was dead.

That singing. His clever little Chickadee. Guiding him to her with song. He'd heard her even before he'd entered the clearing. He'd rushed to the well and threw the cover off, but he couldn't see her. He tried shining his flashlight down, but the light wouldn't reach the bottom. He could hear her, though. He hardly remembered now anchoring a rope and rappelling down to her. He was that desperate to reach her.

She was curled up in a ball in the wall of the well. Clever girl. She'd dug out protection from the rain. Her clothes were still slightly wet, being in a damp well for so long, but at least she wasn't soaked. That's because she'd been smart and dug out the hole.

But she'd harmed herself in the process. The fingers of one hand were a mess. He'd seen the holes in the dirt wall, at least what was left of them. Obviously, she'd tried to climb out by digging handholds, but the dirt had crumbled. He wondered if that's when she'd broken her wrist. Or her ribs. He'd noticed the dried blood on the back of her head. Had Lauren struck her and then pushed her in? Or had she struck her head in the fall? It was an awfully long way down.

Upon reaching her, and when she was done yelling at him, he knew his first priority was fluids and heat. He'd fallen back on his paramedic's training. Since he'd had to wait for the Nighthawks to get to him and rig up the basket, he'd started to grab things out of the pack to warm her up. He'd placed the needle for the IV in her vein and taped it in place.

He'd done the best he could with the available supplies to warm her. Graham knew the best warmth for her would be his own body heat. Despite the cold, he hadn't hesitated to strip off his shirt. He'd laid next to her on the hard ground. Pushing her clothes aside, he'd pulled her into his arms, pressing his warm chest against her far too cold one. It seemed to have worked, somewhat. She had slowly come back to him.

Now that she was safe and he finally had time to process, he was angry. Why did this happen? If it had been Lauren; why?

David and Deputy Ian found him trying to pace out the worst of his anger. "Did you find her?" he asked.

David shook his head. "But there's something you should know. Have you ever been to her place?"

It was Graham's turn to shake his head. "Tell me."

The deputy reported it all to him. "She had pictures of you everywhere. A lot in frames like family portraits. In some, she'd added herself. Photoshopped. Glued in. Whatever. There were more of those than of the real pictures of the two of you. Looks to me like she was obsessed with you."

Graham froze. Obsessed was not a word he would have considered about Lauren. How had he missed it? "Fuck. I never realized. How could I have never seen?"

"None of us saw it. She was good at hiding it," David answered. "But that's not all. There was a journal, the last few entries were full of hate ... toward Natalie."

Graham huffed out a breath running his hand through his hair in frustration. He'd known something was wrong with her, but he'd never gotten the chance to ask her about it. Would she have even told him the truth if he had asked?

"She had convinced herself that you were hers," David continued.

"*Mine*," Graham whispered, remembering what Lucy had told him. Natalie had something Lauren thought was hers. Who would have guessed that it was *him*?

"She believed the only way she could keep you to herself was to get rid of Natalie." *Son of a bitch.* It was his fault. This happened to Natalie because of him. And he'd done nothing to protect her from it. The level of his failure stunned him. He dropped into a chair in the hall.

He'd promised, *vowed* to himself to keep her safe. He'd botched it horribly, in the worst possible way. She could have died.

Knowing that his last words to her had been so horrible made everything exponentially worse. He stared at the ugly tile floor. She could have died thinking he truly meant the callous things he'd said to her. He closed his eyes.

The deputy's cell rang, and he stepped away to answer. David sat beside him. "I know what you're thinking," he said, placing a comforting hand on his shoulder. "But it's not true. You saved her, man! That's everything."

"She was so close to dying. If ... it would have been my fault. I'd failed her," he cried, dropping his head into his hands. Unexpected tears burned in his eyes; he squeezed them shut tightly to prevent them from escaping. "When she told me what that bastard ex of hers had done to her, I vowed I would always keep her safe. I wasn't here. I'd left her alone. I'd left her with those cruel words I'd screamed at her. She could have died with the memory of those harsh words as the last ones she'd ever hear from me.

"She deserves so much better. She deserves tender words. Loving words. She's the best thing that's ever happened to me. She's my guiding light. My true North. And I destroyed it all with my drunken pity party. It's all my fault." A single tear slipped out, sliding down the side of his face. He did nothing to wipe it away.

"No. The fault is Lauren's."

"Lauren did this because of me," he insisted. "This wouldn't have happened to her if she hadn't been with me. If I hadn't fallen in love with her."

"Graham," David commanded. "Stop! She's safe. You saved her. That's what matters. She'll heal and be fine. And you can spend the rest of your life making it up to her. Giving her those tender, loving words."

"If she'll even want to have anything to do with me," Graham said glumly.

"She loves you. Of course, she'll have you."

The deputy returned a glum expression on his face. "Deputies found Natalie's car. No sign of Lauren. There was a small bag and skis in the trunk. Luggage tag had Natalie's name on it."

"She must have written the note Maddie found. Wanted us to believe Natalie had gone away for the weekend," Graham muttered.

"It worked too. For a while," David mused. "If Lucy hadn't followed them that day, we probably would have been searching for her at the cabin." Lauren had planned it all out. David was right. If it hadn't been for the intrepid little girl, Lauren's plan would have worked. Natalie would have died of exposure. And they would have never known what happened to her. That thought froze his blood deep in his veins.

"We'll analyze the handwriting on the note. See if it matches Lauren's." McClintock informed them.

Maddie found them there in the hallway. "She's back. And asking for you."

"I need to talk to her," the deputy said.

David put up a hand to stop him. "Give Graham a moment alone with her first."

Graham shot to his feet and raced down the hall. He peeked behind the ER curtain, and there she was. His little Chickadee. She was awake and sitting up, and she was the most precious and beautiful thing he'd ever laid his eyes on.

He drank her in. She was pale, the scattering of freckles across her nose more pronounced. Dark circles under her beautiful green eyes spoke of her exhaustion. A white bandage peeked out from under her hairline on her nape where she'd been hit. Its stark whiteness a glaring contrast to her dark hair which lay limply across the pillow, the natural waviness absent. Someone had obviously tried their best to scrub most of the blood out of her hair. One hand was wrapped in bandages, the other in a splint. The evidence of her wounds made his heart thump hard in his chest, wishing he could take her pain onto himself.

She spotted him and smiled. That smile lit the darkest places inside of him. Pushing aside the apprehension, he went to her side and dropped into the chair beside her bed. Gently he lifted her splinted hand, placing it in his own hand, his fingers lacing through hers as best he could over the edges of the splint.

"Broken?" he asked, indicating the splint. She nodded. "Ribs?"

"Just bruised."

He saw the tears then, and it broke him. "Aww, Chickadee. Don't cry." He placed his lips on the fingers that peeked out from the splint. "You're safe now."

She nodded again. "I thought I'd never see you again," she sobbed.

He placed a hip on the bed and laid next to her. She shifted to make room, wincing. His heart caught. He gathered her into his arms as gently as he could and held her as she cried. She cried until exhaustion overcame her, and she fell asleep in his arms.

The deputy came in after a while, Maddie and David on his heels. "I'm sorry. I really need to speak with her."

"Chickadee," Graham said close to her ear. He sure as hell hated to wake her but knew the deputy needed answers. "Can you wake up for me?" Slowly she opened her eyes. "Ian needs to talk to you. Do you feel up to it?" She nodded. Graham stayed where he was as McClintock approached. He needed to keep Natalie close.

"I'm sorry to disturb you, Natalie, but I need you to tell me what happened," the law officer began pulling a notebook out of his pocket.

"I'll try," Natalie said quietly. "Some of it is foggy, though."

"Just tell us as much as you can remember. When did you leave your house?" he asked.

"Friday."

"Why?"

"Lauren had stopped by. She said she wanted us to become friends and asked if we could go for a walk."

"And you went with her?" Natalie nodded. "Which way did you two start walking?"

"Towards the school. Away from the lake."

"Did you talk about anything?"

"No, at least not until we got into the woods."

"Go on," he prompted.

"She was acting weird. When we were pretty far into the woods, I asked her if something was wrong ... I think." She placed her bandaged hand on her forehead, her brow creasing as if it hurt to remember.

He saw her peek at him through her fingers. She seemed unwilling to continue. Her eyes looked on him with pity like she didn't want to hurt him by completing her story.

He grabbed her hand and lowered it from her face. "It's okay, Chickadee. I know what she did, who she really is now. You can finish it. It won't hurt me to hear."

She took a deep breath, wincing with pain from her bruised ribs. "She pointed a gun at me then and said I was what was wrong." Graham flinched inwardly at the mention of a gun. Lauren. His friend and confidant all these years. He still couldn't believe she was responsible for all of this. Couldn't believe she would want to harm someone who meant so much to him.

"Did you know what she meant by that?"

"Not at first. Then she explained that Graham was hers and I was in the way. She was ranting about how I had ruined everything." He'd assured Natalie he could handle hearing what had happened, but it still rankled to learn he was the cause of all this.

He'd brought Natalie into his world and had hoped the two women would be friends. He should have paid closer attention. He knew something had been bothering Lauren and should have asked her about it. They could have avoided all the pain. Natalie would have been safe and sound in her house all weekend, not lying broken at the bottom of a pit.

"She led me to the clearing, and then I knew," Natalie continued. "I remembered the well was there. I figured she was going to shoot me and dump my body in the well. I tried to talk her out of it. Tried to reason with her. She'd spent her life helping others. She wasn't a murderer. It wasn't in her nature. I even offered to go away. Leave Graham. She wouldn't listen.

"I tried one last time to convince her she wasn't a murderer. She said something like, 'I'm not.' That's the last thing I remember before waking up at the bottom of the well." Graham squeezed her tighter. She'd begged for her life. That was another image that was now burned into his brain.

His anger surged. He gritted his teeth and contained it, seething inside. Lauren had wanted Natalie dead. She may not have pulled the trigger, but she was still trying to kill Natalie by leaving her in that pit. That, in Graham's book, *was* murder.

"Anything else you need to tell me?" Ian asked. Natalie shook her head, wincing. Her head obviously still hurting her.

"Okay," the deputy said, closing his notebook. "I think I've got everything I need. I'd like to take the clothes you were wearing though. There could be trace evidence on them."

"I'll get them," Maddie offered. She opened the closet in the room and took out a bag that was holding her belongings.

"Wait," Natalie said, spotting her cell phone at the bottom of the bag. "Do you think you need my cell, or can I keep that with me?"

He fished the phone out of the bag. "Don't see why I would need it." He handed it to her. Graham grabbed it since her hands were currently out of commission.

"Battery's dead," Natalie mumbled.

"How 'bout I take it home and get it charged," Maddie offered, taking it from Graham.

"Okay," the deputy said again. "You get some rest. If you think of anything else, let me know."

"Thanks, Ian, I will," Natalie answered.

David and Maddie walked the deputy out.

Since they had a moment alone together, Graham wanted to try to apologize. He struggled to find the right words. Clearing his throat, he croaked, "Natalie ... I—"

Maddie came back into the room before he could rasp out any more words. She went around to the other side of the bed from where Graham was currently sprawled next to Natalie. She laid a hand on her arm, tears in her eyes. "Please don't scare me like that again."

"I will do everything in my power to make sure I don't," Natalie promised.

"Good. I'm gonna hold you to that. Do you want me to stick around, or can I go home to get some rest?"

"Go. I'm probably just going to sleep too. Still so tired." Her eyes drooped even as she said it.

"Okay," Maddie leaned forward and kissed Natalie's forehead. "Love you, little sis."

"Love you, big sis."

After Maddie left, the nurse came in to move Natalie to a private room. By the time they got her settled, she was overcome with exhaustion. Graham laid on the bed beside her again, the nurses having long ago decided that visiting hours didn't apply to him. She sighed and snuggled deeper into his arms, but still didn't drift off to sleep.

"Close your eyes, Chickadee. Rest. There will be plenty of time to talk later," he assured her.

"You ... you're not going to leave me, are you?" she whispered.

His heart skipped a beat and hope blossomed. She still wanted him close. "Not a chance." He squeezed her tighter and laid his head down on the pillow beside hers. He watched over her as she finally let herself drift off to sleep.

Chapter 22

L ATE THE NEXT AFTERNOON, Natalie's core body temperature was back to normal, and she was released from the hospital. Graham was there the entire time. That, more than anything else, helped her to heal.

She could tell he was hurting. Knew he was struggling with finding the right words to say to her. She could wait. She saw in his eyes how remorseful he was. That was enough for her. She didn't want to waste any more time with him now that she had that second chance she'd prayed so fervently for in her dank prison.

Maddie had been there several times throughout the day as well. She'd brought Natalie some of her clothes and was helping her dress in them so that she could leave this awful place. She'd had enough of hospitals to last a lifetime.

Natalie chewed on her bottom lip. Even though she was anxious to go home, she was nervous about what was waiting for her there.

"Something on your mind?" Maddie asked, ever attuned to her sister's innermost feelings. "You seem lost in thought."

"I'm just still trying to process everything," Natalie answered.

"I get that. But I think there is something else bothering you."

Natalie sighed. She needed help categorizing her feelings, and Maddie had helped her sort through some of her darkest thoughts in the years since the tornado. "When I was in that pit, the thing I thought about the most was wanting more time with Graham. I vowed that if I ever got out of there, I would tell him how I felt about him."

"And now that you're out, you're hesitating?"

Natalie nodded, wincing when the bandage on her neck pulled. "I don't know why. I love him. I do. But what if he doesn't feel the same way? Am I willing to risk my heart again? And what if I'm so wrong about him like I was so *very* wrong about Erik? The fight we had that last night, the things he'd said ... it was like I was hearing Erik's voice raging in my head. I don't ever want to go through that type of hurt again. And I have a feeling the hurt that Graham could cause me would be ten times worse than anything I've ever experienced before because I love him so much."

"Okay. First of all—breathe," Maddie ordered her. "Here's what I know. That man moved heaven and earth to get to you. He spent the weekend in a constant state of panic because he couldn't get hold of you. Even after I told him about the note I'd thought you'd written." Maddie's brow furrowed as she clenched her jaw, apparently still blaming herself for not realizing the note had not been written by her sister.

"That was not your fault."

Maddie waved off her assurances. "He knew. He knew you hadn't written it. Somehow, he understood your true nature. You wouldn't have left like that. You would have talked to me. And he knew that you would have texted him back no matter how mad you were at him. He called me several times asking if I'd heard from you. He was so worried. Then yesterday when I called him about Lucy, he knew something was wrong. He could feel it. Only someone who was truly in love could feel that."

"But ..." She snapped her mouth closed when Maddie held up her hand.

"That man loves you more than I've ever seen anybody love someone before. And it's a true love. Don't be afraid to tell him how you feel. I know he feels the same."

"How can you be so sure?" Still, she was hesitant, and she hated that. She started to nibble on her lower lip again.

"Oh, Natalie. You should have seen him. He was desperate to find you, and yet he stayed so calm and focused. He was so amazing with Lucy getting her to tell him everything she knew. We weren't even halfway into the woods when it seemed like he knew where you were. I could barely keep up with him, he moved so fast. He heard you singing long before I did. I don't know how he did it. It's like he could feel you. Like he could see you in his mind's eye. I don't know how to explain it except to say he definitely loves you."

Natalie mulled over Maddie's words. She was still contemplating them as she walked through her front door. Her mind swimming with possibilities as she headed up the stairs to take a much-needed shower. She was distracted momentarily from her thoughts when she spied her cell on her nightstand.

Sitting on the edge of her bed, she turned her cell on. Once it had booted up, she called her dad. Maddie had been in touch, but Natalie had yet to talk with him. He was relieved to hear she was going to be okay and promised to see her at Christmas. He'd decided to divorce their mother and move back to Michigan, but he was going to make the move by way of a cross-country road trip. He wanted to see the sights before he was too old and feeble to see anymore, his words, not hers.

After hanging up with her dad, she scrolled through the dozens of texts and voice mail messages from Graham. Each one growing steadily more panicked. He knew he'd acted horrendously and had apologized profusely for the things he'd said and done that night. His voice sounded agonized as he begged her to forgive him.

But as the days passed, his messages had changed to unbearable worry. Her heart clenched at one particularly distressing voice mail where he begged just to hear her voice. He needed assurance she was safe. If only she could have returned that message. She would have, happily.

She slammed her phone down on the nightstand as anger suffused her. Anger at Lauren, who was still out there somewhere. How dare she try to rob something so special from them. She tried clenching her fists, but the bandages prevented it.

Frustration sent her to her feet, and she stalked into the bathroom and looked at her reflection in the mirror for the first time. Shocked at what she saw. Hollow cheeks, dark shadows under dull eyes. Her hair was a mess. She could still see dirt and blood embedded in the strands. She ripped the bandages off the hand she'd dug so hard with. The nails broken beyond repair. Cuts and bruises all over.

She very slowly and gingerly pulled her shirt over her head and saw the massive bruise over her damaged ribs. God, that was enormous. And ugly, a mass of dark colors. She didn't know how it was possible, but she looked even smaller than she used to be.

She turned her back on her reflection and reached into the shower to turn the water on, letting it warm up as she removed her splint and her pants. Her ribs protested her bending over; she was so tired of being in pain. She popped a few pain killers before entering the shower and let the water rain down over her. The warmth slowly seeping in. Would she ever be completely warm again?

Christ. She couldn't wash her hair by herself, her hands were too messed up.

The tears came then, and she sobbed into the spray. She'd nearly lost everything. Her life. Her love. But she had survived. She was home. Graham was here. Everything was as it should be, except it wasn't. *God!* She couldn't even wash her own hair. The unbearable hopelessness she'd felt after Erik threatened from the corners of her mind. She didn't want to return to that hollowness, but how was she ever going to move past this when she couldn't even do the simple things.

It was after the sobs sent her to her knees that she felt Graham behind her. He wrapped his arms around her and held her as she continued to sob, curling his body around hers. When the worst had passed, he helped her back to her feet and reached for the shampoo. It felt heavenly having his hands massaging the soap into her hair. He soaped and rinsed her hair twice; she watched as the dirt and everything from that awful pit swirled down the drain. Next, he grabbed her loofa and lathered that up too. He slowly ran it all over her body, his other hand sliding freely across her skin, leaving goosebumps in their wake.

He kissed her. Gently. Tenderly. Worshipping her with his lips. When the water started to cool, he turned it off and reached for the towels. Wrapping her in the soft terrycloth, he picked her up and carried her to the bed, gently putting her down.

Graham's eyes surveyed her body, a crease appearing between his brows. He inventoried each and every bruise and cut before reaching for one of his t-shirts. He gently slipped the fabric over her head and helped her put her arms through the sleeves. He was so incredibly tender and gentle she felt the burn of tears behind her eyes. His adoration overwhelmed her, and the tears slipped out one at a time, following each other's trail down her cheeks.

After stepping into a pair of boxers, Graham laid beside her; his remorseful expression making her heart hurt. He wiped her tears away, kissing her soothingly. Rolling to her uninjured side in his arms, she laid her head on his shoulder, inhaling deeply. He smelled incredible. A combination of her soap and the outdoors. She nuzzled her nose deeper into his neck, soaking up every smell, every caress, every moment greedily. Amazed that this incredible man was in her bed and treating her so passionately, so lovingly, while he combed his fingers lightly through her hair. As he gently worked out the knots, she felt her body begin to relax. She soon fell fast asleep, feeling cared for and safe.

Graham was restless, unable to sleep. He held Natalie and listened to her soft breaths as she slept. *Fuck!* He was so lucky. He had this amazing, wonderful woman in his arms, and she was safe. Why, then, was he so restless?

Because you are still acting like a coward. He hadn't found the words to tell her how sorry he was for his behavior that awful night. And he needed to. Soon. She deserved to hear the words. To hear him apologize. Even if, she'd already forgiven him and was lying in his arms. She'd allowed him to take care of her. Touch her. Kiss her. Would she have done that if she hadn't forgiven him? But he still needed to man up and give her the words.

And even more cowardly—he still hadn't given her the most important words. He loved this tiny woman in his arms, yet he still hadn't told her. He'd vowed to tell her the minute she was safe, and she'd been safe for over twenty-four hours, but he was still acting like a chickenshit. Somewhere, deep down, he knew she felt the same way, but his fucking head kept getting in the way.

Unable to sleep and not wanting to disturb her with his restlessness, he slid out of bed. In the bathroom, he spotted her splint. Grabbing it and his pants, he went back to her in the bed. As gently as he could, he wrapped the splint back around her damaged wrist. He left it somewhat loose so as not to wake her. They would tighten it later.

He slipped into his pants and pulled his cell out of his pocket, needing to check on the progress of the search for Lauren. Turning on the display, he saw there was a message from Natalie. He dropped into the small armchair that was nestled up against the dresser. When had he missed a call from her? After he pressed play, he knew.

She'd recorded it for him when she was in that godawful pit. When she thought she would die. Alone. In a deep dark pit. The painful ache in his heart had tears stinging his eyes. The sorrow in her voice hitting him like the tsunami hit the tranquil shoreline, with such a force it was devastating. She was saying goodbye, convinced she would never see him again. He felt shattered hearing her anguish.

Shit! She'd been through hell. No one should have to face their own death alone. Especially not twice like she had. But she had been grateful that this time she could say goodbye. Even if nobody ever found her phone, at least she'd said it.

But the thing that shredded his heart the most was hearing her telling him she loved him. She loved the time they'd had together. She wished for more time with him. Loving him. She felt some regret for the twelve years they had let slip by. She didn't want to die with regret. So, she forgave his shitty behavior from the other night and confessed her love for him. Thanked him for making her so happy these last few weeks. She hoped that when she was gone, he would look back on their time together with nothing but joy because the short time they had been together had been the most joyous of her life.

Graham could hear the underlying anguish in her voice. The sobs she'd tried to choke back. Those sounds had been his undoing, affecting him deep in his core. He dropped his head into his hands, elbows propped on his knees as he listened to the message again. The second time just as heart-wrenching.

Overcome with emotion; he felt the wetness before he'd even realized he was crying.

"Graham?" her voice called from the middle of the bed.

"I'm here," he assured her. He could hear her wince of pain in the darkness as she pushed herself up to a sitting position and threw her legs over the side of the bed in front of where he sat.

"Are you okay? What's wrong?" Her voice was full of concern. For him. Pain wracked her body, and she was worried about him. Just like in her message.

Graham dropped to his knees in front of her wrapping his arms around her waist. He placed his head down on her lap and gathered his courage. "Oh, Natalie. My little Chickadee. Everything is perfect. You're here. You're safe. I love you more than life itself. And I'm so sorry I hurt you."

He looked up into green eyes brimming with tears. Inhaling deeply, he allowed the lavender scent to fill his lungs, giving him strength. "I was a coward and an ass. I should never have spoken to you like that. I didn't mean any of it. I was just so ..."

"Lost," she finished for him.

He nodded, reaching up to cup her face with his hands. His thumbs stroking the tears away from her cheeks. "I let the darkness overwhelm me. I was struggling to understand the death of that boy. Questioning how I could have done things differently. And angry that I was so helpless. And like an idiot, I drank my feelings away. The guilt I was feeling was crushing. Consuming my every thought."

"You know that what happened to that family was not your fault, right?"

"Yes, I know. Logically I knew that. But it still hurt. He was the first victim I'd lost since the tsunami. I handled it poorly. And I hurt the one person who never deserves to be hurt like that. I pushed away the one person I needed the most." He dropped his hands to her lap and carefully took her battered hands in his. Bringing them to his lips, he kissed the tips of her fingers. "You have a magic in you that soothes my soul. You bring light to my darkness. And I am so damn sorry I was so cruel to you. I promise you, if you forgive me, I'll never act that way again. I'll never..."

He broke off when she raised a finger and placed it on his lips. "I know, Graham. You don't have to say anything else. I knew even that night that you were hurting; that you were drunk and lashing out because of how you were feeling. I only wanted to help you through it."

Shaking his head vigorously, he said, "You never have to apologize to me. I was the asshole. Not you. Never you." Graham let go of her hands and hugged her tight to him, burying his face in her neck.

"I love you so much, Natalie. I should have told you a long time ago. I should have told you twelve years ago. You were so extraordinary. I always held you in a special place in my heart. Never forgetting the precious little chickadee with the emerald eyes who, in one afternoon, changed my world forever."

"Oh, Graham," she tried, but he pulled back from the hug, and it was his turn to place a finger to her lips to silence whatever it was she was going to say.

"Let me finish." She nodded, and he dropped his hand, cradling her hands gently in his. He looked down at their hands to gather his thoughts. It struck him then the difference in their sizes. Hers were so tiny, so frail looking. Yet they were the strongest hands he'd ever known. "All these years later," he continued. "That special place in my heart has grown. And these last few weeks with you have filled that place to overflowing until I thought my heart would burst. But it only grows bigger. Filling with you. I love you, Natalie. With everything inside me." He leaned forward and kissed her tiny hands.

Natalie took those hands and cradled his face, drawing it up till he was looking at her. "I love you too," she told him. He didn't know why but he suddenly felt an overwhelming amount of relief. "I think I've always loved you," she continued. "Since I was five years old, and we built our first Lego set together. And it grew and changed when I was twelve years old and started to notice boys." He smiled at that, wishing he'd known back then. "I don't want to be stupid again when it comes to you. This is it for me. I love you, and I will for the rest of my life."

She leaned toward him and placed her lips to his. A simple kiss. Like the one they'd shared twelve years ago.

When she started to lean back, he grabbed her face between his hands. "Wait," he commanded before taking her mouth with his. Deepening the kiss. Pouring everything that was overflowing inside of him into that kiss. This moment so precious, just as it had been that day by the lake. But there would be no storm to interrupt them now. He laid her back on the bed as he continued to revere her mouth. He moved the sheets aside and pressed his body to hers, relishing the feeling of her breasts pressed to his chest.

Graham broke the kiss, carefully peeling the t-shirt off over her head before trailing a path down her throat, across her shoulder, and down to her breast with his mouth. Using tongue and teeth to stimulate every nerve ending she had. When he clamped his teeth around the sensitive bud on her breast, she whimpered. The sound heating his blood to boiling. He wanted to make this special for her. Make it last. But he needed her too much. Needed to be inside her like he needed his next breath.

And so, it seemed, did Natalie. He felt her poor damaged hands at his waistband attempting to undo the button. Leaving her for a moment he tore his pants off then sank into her arms once again. And with one languid thrust he was home. Her heat enveloped him. Her pleasured moans filling his heart. Each one of her inner muscles clenching him, a feeling he savored. Not wanting it to end too quickly, he slowed his thrusts.

Natalie groaned in frustration. He knew she'd been close, but he wasn't ready to let her go quite yet. Slowly, sinfully, he brought her to the peak again. And this time, he let her go, pushing her over the edge as he plunged into her until he too had reached the summit and followed her over, grunting out her name as sheer joy overcame him.

Later, after their heated blood had cooled, they lay in each other's arms, Natalie's head resting on his shoulder. Her broken wrist propped on his chest. Remembering they needed to tighten the splint, he did just that with his free hand. His other hand was too busy drawing lazy circles on her back, relishing the feeling of her soft skin under his fingertips.

"Graham," she said after the splint was tight enough. "I'm hungry." Her stomach growled loudly, affirming her hunger. He laughed and kissed her forehead.

"Okay, you rest," he said as he sat up. "I'll see what I can rustle up for us to eat." He reached for his pants and pulled them on before heading to the door. He looked back at her. She was on her side, facing away from him. The bruises on her ribs standing out in stark contrast to her pale skin. His gut clenched, a panicked itch skittering through his body. He wondered briefly if that would ever stop when it came to thoughts of Natalie being injured.

Chapter 23

THREE DAYS LATER, NATALIE was enjoying lunch with her sister at Jolene's while Graham had gone to Nighthawk to see to some business. He'd been by her side nonstop, and she missed him.

Everyone knew that Lauren was still out there somewhere, so they never left Natalie alone. She was grateful but overwhelmed. Several of her neighbors had already stopped by her place, bringing food, and letting her know they were keeping an eye out for Lauren.

Even here in Jolene's, some of the townsfolk she knew stopped by their table to say how happy they were that she was okay. Most wanted to know every sordid detail, and Maddie was a wiz at deflecting those people. Everyone assured her Lauren would soon be caught.

When the lunch crowd died down, Jolene joined them with another woman. "This is Emma Watterson. She's a friend of mine from college. She just moved to town and is staying with me until her apartment is ready." The sisters graciously welcomed her. Emma was tall, of course, everyone was tall comparatively, but Natalie guessed her to be around five eight. She had nondescript brown hair, but it was the cut that made it stand out. Styled short. Pixie style, Natalie believed it was called. Wispy bangs hanging over her forehead and deep dark eyes, she resembled Audrey Hepburn. She looked lithe and graceful, just like Audrey too. And yet, there was a certain hardened edge to her that made her appear badass.

"So," Maddie started. "What do you do?"

"Emma just received an honorable discharge from the Coast Guard," Jolene answered before Emma could. "You could say she's in-between jobs."

"Really!" Natalie was impressed. She'd never met a woman who'd served before.

Jolene continued to praise her friend's accomplishments. "Emma was one of only a handful of female intelligence officers stationed in Michigan."

Both girl's eyes widened. "That is amazing. Thank you for your service."

Emma blushed. Nice to know the hardened Coast Guard officer could blush like that, made her slightly more human. "So, what was Jolene like back in her college days?" Natalie asked.

"A little like she is now. Just more Southern." The sisters laughed, and Jolene huffed.

"Oh, she still brings the Southern Belle out every now and then."

"It just slips out," Jolene explained. "Can't help it." Just then, Jolene got called into the kitchen to deal with some emergency or other.

"By the way," Emma turned to Natalie. "I hope you don't mind, but Jolene told me what happened," she said, indicating her splint. "I'm glad you're okay. I know Jolene thinks the world of you. She was a mess when they figured out you were missing."

"I didn't know that," Natalie remarked, tears hovering just near the surface. "Thank you for telling me."

"I hope they catch that woman soon."

"We all do," Maddie interjected.

The talk turned to more mundane things then. Men, college, prejudice in the military. "I was stationed at Marquette in the UP until I started my intelligence training in Virginia. I would have liked to have been stationed somewhere a little warmer; Lake Superior is a bitch in the winter," Emma explained. "But it turned out pretty well, for the most part." Her smile faded as her expression turned sad. Natalie wondered if something had happened in her Coast Guard career to make her leave at such a young age.

"Wait," Maddie remarked. "I've seen your picture before. In Jolene's office, right? You were holding some kind of trophy."

Jolene laughed, having returned to her seat just as Maddie spoke. "Emma is an expert in fencing. She's won numerous competitions both as a teenager and in college."

"Really?" Maddie exclaimed. "I always wanted to learn fencing. We did it once in gym class in high school, and I was hooked. I just never got around to learning more."

"I could give you a few lessons if you wanted," Emma offered.

"I'd love that."

Natalie suddenly remembered she was supposed to tell Jolene something. "Graham said he'd be willing to give you a few climbing lessons anytime you want, Jolene."

Emma turned to her friend. "Now you want to learn?"

Jolene shrugged. "I thought it would be a useful skill to have," she said quietly. "Especially after what happened to Natalie."

Natalie snorted. "Lot of good it did me."

"You at least knew enough to try," Jolene uttered.

Maddie turned to Emma and asked, "You climb?"

"Yup," Emma replied. "Been doing it most of my life."

"Do you stick to gyms, or have you done the real stuff?" Natalie asked.

Emma smiled. "The real stuff and the gym. Although, I prefer the real stuff. My dad climbed. We used to take trips together to try lots of different climbs. Different states, different mountains, different terrain; we loved it all."

"That sounds so nice. You and your dad are close then? Do you still get to climb with him?"

Grief touched her face for an instant. "He died a few years ago."

"Oh, I'm sorry."

They grew quiet then. Maddie broke the silence. "Jeez, Emma. You've done it all, haven't you? Is there anything you can't do?"

"Dance," Emma replied, eliciting giggles from the girls.

"Sitting here with us girls must be so boring," Maddie mused.

They all laughed. "Actually, this is just what I needed. Being in such a male-based career, I haven't been able to make many female friends."

"Hey, what about me?"

Emma smiled. "Except for Jolene. Master Chef. Best friend extraordinaire."

"That's more like it."

As the women chatted, the bar started to fill up with the dinner crowd. Jolene left them to see to her duties with her staff. "I can't believe we've been sitting here all day," Maddie remarked.

Natalie put her phone back in her pocket, having just answered a text. "The guys are on their way. I told them to just meet us here. Might as well have dinner too. That way, we don't have to cook," Natalie finished with a wink.

"I'm curious about something you said earlier, Emma," Maddie started. "You called Jolene a Master Chef. Isn't that term usually reserved for those hoity-toity chefs in big fancy restaurants?"

"Jolene never told you about her previous job?" She looked shocked. When the sisters both shook their heads no, she continued, "She was a celebrated chef in a famous restaurant in New York City. Her dishes were revered."

"I wonder why she never told us." Maddie mused.

"I'm not exactly sure," Emma replied. "She's been pretty closed up about things since she left New York and wouldn't tell any of her friends what was bothering her. I always wondered what happened."

They grew quiet then, each lost in thought about their friend. The men entered Jolene's not long after. Natalie felt her heart flutter at seeing Graham. He looked so hot dressed in jeans and a Nighthawk t-shirt. This time it was royal blue which made his eyes an even icier blue.

He made a beeline for her and gave her an intense kiss. Guess he missed her as much as she missed him today. Most of the Nighthawks had joined them for dinner, too, so they grabbed a few extra tables to push together. Thankfully, the owner didn't mind. Natalie introduced their new friend, Emma, to the group.

"Emma climbs mountains. Can you believe that?" Natalie was telling Graham and David. "I have a hard enough time believing I can reach the top of your climbing wall. I can't imagine scaling a whole mountain."

Emma perked up. "You have climbing facilities?" she asked Graham, obviously interested. Natalie guessed that maybe it'd been a while since she'd climbed.

"At Nighthawk, yeah," Graham answered. "We use it to train with ropes and the proper climbing and rappelling techniques. We never know if we are going to have to do any climbing for a rescue."

"Not as good as training on the real thing," David chimed in. "But we're limited here in southern Michigan."

"True," Emma agreed. "Ever been up to Silver Mountain in the UP? There are some nice routes there."

"We have a family cabin not too far from there," Graham informed her. "Don't get up there near as often as we'd like, though." Natalie could see regret flash through his eyes. She knew he blamed himself for ruining their weekend together.

"Tell you what," Graham continued. "Why don't you come out to Nighthawk tomorrow. You can show us what you've got on the wall."

"I would love that," Emma responded excitedly.

"Love what?" Jolene asked as she joined them again.

"Graham's gonna let her use our climbing facilities tomorrow," David answered.

"Ooh. Can I come?"

"Seriously," Emma teased. "All those years I tried to get you to come out with me in college. And *now* you're finally ready?"

"I'm just a slow joiner," Jolene replied good-naturedly.

They agreed to meet here in the morning to take her out to Nighthawk. The rest of the evening was filled with lots of banter and teasing. Natalie felt suddenly overwhelmed. This, right here, was everything. Good food. Good friends. The love of her life beside her. And just a few days ago, she thought she'd never have this again. Her eyes filled with tears.

Graham, ever astute to her emotions, leaned closer to her. "You okay?"

Natalie smiled at him through her tears and nodded. "Just extremely happy."

He hugged her to his side and kissed her forehead. "I completely understand."

Jolene stood up; her glass raised. "A toast," she called, and conversations ceased. "To the Nighthawks without whom we would have lost our dear friend. And to Graham for moving heaven and earth to find her so quickly. Bless your heart." The group erupted with applause and huzzahs.

"I'd like to add my own thanks," Natalie said. "To all the Nighthawks. Thank you for all that you do. You are all amazing." More cheers erupted through the bar, and Graham kissed her again as she sat back down.

After another hour of camaraderie, Natalie felt her strength begin to wane. She loved this time with all their friends, but she was itching to be alone with Graham. "Take me home," she whispered suggestively to Graham.

"As you wish." He stood quickly, nearly knocking his chair over backward. Everyone looked at him. So much for a quiet escape. "I'm taking Natalie home. She still gets tired easily."

"Good night, everyone," Natalie told the group as Graham ushered her out the door. They walked slowly home together, arm in arm.

"I have something for you," said Graham as they let themselves inside.

"Oh? What?"

He pulled a small box out of his pocket. She laughed when she saw the box was made from a colorful assortment of Lego pieces. He opened the top and revealed a little black jewelry box inside. Engagement ring was Natalie's first thought. But there was no way. It was too soon. He wouldn't go that far yet. Would he? He handed her the little black box. She glanced at him questioningly, trying to gauge his expression. But nothing could have prepared her for what lay inside.

Natalie opened the jewelry box to find a starburst nestled in the felt. The little silver star had light beams radiating out from the center, which held a diamond that shone brilliantly as it caught the light in the room. Natalie gasped at the beauty of it as she drew it out of the box. A delicate silver chain was threaded through a small loop at the top.

"Turn it over," Graham instructed.

She felt tears emerge as she read the inscription he'd had engraved into the back. *To my True North. My Light. All my love, Graham.*

"I had it commissioned, and it was finally ready today."

"Oh, Graham. It's beautiful," she bawled as the tears spilled over. "Can you put it on me?" She handed it to him and turned around lifting her hair out of the way. Graham fastened it around her neck, placing a kiss there before she turned around to face him again. "This is the most precious thing anyone has ever given me. Thank you." She kissed him, realizing it was true. Her family had never bothered with sentimental gifts. Too personal. Her parents would have had to actually know who she was to get her something meaningful.

Graham wiped her tears away. "I didn't mean for it to make you cry."

"Happy tears, I assure you. This ... you'll never know how much this means to me. How much you mean to me."

He grinned at her. "I have a pretty good idea. But I'll tell you what, you can show me. In bed. Wearing nothing but that necklace. It's been a fantasy of mine since I ordered it."

Later, much later, as they lay in each other's arms, Natalie decided to broach a sensitive subject. "I know, Graham."

"Know what?"

"I know you blame yourself for what Lauren did."

"I don't ..." she interrupted him with a look. "Okay. Maybe a little."

"You can stop now."

"I know. Rationally, I know that I'm not responsible," Graham admitted. "But she was my friend. I knew something was troubling her, and I never took the time to find out what. Maybe if I had talked to her, she wouldn't have gone over the edge."

Natalie lay half on top of Graham. Her head propped up on her fist so she could look him in the eye. The starburst lay on his chest. "Maybe. But maybe not. From what we've learned about her since she was already a little unhinged."

"I know. But maybe I could have gotten her some help. What if my apathy drove her to it? What if she'd been this troubled from the beginning, and I never noticed. Never cared to look deeper. What kind of friend does that make me?"

Natalie laid her splinted hand against his cheek. "You, Graham, are the best man that I know. Even back in high school. You took the time out of your day to rescue a stranded classmate. Not only that, but you spent time talking to her. Caring. You listened. Truly listened. And now, you've become an even better man. You give so much of yourself to so many people. But the people you care about the most, your friends, your family, they all know that you would do anything for them. I think even Lauren knew that too. It just wasn't enough for her."

He seemed to mull over her words a moment. "I broke my promise," he confessed.

"What promise?"

"The one I made to myself. After you told me about Erik, I vowed to always keep you safe. I never wanted you to go through anything like that again." He sat up then, dislodging Natalie from her position across his chest. He threw his legs over the side of the bed, head in his hands. "I wasn't here. I was lost in my darkness after losing that kid. Feeling sorry for myself, and I treated you so poorly. And then I was so busy rescuing others when the woman I love needed me most. How can I ever forgive myself for that? I failed in every way that matters."

Natalie kneeled beside him on the bed. Her arm around his shoulders. "You didn't fail. You saved me. That's all that matters."

"Yeah, but none of it would have happened if I could have just stayed away from you. I brought Lauren into your life."

"I could have no sooner stayed away from you as you could have stayed away from me. I think we were destined for each other. Look at how you found me."

"You helped with that with your clever little trail," he argued.

"But you knew where to find me. You *knew*. Instinctively. Like you could feel me or something. It makes no sense, but there it is. When I was trying to talk her down, offering to leave you, to go away, she told me that you would just follow me. I knew she was right. You would move heaven and earth to find me."

She moved to stand in front of him, unconcerned with her nakedness. She took his hands and put them on her hips. Then placing her hands on his shoulders, she whispered, "Look at me." His eyes slowly rose, a pained expression on his handsome features. "I am fine. I am safe, and I am fine. I am alive. You did that. And only *you* could have done that. Everybody else would have been looking for me up at your cabin. But you knew. How did you know? Because when it comes to the people you love, you listen to them and pay attention. You knew that note was out of character for me. You knew that me not returning your messages would never have happened. You are a good person. An excellent friend. As you were for Lauren. She was just really good at hiding her true nature."

He drew her closer to him, hugging her tight, his head resting on her breast. "What did I ever do to deserve you?"

She snorted. "Are you kidding me? Your entire adult life has been about saving lives, and you can wonder about what you deserve? The question should be, what did I ever do to deserve *you*?"

He smiled up at her before his eyes turned sad again. "I think it's going to take me some time to come to grips with what happened. With what Lauren did. I hope you can be patient with me."

"I will always be here for you," she said, placing her hand over the starburst nestled between her breasts. "When you feel the darkness, let me be your light." She grabbed his face between her hands, leaned over, and kissed him. He clutched her to him and fell backward to the bed. She giggled as he flipped them and took control of the kiss. Natalie let him.

THE NEXT DAY THEY all watched in awe as Emma scaled the climbing wall like she was taking a leisurely stroll. She tackled the most difficult routes as if she'd been born for it. She was even better than David, and that was saying something. An idea was starting to take root in Graham's mind.

Later, as he watched Emma instruct Jolene in the intricacies of climbing and encourage her all the way up the wall, he knew his idea was perfect. He and David were stretched pretty thin at Nighthawk as their notoriety spread. With Lauren gone, they needed some extra help. Emma seemed like a perfect fit. After running it by David, who agreed, he offered the job to Emma.

"You want me to come work here? For Nighthawk?" Emma asked incredulously. "But I don't have much training in search and rescue aside from water rescues. What possible use could I be?"

"We need a climbing instructor. You, obviously, are the best climber I've ever seen. You see things in the wall that the rest of us can't. I bet you'd have that same instinct during a rescue. I've never seen anyone handle the ropes like you. The rest of the training will come. We'll all work hard in getting you up to speed. That is if you are interested."

"If I'm interested?" She looked to Jolene for guidance, who emphatically nodded her head. "Of course, I'm interested. I've been searching for a new adventure. This seems the perfect fit."

"Excellent," Graham said, shaking her hand. The rest of the Nighthawks crowded around her welcoming her to the team.

"Chow time," David called. The group headed toward the dining hall. "Coming?" David asked Graham as he hung back from the crowd.

"You guys go ahead. I want to put some of these things away." There were a few of the ropes that Graham wanted to set aside to inspect more closely later. It was important that the ropes be inspected after each use, otherwise, an unnoticed fray could be deadly. They'd given them a once over as they coiled them, but some were worrying Graham. He might have to budget for more rope in the future. He sighed when he realized that was a job Lauren usually managed.

"Need help?" David offered.

"Nah. Go get some lunch. I'll be there in a minute," he bent to grab another coil of rope, throwing it over his shoulder. He made his way to the large warehouse that stored most of their equipment. He entered, flipping on the lights, glad he had paid a little extra to have the building heated. He made his way to the back room where they did most of the equipment inspections, passing the floor to ceiling shelves full of supplies.

He walked through the door at the back of the warehouse into the Nighthawk's repair room, glancing briefly around to make sure all the tools were in their proper place. After setting the gear down on the long table in the center of the room, he heard Natalie call to him. "Graham, you in here somewhere?"

"Back here."

She joined him. "David said they need—" She never finished. At that moment, Graham saw a movement behind Natalie.

Moving instinctively, he grabbed Natalie and spun around, his back now to the main part of the warehouse just as the shot rang out. He felt a searing pain in his arm. Natalie screamed. Graham pushed her behind him as he turned to face Lauren.

She was in the middle of the warehouse. Gun in hand. Crazed look in her eyes. "Get back, Natalie!" Graham yelled, making sure to stay in front of her as a shield. Graham placed his body next to the door jamb hoping that would protect him from any more flying bullets, Natalie behind and slightly to the left of him, out of sight as much as she could be. But the windows on either side of the door looking into the repair room were not going to be much of a shield. He knew he should make Natalie leave out the back door, but he also knew she'd never go and leave him to face this alone.

"Lauren," he called. "What are you doing?"

"Shut up! I want her! I want her dead!" Lauren cried firing the gun wildly. The round ricocheting off the metal shelves with a sonorous ring like a bell being struck.

"Lauren, stop! Calm down. Let's talk about this," Graham reasoned. Natalie grabbed the hand he held out in front of her to keep her behind him. He could feel her trembling against his back, her fear palpable.

"No, I want her dead. Why is she not dead? She ruined everything."

"I wish you'd told me, Lauren. Things might have been different if you had just told me how you felt. You didn't have to resort to this."

"No! That little whore would still have gotten in the way. She would still have stolen you from me. You were supposed to be mine. She ruined it." She was gesturing wildly with the gun, pointing it repeatedly at them.

"Natalie has nothing to do with this. This is between you and me. Why don't you put the gun down so we can talk?" he tried.

"This has *everything* to do with that whore!" she shrieked. She was shaking, unable to control her emotions. Dirt covered her clothes and exposed skin, like she had crawled through the mud to get here. Her hair appeared greasy and knotted. She must have been hiding out in the woods since she'd abandoned Natalie's car. What had she done for food? She looked gaunt even with the wild look in her eyes.

"No, Lauren." Graham tried softening his voice. Reminding himself that she had once been his closest friend. "You are my friend, Lauren. I can help you. Let me help you."

She stared at him, breathing heavily. "You're mine," she muttered.

"I know." He took a chance and stepped out from behind the jamb just behind the opening to the doorway, hands raised slightly in front of him. He gestured to Natalie to stay where she was, out of sight. "Why don't you put down the gun so that we can talk."

She looked confused, glancing at the gun as if she didn't know how it had gotten in her hand. "Talk?"

"Yeah, Lauren. Let's talk like we used to. I've missed our chats." It was then Graham noticed the smell. Gas. That last bullet must have nicked the gas line. He needed to get them all out of here. Now. Any spark could ignite the gas building up in the room. Natalie must have smelled it too. She started to move toward him, but he motioned her back.

"Why don't we go outside to talk, Lauren."

"I ... I don't know. I came here to do ... something." She placed the fingers of the hand holding the gun against her forehead. Struggling to clear the confusion. "I can't remember."

"That's okay, Lauren. We can go outside. Maybe that will jog your memory. But first, you need to put that gun down."

She shook her head. "I don ... I don't understand." Her words slurred. Graham's paramedic's training kicked in. Exhaustion, hunger, exposure. Even the gas filling her lungs. Any one of those could be affecting her. Causing confusion. Slurred speech. "I need ... need to do ... something."

"Why don't we go outside," Graham tried again. "We can do it together outside."

"No ... I ..." she broke off again.

Graham tried another tactic. "Lauren, do you smell that? It's gas. We need to get out of the building. There is a gas leak."

"Gas?" she asked weakly.

"Yeah. Let's get out of here before we get hurt. Okay?" He started to take a step toward her. She looked at him, and he stopped moving, standing still in the jamb of the door.

"Don't want to hurt you," she muttered as she started to lower the gun to her side. She looked at him, her glassy eyes baffled. Then her eyes flicked over his left shoulder, spotting Natalie. "No!" Lauren screamed and raised the gun.

Graham turned to Natalie and pushed her toward the backdoor, told her to run as Lauren fired, her shot going wildly crazy. He turned to make a run for Lauren. Hoping to tackle her to the ground before she ignited the gas. But she fired just as he reached the threshold between the two rooms, the shot going wild again as it ricocheted off the metal shelves. That was all it took. One spark from the bullet as it hit the shelf. The intense explosion knocked him off his feet.

Natalie dropped to the ground just outside the door as the explosion rent the air. She lay there, momentarily stunned. Shock and confusion immobilizing her. Her body hurt, and her ears were ringing, but she was alive. She looked to her side, no Graham. She was alone just outside the warehouse. Had he made it outside?

"Graham!" She screamed, looking over her shoulder. She got unsteadily to her feet, looking to the door she had just exited. He wasn't there. Where was he?

Half the warehouse was gone. Debris was everywhere. The room she had fled was still partially standing. The back and side walls still upright. Windows blown out. Door hanging from its hinges. "Graham!" she yelled again. She had to get to him. She couldn't lose him now.

Before she could think about it, she ran back into the building, coughing as smoke hit her lungs. The main part of the warehouse had been destroyed. Little fires everywhere, licking at what was left. She didn't let that deter her. She had to find Graham. She made her way carefully through the debris, lifting what she could out of the way and calling out to him with each step.

She heard coughing before she spotted him. He was under what seemed like half the building. His head and shoulders all she could see. "Graham!" she called, dashing to him. She tore through the debris that was piled on top of him.

"Natalie," he coughed. "Get out of here."

"No, I'm not leaving you." She kept digging, her tears nearly blinding her, until she reached the metal beam that lay across him. She tried lifting it, ignoring her screaming wrist. "I can't lift this. Can you wiggle out from under it?"

"No. My leg is trapped." Natalie cried out and tried desperately to lift the heavy metal again. "Go, Natalie. The rest of the building could come down at any time. Go."

She kneeled down next to his head, shaking her head emphatically as tears coursed down her face. He placed a palm on her cheek. "Please, Natalie. Go. Go get help."

"I'm not leaving. Tell me what to do. How can I get this off of you? What would you do? Please, Graham, tell me what to do," she pleaded, desperate to make him understand. He would never leave her if their situations were reversed. How could he expect her to abandon him?

He must have realized it was hopeless to get her to leave because he sighed. "I'd get something to use as a fulcrum. Find something strong. Something long."

Natalie glanced around her. She spied a long metal rod that used to be part of the ceiling. "How's this?"

"Good. Place one end under the beam and push down on the other end."

"Got it." She shoved the rod with all her might as far as she could under the beam. Grabbing the other end, she pushed down. Nothing. She tried again, standing on tiptoe to get a better angle, using all her body weight. Again nothing. Natalie choked back her sobs and kept trying. Hands joined hers on the rod. The team! They were all there.

"Go help pull Graham out," David said to Natalie. "We've got this." She nodded and ran to Graham's side. She reached to grab him under the shoulders. The other girls joined her to help pull him. "When we tell you, pull as fast and hard as you can." They all nodded.

"He's clear here," Finch called out, making sure as much of Graham was uncovered as they could. They didn't want anything else trapping him.

Four guys got on the rod and pushed. The beam moved a tiny bit. They pushed harder. "Now!" David called, and Natalie pulled with all her might. Wrist protesting. They pulled, dragging Graham as far as the scattered debris would allow until he was free. The men let the beam drop as soon as his feet cleared it. Natalie was beside him in an instant.

"Can you stand?" she asked.

"I think so." She helped him up. He was wobbly and limping slightly, but with the rest of the team's help, he was able to hobble out of the ruined building. Stopping briefly, he turned to David. "Lauren. She's in ..."

"On it," he said, calling to Jude and Evan to help him look for her.

Natalie put her shoulder under his, her arm around his waist as she helped him half walk half hop away to a safe distance from the warehouse. He plopped himself in the grass, staring at the building in disbelief. The magnitude of the destruction was overwhelming. Natalie knelt beside him, checking him over for injuries, so beyond grateful he was alive. "Your arm is bleeding."

"Shot."

"What? She shot you?"

"Well, the ricochet did. Don't worry. It's just a scratch," he reassured her.

Natalie turned to Logan, who was carrying a med bag, demanding the supplies she'd need to clean his arm. She knew Logan was a paramedic like Graham, but she had to do something, or she'd fall apart. She ripped his shirt sleeve as much as she could and reached for the antiseptic wipes tearing one open with her teeth. Her injured wrist wasn't cooperating, unable to make her fingers grasp anything. She cleaned the blood away to find a deep gash in the upper part of his arm. As Logan saw to his leg, wrapping a cold pack on his ankle with an ace bandage, Natalie kept cleaning. She bandaged it, not sure if it needed stitches or not. Then she started to look for additional injuries.

"Chickadee," Graham said, grabbing her hand as she fussed. "Stop. I'm fine."

"O ... okay," she stammered at a loss as to what to do next. He pulled her to his side, his arm around her. He kissed the top of her head. Together, they waited for the others to find Lauren.

It wasn't long before David was walking toward them, grief in his eyes. "We found her," he reported quietly. "It looks," he stopped and took a deep breath. "It looks like she was killed instantly in the blast."

"Oh, God," Natalie gasped. Even though the woman had had almost killed her, she shouldn't have died in such a horrific way. Everyone stood around, different levels of grief affecting them. Lauren had been a member of the team from the very beginning. It was going to take Graham and the team a long time to understand and accept everything that had happened. Natalie's heart went out to all of them.

"She tried to kill Natalie again," Graham told David. "I tried. I tried talking her down." David placed a comforting hand on his brother's shoulder as they waited for the authorities to arrive.

Hours later, after all the interviews from the sheriff's department, after the coroner took Lauren away, after Logan had rechecked her handiwork on Graham's arm and added a few stitches, Natalie paced in her kitchen. She needed to find something to distract herself. Otherwise ... well, she didn't want to think what she'd do.

Upon arriving home, they went directly to the shower. Washing the remains of the horrific day off of them. They made love against the shower wall. Quick, fast, and furious. Both needing to release the pent-up adrenalin. It had been intense but exactly what they had both needed. Each wanting to reassure themselves the other was alive and unharmed.

But now, she paced as Graham spoke on the phone to his parents, reassuring them he was fine, and that Natalie was fine. How sweet of them to ask after her too. Graham found her at the kitchen island, absentmindedly folding and unfolding a dish towel over and over. He wrapped his arms around her from behind. She placed her hands on his arms where they crossed in front of her.

"Come, Chickadee," he said gently. "You're supposed to be icing that wrist." She had tried to hide her pain for as long as possible, but of course, Graham had noticed. He insisted the paramedics look at it. They had wanted her to go to the hospital for more x-rays, but that was not how she wanted to spend the rest of the night. She promised she'd get it looked at on Monday.

Letting go of Natalie, Graham reached into the freezer for the bag of peas. He steered Natalie into the living room, made her sit, and place her wrist on the arm of the couch, then covered it with the frozen peas. God, that hurt. But the longer she sat, the more the pain eased.

Graham had turned on the fireplace before joining her on the couch. He grabbed her uninjured hand and laced their fingers together as she laid her head on his shoulder.

"I'm sorry about Lauren," Natalie said softly.

Graham sighed. "Yeah."

"No matter what she was at the end, she didn't deserve to die that way."

"You're more forgiving than I am." He rose swiftly, his turn to pace. "I just can't believe what she did. I can't wrap my brain around it. The woman I knew was not the woman in that warehouse. How did that happen? How could something go so horribly wrong in her head?"

"I don't know," Natalie replied quietly.

Still pacing in front of the fireplace, he continued, "When I smelled that gas, the only thing I could think about was getting us out of there. Getting you out. Even getting Lauren out. She was having so much trouble grasping reality. It's like she kept phasing in and out of madness."

Graham had tried so hard to reason with her, but the madness had consumed her. "She was almost back. There at the end. She was almost the Lauren I knew again. The moment I saw her eyes flick to you, I knew that was it. It was over. Then it was all about getting you out of there. I thought once you were out of the building, I could tackle Lauren and seize control of the gun. But it was too late."

Natalie stood, dropping the peas to the coffee table. She walked over to stand in front of Graham. Placing her hands flat on his chest, she told him, "You did everything you could. Like you said, the madness had taken control of your friend. Now, you need to remember that she was once your friend. Remember the good times. Don't let her madness cloud your good memories. Otherwise, you'll never be able to forgive."

He looked down at her, and she could see the love he had for her in his eyes. "When did you get so wise?"

She smiled and placed her ear to his chest, wrapping her arms around his waist. She listened to his heartbeat, thankful she still could. Quiet tears fell from her eyes, and she squeezed them shut. "I love you, Graham," she said with a hiccupped sob.

He placed a hand under her chin and drew her head up to look at him. "Hey." He kissed her, a soft peck on the lips. "I'm okay, Chickadee."

"I know."

"I love you," he said just before he lowered his lips to hers again. Taking her mouth more deeply this time. He gathered her closer, pressing her into his hard body, leaving Natalie trembling in his arms.

When they both lay gloriously sated in front of the fireplace, Graham thought about how easy it was to love the woman who lay in his arms. At that moment, he made another vow to himself. He vowed to always let his little Chickadee, his north star, know how much he loved her. He vowed to show her and tell her every day. The woman who was his heart's home would always know she was loved.

"I love you," he whispered in her ear from behind her as they both basked in their love.

Epilogue

Logan

EVERYBODY TRICKLED INTO JOLENE'S the day after the explosion in the warehouse. They all needed to come to grips with the loss, both of their friend, and the loss of the equipment in the warehouse. Logan stared into his beer, trying to block the memories of his losses. The years pass, but the ache remains. Losing a coworker, while tragic, was nothing like the loss that haunted him still.

An image on the big screen tv behind the bar momentarily caught his attention. A woman was being escorted into a courthouse surrounded by news media who all wanted a piece of her. The story was of no interest to him. It was the woman, or more precisely, the woman's hair. Beautiful long blonde waves cascaded down her back shone in the sunlight. Hair so similar to a girl from his past. One he had loved and lost but never forgotten.

He took another swig from his beer and turned away from the tv screen. He didn't need to be reminded of what he'd lost. It haunted him every day.

"That woman is so courageous. I don't know what I'd do if I was ever faced with that situation," Natalie said, her eyes glued to the tv.

"What situation is that?" Logan asked.

"The school shooting." He raised an eyebrow. He hadn't heard anything about a school shooting.

Emma jumped into the conversation. "You're a teacher, Natalie. Do you ever think about something like that happening at your school?"

"I try not to, but it's hard when we have to drill the procedures of what to do in the event of an active shooter. Since I teach elementary, those drills can be pretty scary for the kids. And yet, the more we do them, the more the kids have grown desensitized to it. But what that woman went through, I can't imagine." She shivered, and Graham placed his arm around her shoulders, pulling her in close and kissing her on the top of her head.

"So, what happened with that woman?" Logan asked.

Natalie glanced at the tv again before answering. "She was shot by one of her students, who then kept the entire class captive for hours. She managed to talk him into surrendering himself, saving her students. She's a hero."

Logan glanced back at the tv hoping to get another glimpse of the blonde woman, but they had moved on to a different story. He'd always heard stories of the hero teachers who protected their students, but for some reason, this one had him wanting to learn more. Maybe it was her resemblance to the girl from his past. The girl he'd spent the last fifteen years trying to forget but knowing she would always live in his heart.

Graham sat surrounded by his Nighthawks, each of whom was mourning both the loss of Lauren and of the warehouse. The equipment and supplies in the warehouse were uppermost in his mind at the moment. While the loss of a friend was devastating, he couldn't help the direction his thoughts kept turning. Losing the warehouse and everything in it would cripple the Nighthawks. Insurance would cover some of it, but not enough. The loss was extraordinary. Graham felt like he was going to have to start all over again.

He and David had talked by phone late last night after Natalie had fallen asleep. They needed a plan to recover from the financial loss. They had investments that they had been hoping to build up, after withdrawing a huge chunk the previous year to build the climbing gym. Maddie had even offered her expertise to help them figure out where they would get the money from. Of course, there were always loans. Graham groaned inwardly at that thought. He didn't like the idea of being in debt to any bank. They would just have to increase their fundraising efforts.

In an effort to cheer themselves up, he and Natalie had adorned the duplex inside and out with Christmas decorations. It had worked for a while. Natalie, of course, with her creative brain, was a wiz at knowing exactly where to place everything. But she wasn't bossy. She let him put whatever he wanted wherever he desired. They even ran out to buy a tree together and listened to cheesy Christmas tunes as they trimmed it with the ornaments Natalie had collected over the years. She had a story for almost every ornament, and Graham enjoyed listening to her tell each one.

But as the house became more festive, reality threatened to intrude. After putting all the empty boxes back into storage, the two of them decided to meander over to Jolene's. Maddie joined them for the short walk. It seemed as though Jolene was trying for some cheer as well; the bar looked like Christmas had thrown up inside it. Streamers of all colors draped across the ceiling, and ornaments hung everywhere over their heads. There was a huge tree in the corner draped in tinsel and red and green bulbs. The old-fashioned jukebox next to the bar had been filled with Christmas CDs.

They took their usual spot, and as more friends joined them, more tables were pushed together. Laughter was in short supply, but they each put forth the effort. Maddie stood once everybody had arrived, glass raised in front of her. "I'd like to make a toast," she announced as everybody grew quiet. "To my superhuman sister, thinking she could lift a two-thousand-pound beam. And with a broken wrist to boot!" Everyone cheered. Glasses clinked.

David stood. "To my brother! Thanks for not dying!" More cheers and clinking glasses.

The toasts and the jovial intention they were given seemed to do the trick. The mood around the group of tables improved. The jokes and teasing started up then. Finch kept asking Natalie to flex her bicep muscle and feigning a faint every time she appeased him. She was one of them now. No longer immune to their teasing.

Suddenly a hush came over the surrounding tables. Even his friends stopped talking, staring eyes wide at whoever had just come through the door. Graham turned slightly in his seat and groaned. Marcus Rayne. What in the world was he doing here?

The actor spotted them and approached. Graham stood and shook his proffered hand. "I was told I could find you here," Marcus started. By whom? Everyone he knew was here. "I hope I'm not intruding."

Graham couldn't seem to find his voice for some stupid reason. Natalie stepped closer. "Not at all, Mr. Rayne. Won't you join us?" Someone moved to pull another chair over. "I'm Natalie Ghannon."

"Ahh," Marcus said, shaking her hand. "The girlfriend." Natalie blushed. "And it's Marcus, please." She nodded and sat back down as he took the new chair at the head of the table on Graham's right.

Finally, he found his voice. "It's nice to see you, Marcus. What brings you to our neck of the woods?"

"Well, you do," he answered. "I've had my people keeping an eye out for every and any media report that contained your name. I'm not entirely proud of that, but my curiosity about you and your Nighthawks overwhelmed my common sense." Somebody, probably Jolene, placed a beer in front of him. He picked it up and took a deep sip. "Wow. That is just about the best thing I've ever tasted!"

Jolene leaned over to Emma and whispered, not too quietly, "He likes my brew. Bless his heart!" Everyone chuckled.

"You made this?" Marcus was asking Jolene.

She nodded, obviously afflicted with the same tongue-tying disease that had stricken Graham. "She owns this place," Emma informed him.

"Then you must be the infamous Jolene?" She nodded again. "Well, Jolene, I do declare this is one tasty brew."

"Bless your heart," she said, finally finding her very southern voice. "Can I get you something to eat?"

Finch spoke up then. "You think the beer is good; you should try her burgers."

"Okay. A burger then." Jolene hurried to the kitchen to rush her cook into making him his burger.

"So, who all do I have the pleasure of sharing my meal with?" Marcus asked.

Graham went around the table, naming every one of the people who meant the world to him. New and old. When he got to Logan and Tin Man, Marcus recognized them. "I remember you two. You were on that cliff too. Thank you for all you did that day. I might have been too addled with pain to thank you properly then." They both nodded, accepting his gratitude.

Jolene returned with the burger just then. "This looks like a masterpiece," he said before taking a bite. His eyes rolled back into his head as he moaned with pleasure.

"Told you, bro," Finch teased.

"Seriously, I must have died and gone to heaven. Good beer, awesome burger. Are you some kind of kitchen savant?" Marcus said to Jolene.

She, of course, blushed again with another 'bless your heart.' Conversations among the group commenced as Marcus finished his burger. But as he sighed in contentment and wiped his mouth on a napkin, conversations died out. Everyone was curious as to why the famous actor was in Lake Haven.

"As I've already admitted," he started, "I've been watching the media reports. I've read every internet story I could find. Including what happened to you last week, Natalie. I'm relieved you are okay."

"Thank you," Natalie replied, bewildered he knew anything about her.

"And I know what happened yesterday." The bar was so quiet one could hear a pin drop. Even the jukebox had gone silent. "And I'm sorry, both for the loss of your friend and for the equipment. And that brings me to the reason I am here." He paused for another pull on his beer.

"I have a deal for you. I'll donate all the capital you need to rebuild and resupply on one condition." As any true actor worth his salt would, he paused for dramatic effect. "You let me write, produce and star in a movie about your life."

Graham could hear gasps of all sorts from all over the bar. It seemed the whole town was listening. He looked over at his brother, who was sitting on Marcus' other side. They stared at each other in shock. It was everything they could ask for. It would solve all their current financial problems.

Marcus stood. "I'll give you a moment to talk it over with your," he paused, glancing at each person around the grouping of tables. "Family," he finished.

And wasn't that the truth. These people were his family as much as David was. And he was so grateful for each one. Even his new friends. Sure, he'd started a family of sorts when he launched Nighthawk, people he would trust with his life. They had respect and camaraderie, but now they have love. Natalie had done that for him. And she came with her own family, which rounded them out.

Therefore, turning to his family, he asked, "Well? What does everyone think?" They all started talking at once. Then laughed. "Okay, one at a time. David?"

"I admit, it's tempting. It would answer all our prayers. But are you sure you want to expose your life to the world like that?" Graham nodded and turned to the next person. "Maddie?"

Shocked, she said, "I get a say? But I'm not a Nighthawk."

"You're as good as one. And you're family."

She blushed. "Umm. Okay. I agree with David. You wouldn't have to turn all your focus on resupplying and fundraising. You could continue with the training seminars and search and rescues. And expanding the facilities and classes you offer. God knows you and more like you are all needed out there."

"Finch?"

"Do it. Why not? What could it possibly hurt?"

Graham listened to each and every one of them.

When he reached their newest member, Emma, he was impressed with her thoughts and thought her ideas had merit. Finally, he turned to Natalie. "This involves you as much as me since you are part of my life story."

He knew she'd been thinking along those lines too. "I think ... I think it could be a good idea. If we make the condition that Emma suggested, then we can make sure it doesn't get screwed up. We could have a hand in how your story is told. You could make it so you would get final say on any script. And you could be a consultant during filming, so they don't get the details wrong." Graham mulled that over. That was true. He could make Emma's condition as well as insist on having the final say on the script. It had possibilities. But would Marcus agree to his conditions?

But of course, Natalie had more thoughts. "What you do, Graham. All of you. Saving lives. Helping people during the worst times in their life. That is important work. If Marcus did this movie, it would bring attention to all organizations such as yours. There could be a boost of generosity from the public. Police, fire, paramedics, search and rescue, this could help them all. People need something to root for. Everyone still talks about the overwhelming support all the first responders received after nine eleven. All across the country. If this movie were made and done right, it could go a long way toward bolstering support again. This time all over the world."

Natalie continued, not quite done with all her thoughts. "Marcus Rayne, because of his Titan superhero movies, brings with him a certain audience. Young boys and girls. Imagine those kids watching their hero on the big screen saving lives without superpowers. Imagine them saying, 'I could do that. When I grow up, I want to be just like Graham Whitaker!'" Leave it to Natalie to get to the heart of things. Not once was she concerned about the consequences to her own life.

He brought her hand to his lips, his love for her overflowing. "You have the kindest heart."

"Can I change my answer?" Finch called out, raising his hand. The group erupted in laughter.

Graham looked to his brother again. He wouldn't do this if he weren't completely on board. David gave his trademark thumbs up, and Graham flagged Marcus - who was signing autographs and taking selfies - over.

"Okay," Graham started when Marcus sat down with them again. "We agree, but we have a few conditions of our own."

"Name them."

Graham laid the conditions out for Marcus. "First, I, rather we, get final say on any script. Second, one of us will act as a consultant during filming. And third, you go through the training that I require of all my Nighthawks."

Marcus mulled it over for only a minute. Finally, he held out a hand to Graham. "Deal!"

CONTINUE READING FOR A PREVIEW OF THE NEXT
NIGHTHAWK SEARCH AND RESCUE BOOK

ANNIKA'S AURORA

Also By

Books In This Series

Nighthawks Search and Rescue
Nadia's Nemesis (Nighthawk Prequel Novella)
Natalie's Nighthawk
Annika's Aurora
Emma's Element
Sutton's Shadow
Hollynn's Horizon
Sophie's Song
Jolene's Justice (Coming Soon)

Acknowledgments

Dear Reader,

Thank you so much for taking this wild ride with me and allowing me to tell this story that means so much to me. I appreciate you taking the time out of your life and offering a piece of yourself to these words and these pages. Your enthusiasm and love for my characters makes this job a joy to do and your support means the world to me.

Did you enjoy Graham and Natalie's story?

People are often hesitant to try new books or new authors. Honest reviews of my books help bring them to the attention of other readers and encourage them to make that leap and give it a try. If you've enjoyed this book, I'd be eternally grateful if you could spend just a few minutes leaving a review on any or all of the following sites to help this story find the readers who would enjoy it. Goodreads, Bookbub, Amazon. Even the short reviews really make an impact.

I would also like to acknowledge the following without who this book would not be possible.

Laetitia Treseng of Little Tweaks and the OG of beta readers, whose advice and prodding have gone a long way to fluff up this story.

Jenni Bara and AJ Ranney, the best beta readers who never hesitate to tell me the truth. I look forward to reading your future books as well.

Roxx Tarantini, my editor who tirelessly works to clean up my manuscripts. I always thought I was good with the commas. Who knew I was so wrong?

My family, who more often than not, leave me alone long enough so that I can commune with the voices in my head.

About Author

Amanda Zook has been an avid romance reader since middle school when she delved into Gone with the Wind and has finally decided to liberate the stories that live in her head. After growing up in the Sweetest Place on Earth (Hershey, Pennsylvania) she attended college at a small liberal arts school majoring in English (what can you do with an English degree?). She met the love of her life there and followed him to the Jersey Shore (no, not the MTV reality show) where they lived for the first 20 years of their marriage, before moving halfway across the country. Amanda now lives in the Southwest corner of the mitten state on the shores of Lake Michigan (no sharks, no salt, no problem).

She is a wife, a mother of teenage twin girls and can now add published author to her list of achievements.

You can find her on Facebook, join her reader's group, Amanda Zook Books, Instagram , and TikTok.

Visit her website for all the latest news and sign up for her newsletter for freebies. www.amandazook.com

or email her at amandazook@amandazook.com